The Hallowed Isle

Book Two:
The Book of the Spear

Other Books in
The Hallowed Isle *cycle by*
Diana L. Paxson

The Book of the Sword

Wodan's Children *Trilogy*

The Dragons of the Rhine
The Wolf and the Raven
The Lord of Horses

With Adrienne Martine-Barnes

Master of Earth and Water
The Shield Between the Worlds
Sword of Fire and Shadow

THE HALLOWED ISLE

BOOK TWO:
THE BOOK OF THE SPEAR

DIANA L. PAXSON

AVON BOOKS, INC.
1350 Avenue of the Americas
New York, New York 10019

Copyright © 1999 by Diana L. Paxson
Published by arrangement with the author
ISBN: 0-380-80546-4
www.avonbooks.com/eos

Library of Congress Cataloging in Publication Data is available from the publisher.

First Avon Eos Trade Printing: April 1999

AVON EOS TRADEMARK REG. U.S. PAT. OFF. AND IN OTHER COUNTRIES, MARCA REGISTRADA, HECHO EN U.S.A.

Printed in the U.S.A.

OPM   10   9   8   7   6   5   4   3   2   1

In Memoriam
Paul Edwin Zimmer

ACKNOWLEDGMENTS

My special thanks to Heather Rose Jones, who took time off from her doctoral studies in Welsh philology to advise me on the mysteries of fifth-century British spelling. I would also like to thank Winifred Hodge for her comments and for correcting my Anglo-Saxon.

For those who would like an excellent historical overview of the Arthurian period, I recommend *The Age of Arthur* by John Morris, recently reprinted by Barnes & Noble. There are many works on the Anglo-Saxons, but I suggest in particular the fine series published by Anglo-Saxon Books, 25 Malpas Dr., Pinner, Middlesex, England.

Through the fields of European literature, the Matter of Britain flows as a broad and noble stream. I offer this tributary with thanks and recognition to all those who have gone before.

ALBA

PICTS

ALTA CLUTA

DUN EIDYN

VOTADINI

MABONSTONE

LUGUVALIUM

ISLE OF MAIDENS

B
R
I
T
A
N
N
I
A

EBURACUM

MONA

LINDUM

DUN AMBROS

GUENET

DEVA

ANGLES

DEMETIA

VENTA
ICENORUM

MARIDUNON

VENTA
SILURUM

GLEVUM

CAMULODUNUM

VERULAMIUM

ISCA SILURUM

MONS BADONICUS

CALLEVA

LONDINIUM

AEGELES FORD

TANATUS IS.

AFALLON

DUN TAGELL

DUMNONIA

SAXONS

CANTUWARE

CANTUWARA BUR

ISCA
DUMNONIORUM

VENTA BELGARUM

HAESTA'S

PORTUS ADURNI

SORVIODUNUM

DURNOVARIA

PROLOGUE

In the beginning was the breath.

   When the first Fire met primal Ice there came a wind, released by their meeting, feeding the flame. By virtue of that third element, the breath of life and the spirit that moves through all the worlds, matter and energy interacted.

   It moves upon the face of the waters, and life begins to stir; the trees of the forest exhale it; the newborn babe breathes it in and becomes a child of time.

   In the beginning was the Word.

   Invisible, essential, it moves through all that lives, knowing everything, itself unknown. Aware, it wills the world to change and grow. Conscious, that will is borne on a breath of wind in the form of sound. . . .

   In the morning of creation the god who gave men breath hangs on the Worldtree. Nine nights and days he hangs suspended, neither eating nor drinking, until out of his agony comes understanding, and he calls forth the primal energies of the world in sacred sounds. One by one he calls them into manifestation as Runes of might and power. And then he gives them to the world.

   The Breath carries the Word.

   In a northern forest, a rune-master chants, calling the wind. All

I

through the night the wild storm rages. He stands to face it, hair streaming, garments blown to ribbons, shouting out the names of his god. When dawn breaks and the wind grows gentle, he sees before him the limb of an ash tree that the storm has speared into the ground.

Whispering a prayer of thanks, he pulls it free, finding it exact in weight and balance for his needs. From fallen wood he builds a shelter at the foot of a hill, and there, for nine nights and days he labors, eating nothing, drinking only from the sacred spring.

Carefully the wood is smoothed and polished, all irregularities planed away. As he works, he sings of the sun and rain that nourished the tree, the earth that bore it, the wind that ruffled its leaves. When he is finished, he holds a smooth shaft, almost as long as he is tall.

With his graving tool, he carves into the ashwood the angular shapes of the runes. One by one he carves them, chanting their names so that the wood vibrates with the sound. With the sounds come images, each rune name is a doorway to another realm. With blood and breath and spittle he colors and consecrates them, and as each one is added, the shaft gains power.

On the eighth night he is finished. To his eyes, the rune staff seems to glow. Now, it contains, but does not yet direct the power. In the dawning of the ninth day, he draws forth from its wrappings the one thing he himself has not made. A cleanly polished leaf-shaped blade of translucent, smoky stone, it came to him from his father. But it is far older.

When he holds it images come to him of hide-covered huts beneath a northern sky, and he feels the icy breath of eternal snows. The soul of the shaman who made that blade still guards it, whispering of ice and fire and monstrous enemies. Since the time when the fathers of the fathers of his people first spoke in human words, this blade has warded them; it comes from a time even before they knew the runes.

Handling it with reverence, he eases it into the slot that he has carved into the shaft, bedded in glue made from the hooves of stallions. With the sinew of wolves he wraps it, and ties two raven feathers so they will flutter in the breeze.

When he is finished, the wood feels different. It is not only that the balance has shifted. The power that was inherent now is focused.

As the ninth night falls he climbs the hill. The wind that has sprung up with the coming of darkness is whispering in the trees.

He turns to face the breeze and it blows stronger. With both hands, he holds up the spear. Wind shrills down the shaft.

"Gungnir I name you, to Woden I offer you, to bear his word and his will throughout the world!"

THE WILD HUNT

A.D. 470

WIND GUSTED AROUND THE FEASTING HALL, SHRILLING through the thatching and shaking the pillars. Oesc, leaning against the posts of his grandfather's high seat, could feel the wood trembling beneath his hand. *Maybe this will be the storm that destroys us,* he thought with a shiver in which excitement mingled with fear. *The wind will knock down the hall and then the sea will pour in over the fields and wash us away . . .*

Storms were common at this season, when the forces of winter fought a rearguard action against the advance of spring, but in all his nine years Oesc could not remember so mighty a wind. For generations the Myrgings had held this land, stubbornly clinging to their homes when other tribes passed away. Men spoke of gentle winters and good harvests when they sat around the fires, but since his birth, it seemed, the weather had been bad, and this was the worst year of all.

A cold blast whipped up the flames in the long hearth as the door opened. Several drenched figures pushed through and slammed it shut, stamping their feet and shaking themselves like wet dogs. Oesc listened with interest as they swore, testing the forbidden words with a silent tongue.

"The etins are pissing up a storm, curse them!" exclaimed Æthelhere, flinging his cloak at one of the thralls. "I swear the rain is coming in sideways, straight from the sea!"

"—And cold as the milk from Hella's tit, too!" echoed Byrhtwold, following him. Their boots squelched, and water ran down their necks from their wet hair.

"What of the tide?"

Oesc looked up at his grandfather, who had been sitting motionless since noon, listening to the wind.

"It will be high just past sunset, lord," said Æthelhere. "If the wind has not dropped by then—" He grimaced and shook his head.

He did not need to say more. At this season the wind, adding its power to that of the tide, could turn back the Fifeldor in its course. The storm tides and the flooding river between them would drown the newly planted fields.

"The Norns have cast for us an evil fate . . ." muttered Eadguth. "If foes attacked us I would go forth in arms, old as I am, but no man can hold back the sea."

Oesc looked up at his grandfather. Eadguth had always seemed eternal. Now the boy saw the sunken eyes and furrowed brow, the transparent skin on the thin hands, and knew that the Myrging-king was *old*, not as a standing stone is ancient, its rough surfaces weathered by the years, but like an old oak, decaying from within until it has no strength to withstand the storm. Already this wind had torn limbs from several of the trees that had rooted themselves in the wurt-mound on which stood the royal hall. What would it do to the old man? He crept closer and clasped his arms around Eadguth's leg as if his young strength could root him into the ground.

The old man's hooded glance turned downward and his lips twisted.

"Is it a curse on your line, boy, that has doomed you to find rest nowhere? I am glad that your mother did not live to see this day. . . ."

Oesc let go and sat staring. He did not remember his mother, a fair woman with eyes the rich brown of tree bark in the sun, so men said, who had run off with an Anglian adventurer called Octha and crept home again, heavy with child, when her man went over the sea to join his father in

Britannia. Eadguth's sons had died in battle, and his daughter had been the apple of her father's eye.

"Or is it you who are the doom-bringer?" The king's gaze sharpened. "Doom to your mother in child-bed, and now the doom of my land?"

Oesc edged carefully away. He knew Eadguth's black moods too well. When he was smaller he had tried to say he was sorry, though he did not know what for, and only been beaten harder. He looked like his father, said the women. Perhaps that was why. But the old man, he could see, was too weary to strike him now.

Byrhtwold glanced from his king to the boy, pity in his eyes, and gestured toward the door. The old warrior would never criticize his lord, but he had showed Oesc what kindness he could. Nodding his thanks, the boy reached the shadows behind the row of pillars and slipped down the aisle between them and the bed boxes until he reached the door.

His grandfather, king of the Myrgings and lord of their land, was the supreme power in his small world, but Eadguth had ever been a chancy protector. Still, he was not the only power. Oesc slipped through the door, straining to hold it against the wind, seeking the one person by whom he had never been betrayed.

Before he had gone three steps he was soaked to the skin. The storm was driving down from the north, cold as the seas from which it came, lashing the land with rain. With each gust the big oak tree beyond the palisade thrashed wildly; the ground was littered with leaves and branches. Bent nearly double, Oesc splashed through the puddles, shielding his eyes with his arm. Even so, the wind slammed him against the weaving shed and sent him sprawling beside the storehouse before he came under the lee of the log palisade and crept along it to his goal.

Hæthwæge's hut was partially sheltered by the wall; the horse's skull on the post before the doorway rattled in the wind, and the raven feathers tied beneath it flapped wetly, but here Oesc could stand upright. He took a deep breath and wiped his eyes before knocking at her door. The moments seemed long before there was an answer. Surely, he thought, on such a day she would stay indoors, although the wise-folk were not like other men, and if her magic required it, even a woman who was a wicce might brave the storm.

The weight of the spindle drew out the thread, spiraling ever round and round like the turning of the seasons, the lives of humankind. Half-tranced by the motion, Hæthwæge did not at first distinguish the knocking from the sound of the storm. It was the flare of emotion that got her attention, rather than the sound. In another moment she sensed a pain more of the mind than the body, and recognized, as one identifies the pungence of bruised pine needles on the wind, that Oesc was waiting there. She twisted the thread through the notch in the shaft of the spindle, and before the knocking could come again, opened the door.

As the boy started to ease around it, the wind gave him a sudden push that propelled him the rest of the way inside. He fell to his knees, blinking at the darkness.

"Child, you are wet through! Take off your shoes—you are already making a puddle on the floor."

The words were harsh, but the tone was not. Hæthwæge had been Oesc's nurse when he was little, and knew that he was used to her scoldings.

The fire flared in the draft, showing her a boy whose hands and feet seemed too big for his thin frame, his fair hair plastered dark and flat by the rain. She took up a cloak and wrapped it around him. He sank down on the three-legged stool beside the fire, nose wrinkling at the smell of wet wool as its heat began to absorb the moisture from his clothes.

Hæthwæge took up her spindle again and began, humming softly and watching him from the corners of her long eyes, to spin. Oesc eyed her curiously, knowing that a wicce's spinning was sometimes more than yarn.

"It is black wool and white," Hæthwæge answered his unvoiced question, "carded together. Opposites entwined balance the magic."

"What do you use it for?"

"For healing, mostly. I can use this yarn to take a sick man's measure and seal it with a drop of his blood. Then I bring it home and sing over it, and the magic works as well to heal as if the man were here."

To heal, or, of course, to harm. . . . Those hanks of yarn measured trust as well. In the dozen years she had lived with the Myrgings, Hæthwæge had treated almost everyone in the king's household. She glanced at the boxes and sacks crammed into the space above the boxbed and around the room, trying to remember how many twists of grey yarn she had stored there.

"Can you use the measure to change my grandfather's mood?" Oesc said suddenly.

The twirling spindle stilled. "Has he beaten you again?"

Oesc shook his head. "I almost wish he had. He talks like one doom-fated, and blames it on me. Is it true, Hæthwæge? Is that why my father never came back for me?"

For a moment she considered him. She had known that one day he would ask her this question, and understood as well how careful she must be in her reply, so as not to alter the twinings of wyrd and will.

"Doom-fated you are, and so is Eadguth, and so is every man, all the more when they are god-descended, the children of kings. Eadguth traces his line to Ing the son of Mannus, but your father's family comes of Woden himself. When you were born, I cast the runes, and told your grandfather that he must lift you in his arms and give you a name." She fed out more yarn from the distaff and set the spindle to turning once again.

Oesc nodded. No doubt he had heard the maids gossiping when they thought he could not hear. Until the head of the family accepted the child, it had no legal existence. Her throat ached with pity for the boy whom she had taken as an infant from his dying mother's side, sensing his potential, and impelled by her god. She could not leave it there.

"I told him that you were the hope of his house, that if he gave you to the wolves, it was not Octha's, but his own line that would fail. And yet I do not see you sitting in Eadguth's high seat here. You will have a kingdom, but it lies elsewhere.

The rune that goes before you is Sigel, the sun-road that leads to victory."

"Does my father know?" Oesc asked sullenly.

"A message was sent, but even I cannot tell if it ever found him. He has been fighting in Britannia. Perhaps he felt you would be safer here. And remember, the wandering shope who sang at last year's Yule feast told us that Uthir the British king had taken him prisoner."

"Perhaps he's dead . . ." muttered the boy.

Hæthwæge shook her head. "I have *seen* the two of you together. Your time will come."

Oesc sighed and let the blanket slip from his shoulders. His damp clothes were beginning to steam in the heat of the fire.

"Well, if it's not my fault, why does the king lay the blame on me?"

"Do not judge him too harshly. He is an old man. Since his own grandfather was slain by Offa of Angeln on the banks of the Fifeldor things have gone badly for the Myrgings. Now he sees his land being eaten away by flood and storm. When he goes to his fathers, the shopes will not sing that the harvests were good in his reign, and no one will lay offerings at his grave. Of all dooms, that one weighs hardest on a king."

As Hæthwæge played out more wool the thread broke suddenly, sending the spindle rolling across the floor toward the rune-carved spear that leaned against the wall, its head shrouded in a piece of cloth.

Hah, Old Man! she thought, *Has the time come for you to take a hand?* For a moment it seemed to her that a faint radiance played about the spear. A dozen years ago it had been entrusted to her, at the same time as her visions had instructed her to take service with the Myrging king.

Oesc bent to retrieve the spindle, his troubled gaze meeting her own, and carefully set it beside her stool.

"My grandfather hates me, and my father doesn't even know my name," he said bitterly. "Who will protect me?"

Hæthwæge twitched, feeling the first brush of power against her mind, subtle as the draught that stirred the fire.

"Look to the father of your fathers," she answered, her own voice sounding strange in her ears. Sight darkened as more words came to her. "Not the god of the land, but the one who hunts on the storm. He is coming—do you hear him?" She pointed northward, head cocked, listening.

The fire hissed, and above that came the sound of the rising wind, gusting through the branches of the trees beyond the palisade with a sound like surf on some distant shore. And beyond that . . . deep as her own heartbeat, the drumming of hooves.

Oesc's voice came to her as if from a great distance. "I don't understand—"

"Come—" The wicce rose from her stool. Without needing to think about it, she took the spear from its corner and started toward the door.

She could sense the boy's confusion, but to her spirit the hoofbeats were growing ever closer. If the boy's presence had been a scent on the breeze, what was coming now was the wind itself, a storm of terror and delight that could whirl consciousness itself away.

Hæthwæge pulled open the door. Wind swirled around her, insistent as a lover, plucking the pins from her hair. She felt the spearshaft vibrate in her hand and laughed.

I am coming, I am coming, my lord and my love. . . .

Laughing, she walked into the storm to meet the god, in that moment scarcely caring if the boy followed her.

Outside, dusk was falling fast. Oesc splashed through the puddles to catch up with Hæthwæge, raising his arm to shield his eyes from the driving rain. It came in flurries, as if the storm clouds were being broken up by the force of the wind. Head high, her hair streaming out behind her and with every moment growing darker in the rain, the wicce strode across the yard to the eastern gate. Oesc knew her as a woman just past middle life, her shoulders rounded and her body thickened by the years. But now she looked taller, and young, and by that he understood she was already in trance.

Below the mound that raised the village above the floods stretched a level land of wood and marsh and field, dotted and channeled by pond and stream. To the west, a little light shafted below the scudding clouds, touching the Law-Oak and the Field of Assembly where the tribal moots were held with a sickly yellow glow. In the distance he caught the pewter gleam of the sea. That last light gleamed on water that was closer as well, for from here he could see that the slow curve of the river had become a crescent grin of silver water that with every moment nibbled away more of the sodden fields. Monster-gate, they called it, but now it was not the etins who lived in the North Sea but the waters themselves that were devouring the land.

Beyond the palisade that sheltered the workshops and the king's hall, the long-houses of the villagers clustered closely along the slope. Oesc saw Hæthwæge disappearing between the last two and hurried to follow her. To the east stretched the home pasture, but on the west side, the marshes came nearly to the base of the mound. A narrow causeway, in this season half underwater, led through it. Picking his way carefully, Oesc followed the wisewoman. He could guess where she was heading now. In the heart of the boglands lay the dark pool where the Myrgings made their offerings under the staring eyes of the carven gods. Except at the time of sacrifice, most folk avoided it, but Oesc had gone there once or twice with Hæthwæge when she was gathering herbs.

Though the rain had diminished, by the time he caught up with the wicce, water from swinging branches had drenched him as thoroughly as the storm. Together they pushed through the screen of alder and willow that edged the pool, and at that moment the sun set and the clouds closed in once more, as if the mists of Nibhel had overwhelmed the world.

The wind stilled. Oesc shivered and drew closer to Hæthwæge. Reason told him that the horse whose hide and head were suspended on a framework of poles above the water was quite dead, but the water had risen, and it seemed now to be standing in the pool.

"What is happening?" Instinctively he dropped his voice to a whisper.

She turned, and this time she saw him, though her pupils were still dilated so that her eyes seemed to open on darkness.

"Wait." A tremor ran through her body. "Soon, he comes." With trembling fingers she unwound the cloth from about the head of the spear. The smoky stone glimmered in the shadows as if it shone with its own light.

Faint with distance, he heard a long horn-call. The raven feathers tied to the shaft fluttered in a sudden wind. Then came the hoofbeats. Men were riding on the wooden causeway that led through the marshes, he thought, but the sound grew rapidly louder. No horse could gallop safely on the rain-slick logs, nor could they cross other than in single file. What he heard now was the sound of many horses—or was it thunder? Was that the shrieking of the wind or the bitter answer of many horns?

He could not tell, but the sound sent a chill deep into his body. He crouched at Hæthwæge's feet, wishing he could burrow into the earth for protection. The animal heads spiked upon the offering stakes swayed frantically, and the horsehide heaved above the ruffled waters, straining toward the attenuated images of the gods.

In the next moment the tumult he had heard approaching was upon them. The last of the light had gone; he could make out only a confusion of shadows. Was it his imagination that shaped them into skeletal horses and wild riders who brandished spears or swords, or worse still, into wælcyriges, warhags riding slavering wolves with serpents for reins. He bit back a cry as a gust of wind sent the horsehide flapping into the air to join them.

He cowered beneath their keening until Hæthwæge's hand on his shoulder made him look up again. The horrors had passed. The shapes that swept above him now, limned in their own light, were of a nobler kind.

"Behold, son of Octha, your fathers of old—Wihtgils, Witta, Wehta, and their sires before them. . . ."

Shaking, Oesc got to his feet and raised his arm in salute. The names rolled on, but he could not hear them. All his being was focused on those luminous shadows, grim or kindly, that looked on him with a considering gaze as if deciding whether he was worthy to continue their line.

And then, though all around them the trees still bowed to the storm, the air above the pool grew heavy with a sense of presence. Oesc remained standing, but he shut his eyes tightly. Whatever was coming now was something he was not yet ready to see. But he could not keep from hearing, though he never knew, then or thereafter, if the words had come to his mind or his ears.

"So this is the boy—" a deep voice seemed to say.

"Since his birth I have warded him," Hæthwæge answered. "When will the future I foretold for him come to be?"

"That is Verdandi's business. But when that time comes, he will have to choose . . ."

"What are his choices?"

"To stay here and live long in a dying land, or to risk all across the water. . . ."

"But the runes spoke of victory—" the wicce began. That other voice interrupted her.

"To endure the turning of the seasons is as much a victory as death in battle. The one is the path of Ingvi, but the other is mine. If he chooses Me his name shall be remembered in a new land, and he shall sire kings."

"Is that your will, lord?" Now it was Hæthwæge's voice that trembled.

"I will what shall be, but it is not for me to choose how it shall come to pass—that lies with the boy, and with you."

Oesc had the abrupt sense of being the focus of attention, like a mouse trapped between a wolf's paws. He scrunched his eyes shut even more tightly. For a moment more he was held, then the pressure was released with a hint of laughter.

"I do not force you," came that whisper from within, *"but the Norns will force the choice upon you, my son, and soon."*

"I have chosen you, High One, since I was young—" Hæthwæge said then.

"It is so, nor have I ever been far away."

If there was more, it was not meant for Oesc's ears. He sank down at the woman's feet, and only afterward, when the god and those he led had passed, did he realize that his face was wet, not with rain, but with tears.

The wood seemed very silent. Oesc stood up, wiping his eyes. Then he stiffened, hearing once more the sounds of hoofbeats and horns.

But this was no spectral hunt—he could tell the difference

now. Those were mortal horses whose hoofbeats he heard ringing on the wet logs, and mortal lungs behind those plaintive horns.

"There are riders, Hæthwæge! Riders on the causeway!" he exclaimed. "Hurry, we must get back to the hall."

She nodded, shrouding the spearhead once more, and he saw her face still luminous with memory. But as she turned her awareness back to the human world the lines deepened in her skin and she became merely mortal once more.

"So, it has begun. . . ."

Oesc peered through the door to the great hall, which only this morning had seemed so huge and empty. Now it was filled with men clad in well-worn war-gear and battered finery, with a liberal splashing of mud over all. The folk who served the hall were bustling around them, taking wet cloaks away and bringing beakers of heated ale.

"May Freo bring you blessings," said their leader, accepting a horn of mead from Æbbe, the king's widowed sister, who had ruled his household as long as Oesc could remember. He must have been handsome once, thought the boy, but now one eyelid drooped and the left side of his face was stiffened by a long scar.

"But where is your neice, Æbbe? Should it not be she who gives the welcome?"

"There is no other Lady in this hall," said the woman, taking a step backward. "And what unholy wight has taught you my name?"

The stranger frowned. "Did Hildeguth remarry, then? I suppose she thought I was dead—I've thought I was dead a few times myself, these past years!" His hand moved to touch his scar. "Have I changed so much, Æbbe, that even you don't know me?"

"It is my daughter who is dead," came a harsh voice from the far end of the hall, "killed by the seed you planted in her belly, and if you had not already claimed guest-right I would drive you from my door!" Leaning on his staff, Eadguth limped forward to his high seat and took his place there.

Oesc stared from one to the other, aware of every heartbeat

that shook his chest, understanding without quite believing who the newcomer must be.

Octha, son of Hengest . . . his father.

Octha straightened, the muscles of his face stiffening into a battle-mask. "And the child?" he asked in a still voice. "Did it die too?"

"Shall I tell you it died in the womb?" Eadguth spat, "or that I set it out upon the heath for the wolves?"

"You shall tell him the truth, old man," said Hæthwæge, gripping Oesc by the shoulder and pushing him before her into the light of the fire. "Sore though it grieved you, you have reared up his son!"

For a moment longer the warrior's glance clashed with that of the king. Then Octha turned, his face changing as he looked at the boy.

"Come here—"

With feet that did not seem his own Oesc stepped forward. Octha knelt and gripped the boy's face between callused hands. After a moment he swallowed.

"You have your mother's eyes . . ."

Oesc nodded. Hæthwæge had told him so.

"But I see Hengest in your brow . . . What do they call you?"

"I am Oesc, son of Octha—" His voice wavered only a little.

"My son!"

Powerful arms closed around him; Oesc smelled horse, and wet wool, and the strong scent of the man. It was very strange. Not so long ago, Woden had also called him son—from being fatherless he seemed suddenly over-supplied with kin. He took a deep breath as Octha let him go.

"I am going back to Britannia, where the cows grow fat in green pastures and apples hang heavy on the bough. Will you come with me?"

Soon, Woden had told him, he would have to choose. Oesc looked into his father's storm-grey eyes, but when he spoke, he knew he was answering the god.

"Yes, father, I will come."

*   *   *

Since Octha's arrival three days had passed. The storm had moved on, but on the Field of Assembly scattered pools mirrored the blue sky. Only a few rags of cloud still clung to the southeastern heavens. As the people gathered, the green grass was being trampled to a muddy brown. But perhaps it would not matter, thought Oesc as he watched them from his place at his father's side. If the moot voted to follow Octha over the sea, the cattle would be slaughtered or sold and there would be no need for pastureland.

The thought awakened an anxious flutter in his belly. He knew there were other lands, for he had heard the shopes and gleemen sing of them, but Eadguth's hall was the center of his world. Most of the Myrgings had gathered, women and children forming a larger ring around the chieftains and heads of families. He looked around him for Hæthwæge, then remembered that the wicce had told him she had no need to watch. She had already seen this wyrd when she cast the runes.

Why did she not inform Eadguth, then, and save us all the trouble of deciding? he wondered, but as the wisewoman had often told him, you might predict the sun's rising, but you had to wait for it to happen just the same.

A bench had been placed for the king beneath the oak tree. His *witan*, the tribal elders, sat around him. Sunlight glowing through the young leaves dappled his white hair. Eadguth Gamol, they called him, Eadguth the Old, for of all the kings of the north, only Healfdene of Sillende had reigned longer.

His other grandfather, Hengest, was old too, thought Oesc. But he ruled a confederation of war-bands, like the sea-kings of Frisia. Eadguth was bred and bound through many fathers to his kingship and his land.

A murmur ran through the crowd as Geflaf, leader of the king's sword-thanes, stepped forward. He raised a great silver-mounted horn to his lips and blew, and as its echoes faded, the people also became still.

"Hear, ye chieftains and people of the Myrgings here assembled. A stranger, Octha son of Hengest, has come among us. The witan has called you to hear and consider his words."

"He is an Anglian of royal kin, and our enemy!" cried the chieftain of one of the older Myrging clans.

"He is not of the kin of Offa the king-slayer, but a lesser line, and has never borne arms against us," came the reply.

"Our kin serve in his father's war-band," said one of the Jutes who had settled among the Myrgings, taking up farm-steads left vacant after the Anglian wars. "Let us hear what he has to say."

For a little longer the clamor continued, but eventually it became clear that the mood of the moot was in Octha's favor.

Another murmur arose as he stepped forward, Oesc at his side. By now, of course, everyone had heard the rumors that the mysterious father of their Lady's son had reappeared. Oesc hung back as he realized that they were staring at him as well, but Octha's grip was firm.

He is using me to show them he is not an enemy, the boy realized suddenly, and allowed himself to be pulled along. For most of his short life he had been at best an embarrassment to his mother's kin; to stand forth before the people as one with a right to honor seemed very strange. For the first time, it came to him that he too might one day be a king.

"Men of the Myrgings!" cried Octha, "and all of you—be you Jute or Saxon or Frank, who by marriage or alliance have become part of this tribe. I come here as your ally, for it was a princess of your people who gave me my son!"

Someone started a cheer, and Oesc felt the hot color rise in his cheeks.

"Then why have you waited till now to claim him?" came another voice.

"There's many a man who goes off to war childless and returns to learn he has an heir. For ten winters I have battled in Britannia; I have slain many princes of their people, and cut down those who thought themselves the heirs of Rome. At first we fought for treasure, but now we fight for land. The British have little strength to resist us—their king is a sick man, and he has no son. The land lies undefended, ripe for the taking. To hold that earth men must till it, and so I come to you.

"Follow me to Britannia—bring your wives and your children. Bring your axes and your ploughs."

"Why should we abandon the hearths of our mothers and the howes where our fathers lie?" came the cry.

"Because this land is drowning!" responded Octha. "Look around you—the fields are blighted by bad weather and your cattle are dying. Each year more of your shores are eaten by the sea. In Britannia there are wide fields, fruitful and flourishing—good harvests of oat crops and broad barley-crops, white fields of wheat-crops and all that grows in Middle Earth."

"But they are not *our* fields. Will they bear for us if we do not know the names of the wights that dwell there?"

"Those fields have borne fruit for all the tribes the Romans settled in that land," said Octha. "Warriors from Iberia and Sarmatia and Gallia and other lands who took up farming after their time in the legions was done. Our cousins the Franks get good crops from the lands they have won in Gallia. Till the fields and make the offerings, and when your time comes, lay your bones in the soil. By blood and toil shall we claim Britannia and make it our own."

"We will go!" said one of the Jutish chieftains, a man called Hæsta. "There are men of my blood already in Hengest's warband. They have said that Cantuware is a land of good soil and good grazing, where the cows give milk thrice a day at this time of year."

"And it breeds good fighters—" an older man spoke up, lifting an arm scarred and twisted by an old wound. "In my youth I too have been to Britannia, but all I got there was steel. It is well enough for warriors to take such chances, but I will not risk my family in a land whose native folk are awakening at last, determined to get back their own."

"Better to die by steel than starvation!" exclaimed another, and suddenly everyone was arguing.

"What says Eadguth?" someone cried at last. "What is the word of the Myrging king?"

Slowly, silence fell. When it was quite still, the thrall Cubba, who was even older than the king, assisted Eadguth to unfold his gaunt frame from the chair. The king came forward, leaning on his staff. For a few moments he looked around him, and those who had cried the loudest for emigration found it hard to meet his eyes.

"The gods have given me long life. For more than forty winters I have been your king. . . ." His voice did not seem loud, but it carried.

"In those years I have seen many things. I have seen five summers when the rains were so scant that the river sank down till its banks gaped like toothless jaws. That time ended. So will this. I have seen blizzards that heaped snow halfway up the walls and held us prisoner from one moon to the next. That time ended—this will too. And I have seen harvests so plentiful we had not the barns to store it all. And those times also came to an end. You cry out now like children who cannot go out to play because of the rain. And I say to you, neither will this time last."

He spoke slowly, a kindly grandfather chiding willful boys, and here and there a man would hang his head with a shamefaced grin.

"A man's mood changes, sometimes happy and sometimes sorrowful. Our holy mother earth has also her moods and changes. Will you desert her because now she is weeping? For men who have been uprooted from their homelands perhaps it is true that one land is as good as the next. But the Myrgings have been here since Mannus himself walked the earth. We are a free land and a free people, bound only to this soil."

Carefully, Eadguth bent and grasped a handful of muddy earth. He held it high, and the water squeezed out between his fingers and ran like brown blood down his hand.

My mother's bones lie in this earth, thought Oesc. *If I leave here, I will have lost her entirely.* But his father still stood beside him, and his bones were clad in warm and living flesh.

"Will you leave this holy earth, blessed by the blood of your fathers, for an alien land? Perhaps, as Octha says, in time it will accept you. But I say this—it will not be in your time, nor in that of your children. Stay, men of the Myrgings and those whom we have welcomed here. Stay, and defend the land that has nourished you."

Some of the men knelt in reverence and set their hands on the wet grass, but others were still standing, brows bent in thought.

Geflaf stepped forward once more. "The Myrging-king has spoken. Go now, carls and eorls, free men of our nation. Speak together, and when the sun is sinking toward the sea, return and say what your decision will be."

He turned away, and the men drew into knots and clusters as they began their debate.

"What now?" asked Octha, watching King Eadguth make his way slowly back toward the hall.

"Now we wait," answered Geflaf. He also was watching his king, and Oesc saw sorrow in his gaze.

That day seemed very long to Oesc, longer even than the day before the Midsummer festival. He tried to fill it by showing his father where Hildeguth was buried, and the best place to catch fish below the whirlpool, and even the god-images in the sacred bog, but he could tell that Octha's attention was elsewhere. And as the sun drove her wain across the fields of the sky his distraction grew, until the time came to turn their steps back toward the great oak tree.

Away to the west the sky was glowing in shades of amber and rose. Broad bands of light rayed out from the setting sun as if showing the way to Britannia. But a great peace lay on the Myrging lands. Even the sea lay still, its waters a lucent blue, and each leaf and blade of grass seemed to have caught the sunset's gold. Did it seem so fair, wondered Oesc, because he might soon be leaving it? Then he looked again and thought, *But perhaps we will not be going. It is too beautiful. On such an evening, no one could make the choice to go.*

Once more King Eadguth came forth and sat in his carven chair, gazing at his people with hooded eyes. Once more the people gathered around the great tree.

"Men of the Myrgings," said Geflaf when they were quiet. "The sun has finished her course and it is time to choose our own. Are you ready to decide?"

"Aye," came the response from many voices.

"Then let the leaders of your clans and families stand forth and say your will."

Hæsta was first to step out from the crowd.

"I speak for the Jutes who dwell along the Fifeldor. For a generation we have guarded your northern border. We do not fear fighting. But the fields will not bear for us. We vote to seek the new lands across the sea."

There was a murmur at that, for the Jutes made up a sizable portion of their fighting men. A Myrging thane came forward next, and said that he would stay by his king. One by one others followed and spoke the will of their clans. And though there were some who swore to stay in the Myrging homeland, it became clear that those who had been convinced by Octha's words were in the majority.

"I would stay, but I see the choice being made for me," said one farmer, whose rich fields lay inland, away from the sea. "We cannot stop those who decide to leave us, and how can we defend ourselves against our enemies if only a tithe remain?"

A mutter of agreement swept through the people, and after that most of the men who stepped forward said that they would follow Octha. Now, only a few chieftains from the oldest families spoke for staying, and Eadguth's sworn swordthanes, who said that while he lived, they would remain by their king.

Geflaf turned to his lord with troubled gaze.

"My king, the will of the moot is clear. Will you not change your mind and agree to lead us to the new land?"

Eadguth rose from his chair and set his hand against the rough bark of the great tree.

"Will you uproot this oak and carry it over the sea?" His voice grated painfully. "It is too old, too deeply rooted, and so am I. Go if you will—I cannot prevent you. I will remain with my land."

Oesc looked at his grandfather and felt a tremor beneath his heart as if someone had struck him there. *He looks like a dead man.* Suddenly he wanted to run to the old man as he had when he was little, before he understood why Eadguth hated him. But his father's hand was on his shoulder, and he did not move.

Once more Eadguth's dark gaze passed over his people, then he turned and started back toward his hall. His house-thanes fell in behind him, but their faces were grim.

But those who had voted to go with Octha pressed around him, clamoring with questions about the new land.

Oesc woke from a nightmare, fighting for breath. The bed-clothes were strangling him—he fought free and lay gasping. In the hall, his own harsh breaths were the only sound, but outside he could hear birdsong. It must be dawn, he thought, blinking. Through the parted curtains of his bed-closet he glimpsed a faint glow from the long hearth and beyond it a colder light. He pulled back the curtains and looked out into the hall.

Along the hearth he could see the humped shapes of sleeping men. But beyond them, the little side door stood open. What clumsy thrall, he wondered, had left it so? Æbbe, who always rose early to supervise the thralls as they got break-fast, would have a thing or two to say about that when she knew.

But now he was curious. Who had gone out so early? He pulled his tunic over his head and tied on his shoes, and then, because the air was brisk, took his cloak from its peg as well. Silently he made his way between the sleeping men and sought the door.

Beyond the threshold the muddy ground showed many footprints, dusted by a light frost that was already melting in the growing light. But across that sparkling veil two sets of tracks showed clearly, and the larger prints were punctuated by the round mark of a staff. For a long moment Oesc stared, a cold feeling growing in his belly.

"Close the door, boy," came Æbbe's voice behind him. "You are letting in the cold."

"Æbbe—" he said, turning, "why has the king gone out so early?"

"What do you mean, child? Old men sleep late—he is in his bed still!"

"Look, are not those his footprints? Where did he go?"

For a moment she stared over his shoulder at the marked ground, and then, without a word, hurried back into the hall. Oesc sank down on a bench, shivering, but it was not from the cold. In a few moments the old woman returned with Byrhtwold and Æthelhere behind her. When they started out across the yard, Oesc followed.

The trail led toward Hæthwæge's hut, and when they picked it up again, there were three sets of footprints, one of them a woman's. Near the side gate they lost the trace, but the young warrior who guarded it, confronted with his king's senior thanes, confessed that his lord had passed through just as the first pallor that precedes the dawn was brightening the sky. The thrall Cubba was with him, and the wisewoman.

"I thought they were going out to make some offering to the gods. He told me to keep silence and stay at my post," said the warrior, "but my shift is almost over, and surely I do not break my oath to tell *you*. . . ."

"No doubt that is it," said Æbbe with a sigh. "I will go back to the kitchen—the king will be wanting his breakfast when he returns."

"I will go out to meet him," said Æthelhere. "It is not right for the lord of the Myrgings to go about without an escort."

Byrhtwold nodded, and when they passed through the gate, Oesc followed the two thanes down the hill.

Here and there a scar upon the frosted grass marked the trail. It led toward the Law Oak. As they came around the edge of the woods they stopped short, staring, for an untimely fruit was dangling from the oak tree's limbs.

It was King Eadguth's body that was hanging there. Blood from a rent beneath his breast had stained his tunic, and the thrall Cubba lay below him, a knife in his hand and blood from his slashed throat soaking the ground. *An ætheling can look on anything, even his doom,*" Eadguth had once told him, but after Oesc had taken one look at his grandfather's purpled face and staring eyes, he fixed his gaze firmly upon the ground.

"Ah, my dear lord," said Æthelhere, shaking his head. "This is ill done, to go before me with only this thrall to escort you. Still I think your start is not so great I cannot overtake you."

"Why did he do this?" asked Byrhtwold. "We would have stood by him to his life's end."

"And so you have done—" came another voice. They turned, and saw that Hæthwæge was standing there, leaning on a staff whose top was swathed in a blue cloth. "Do you not understand? He had no son to follow him, and those who vowed to stay here are too few to defend the land. By his death Eadguth has freed them from their oaths and made offering to Woden for their protection. This was a noble sacrifice."

"By the knife of a thrall?" asked Byrhtwold.

Hæthwæge shook her head. "Cubba took his own life, but Eadguth's blood was shed by Woden's own spear." She lifted her staff, and Oesc's skin pebbled as he recognized the rune-carved shaft beneath the wrappings.

"This is the last and greatest act of a king," said Æthelhere, "to give his breath to the god and his blood to the land that his people may live."

VERVLAMIVM

A.D. 473

A DEAD HORSE LAY STIFF BESIDE THE ROAD. THE RAVENS, BUSY at their feasting, waited until the approaching riders were upon them before fluttering aside, cawing their mockery. Beyond them the Roman road ran straight southwards, where a thin haze of smoke stained the pale morning sky.

"We move from before your feet," they seemed to say, "but one day you will be our meat!"

Oesc suppressed a shiver; then his mare, scenting the carrion, tossed her head, and the boy reined her sharply in. His grandfather in the old country had not had the wealth to give him a pony, and in any case it was not the tradition of his people to fight mounted. But Britannia was a large island, and in the three years since Octha had brought him across the sea it seemed to Oesc they had ridden over most of the eastern half that the Angles and the Saxons and the Jutes and tag ends of other tribes were making their own. Through necessity, he had become an adequate horseman. He lifted his chin and straightened his shoulders in unconscious imitation of his father, sitting his big grey easily at the head of the column.

Most of the Myrgings had been settled in Cantuware, along with the Jutes and Frisians and others who had answered Hengest's call. But the best of the warriors had left the rich fields of the south coast, settled for a generation already by men of the tribes, to ride north with Octha, where there were new and perhaps even richer lands to be won.

Hengest had wanted the boy to stay with him in Cantu-ware, but there had been no question, really, what Oesc would choose. He had spent most of his short life mewed up with one grandfather, and the other was past eighty, so ancient that many assumed he must be dead by now. No boy could resist the chance to ride with the men and share their glory. It was only sometimes in the night that he regretted the well-built hall and the peaceful fields of his homeland, and the gulls soaring over a sea that glittered with a golden treasure no Roman hoard could match in the light of the setting sun.

Oesc wondered now if he had made the right decision. Men of the German tongue held half the south and the fenlands on the eastern shore, and three years of campaigning had made the beginnings of an Anglian realm south of Eboracum. Only the valley of the Tamesis still separated the English lands. But Leudonus of Alba, having married the British king's daughter, had thrown all his strength into the reconquest of the north, and six days since, had brought the Saxons to battle on the banks of the Abus, and won.

Oesc kicked the mare's stout sides and drew up beside Colgrin, an Anglian who with the Jutish Baldulf was second only to his father in the band.

"Have the scouts come in? Is Leudonus following?" He glanced back, where the Saxon column, dissolving into its own dust, seemed to extend all the way back to Eboracum. Hæthwæge was back there somewhere, in the wagons with the wounded. Beyond them storm-clouds hung heavy in the sky.

Colgrin shook his head, the grey hair hacked short where they had bandaged a slash from a British sword. "Nay, lad, he will not catch us—we gave him too sound a savaging."

"But he is following . . ." Oesc repeated.

"Not yet . . ." the older man admitted. "There's no need to fret. By the time his men can march, we'll be safe behind Verulamium's stout walls."

"How long till we get there?"

Colgrin pointed to blue smudge that lay across the road on the horizon. "Verulamium lies just beyond those hills."

Oesc squinted ahead, and then, as a breath of cool air touched his cheek, looked back again. The curdled clouds were rolling after them, a visible expression of Leudonus' wrath. If the storm hit before they reached shelter the wounded would suffer. He looked at his father's straight back, frowning.

Colgrin, following his glance, sighed. "Not even the greatest of leaders can make the best decision always. And sometimes all choices are flawed. Octha thinks like a warrior, and takes a warrior's chances. Woden loves a brave man, and will give him victory."

"I know...." Oesc nodded, but for the first time it occurred to him to wonder in what way the choices of a warleader might differ from those of a king. The wind blew once more, ruffling his pale hair, and with it came the first spatterings of rain.

The gates of Verulamium were open. Oesc, watching from the walkway atop the old Roman wall, gazed past the tower of the gatehouse to the British army encamped outside. But it was not Leudonus and his blood-stained veterans who were beseiging them. The forces outside the gate—dark-haired Romans in their grandfathers' breastplates or bright-haired British with checkered mantles over their mail, were men of the south and west, under the command of their dying king.

Octha's face had darkened when he heard that Uthir had come against him. He remembered his captivity in the Tower. And then he had told them to unbar and open the great gates that guarded the western route into the town.

"Why not just send Uthir an invitation to charge through?" Baldulf had exclaimed when Octha gave the order.

"That is what I am doing," answered Octha, grinning through his mustaches. "Or did you fancy spending the winter starving behind these walls? Inside the town they will not be able to use their horses, and we can overwhelm them."

"If they come—" said Colgrin.

"If they do not, it will not matter whether the gates are open or closed!"

And Oesc had heard the sharp silence, and then Colgrin's explosive laugh. But the British army, nestled in tent and brush shelter around the city, neither attacked nor lifted the seige.

As he had every day since the British came, Oesc watched them from the guard tower, curious, after all the stories he had heard, about this enemy. Sometimes the wind carried the swift, lilting gabble of the British speech, or the more sonorous cadences of Latin, but mostly he learned by watching. He had become accustomed to the diversity of the Saxon forces, composed of men from all the tribes of the north. But these Britons were more varied still, and in their faces he saw the mosaic, in miniature, that was the Empire.

To the Saxons, they were an accustomed and worthy enemy, but from time to time Oesc, seeing the British king being carried through the camp, would remember how his other grandfather had clung to his land, and feel ashamed. But when he saw his father again the feeling passed. Octha, his skin ripened to bronze by the weather and his body honed to muscle and sinew by the summer's campaigning, was now at the height of his powers, as great a hero as Sigfrid Fafnarsbane, of whom the shopes liked to sing.

Eadguth had been a landking, bound, blood and bone, to his native soil. Octha son of Hengest was a conqueror.

That night the Saxon chieftains met in the dining room, its walls painted in red ochre edged by a design of twining vines, of the house where once Catraut, the British prince who had been the city's chief magistrate, had entertained his peers. Its owner was fled long since—Oesc, bringing in more ale, wondered if he might be even now in Uthir's camp, gazing longingly toward the walls that hid his home. Most of the notable men of the town had escaped, or been killed when the Saxons marched in. But Octha had the authority to forbid looting, and if the common people had not accepted the warriors billeted among them with gladness, neither did they show active hostility.

"How long will we stay cooped up here?" asked one of the

younger chieftains. "If we wait too long, Leudonus will come to his good-father's aid!"

"If he does so, I will close the gates—" The golden torque around Octha's neck glinted as he laughed. "But I do not think the British will maintain the seige so long."

"It is true. The British king is a sick man," said Baldulf thoughtfully. "And a military camp is no good place for healing."

"And unless you count Leudonus, he has no heir," said one of the others. "When Uthir dies, the British will be easy prey."

"Easy prey?" exclaimed Colgrin. "Is that the word of a warrior? The weaker Uthir becomes, the less honor there will be in defeating him. I say we should attack them now . . ."

But Octha was looking at the doorway, where Hæthwæge had appeared. "I called her—" He answered the question in the chieftains' eyes. "In the old days, the priestesses always went with the warriors. Hæthwæge is alone, but she was trained by the Walkyriun. Sit—" he gestured toward one of the benches, and then to his son, "bring her ale."

Hæthwæge accepted a sip from the cream-colored clay cup, but she did not sit down. Oesc's words of greeting stuck in his throat. He had grown too accustomed to her care for him, he thought, and forgotten what she was. Her eyes were wide and lightless, as if she had fared halfway down the road to the Otherworld already. As always when she worked magic, her face seemed simultaneously ancient and young.

"Wise One," Octha said softly, "our enemies surround us. Speak to the spirits and give us good counsel."

"I must have a high place . . ." she whispered.

Octha nodded soberly. "It shall be so—" He gestured to the others. Silent now, they rose, and as they moved down the empty street Oesc followed them.

Hæthwæge stared up at the dark bulk of the gatehouse of Verulamium, stark against the sky, its towers looming to either side of the arched gateway. The night was very still. It was only within that she sensed the slow stirring of power.

Somewhere not too far away someone was working magic—perhaps it was the British witega they called Merlin.

They say you are strong to foretell the future, gealdor crafty. But I too am witege, and tomorrow you shall see that I too can sing battle spells. She moved into the darkness of the doorway, frowning. For a moment her questing spirit had touched something stronger and sharper, like the mind of a god.

The planks of the stairway rang hollow as they climbed, feeling their way along the curving wall, but when they emerged at the top they breathed freely beneath the starry vault of the heavens. To one side glimmered the lamps of the city and on the other the watchfires of their enemy glowed like red eyes in the darkness. A faint breeze stirred men's hair as if the night were breathing.

Hæthwæge sank down upon the bench beneath the parapet and pulled down her veil. One by one, the warriors sat on the cold stone walkway until only Octha remained standing, his speech becoming the chant of ritual.

"Wicce, hear me . . . to this high place I have brought thee. From here thou mayest soar between the worlds."

"This deed I will dare," her own voice came hoarse to her ears, "but the way is long and weary. It is your prayers I carry—let your power carry me. . . ."

Octha nodded, and began to strike the palms of his hands rhythmically against his thighs. The other men followed his example, swaying gently as the soft vibration pulsed in the air.

> "Wicce, Woruld-Aesce ymbwend,
> Wisdom innan thin hyde gewinn.
> Wicce . . . Wicce . . ."

The word, repeated, became part of the soft susuration of flesh on cloth, a whisper of sound that lifted the hair and the spirit and whirled them away to journey around the World-tree to the worlds it contained and gain access to the wisdom they held. *Wicce, to the Word-Ash win . . . Wisdom, shape-strong, find within. . . .*

Hæthwæge took a deep breath, and then another, letting her limbs relax against the parapet. Awareness extended into the stones, all the way down to the foundations of the tower and then back up again. As her consciousness changed she fancied she could feel it swaying, even though there was only a little wind. She focused on the singing, and with each repetition felt the links between body and spirit loosen, until like a boat that has slipped its mooring, she fell inward and away.

Images whirled past her—the tower and the army encamped around it, the undulating bands of field and forest, still under starshine, with the rivers, black and shining, veining the land. Then these too dimmed, and there was only the great plain of Middle Earth, and in its midst the huge column of the Worldtree, its radiant branches brushing the skies.

But the will that carried her drew her downward, diving into darkness beneath one of the three great roots of the Tree. Around and around her spirit spiraled, past mist and shadows, past the roots of great mountains where rushed the icy streams. Through the heat of Muspel's fires she journeyed, and sped by the cool grey mirror that was the Well of Wyrd. And still her way led downward, around, and deeper within, until she saw the great gorge of the worldriver and the last bridge, and beyond it the land where the Dark Lady rules and the apples of the blessed and the wild hemlock grow.

One final gate remained to pass. She dropped into darkness, and for a time beyond time, knew no more.

A long time later, it seemed, she became aware of a quiet voice calling her name. Unwillingly she forced her mind to focus. It was Octha, using the same calm voice with which he commanded his warriors.

"Wise One, say then, what dost thou see?"

At the words, images began to dislimn from the darkness. She struggled to make her lips form an answer.

"A dark plain, and a dark lake, and a black swan swimming . . ." she murmured, her voice sounding thready with distance. "My raven flies before me, and around me glimmer the pale faces of those who have gone before."

"Our enemies surround us. How shall we bring them to battle?"

In the pause that followed, her breathing came and went like the wind, fluttering the fabric of the veil. The scene before her blurred. There was still water, but in its midst now she could make out an island. From the woods that surrounded it she could hear the yammering of hounds, and in another moment she saw them, leaping up and down on the shore. What were they barking at? She strained to see, and presently became aware that she was speaking once more.

"I see a wolf brought to bay upon an island. The dogs wait on the shore. They will not swim across to meet the wolf's sharp fangs. He gazes around him and sees where the circle is weakest—where the old pack-leader watches—there he will make his fight." She drew a deep breath. "Wilt thou know more?"

"Will the British king die?"

"All men die!" the answer came to her immediately. "And this one is half-dead already."

"And will our sons inherit the land?" Octha added then.

Hæthwæge took a deep breath, releasing the vision, observing the ebb and flow of image until at last there came something she could put into words.

"I see the wolf and the dog running in one pack . . ." more visions came to her ". . . I see the wheat crop and the barley crop growing in one field . . . his seed shall rule men's hearts, but yours will rule the land. . . ."

While they were still chewing on that answer, another voice, that she recognized as Baldulf's, spoke.

"And what about the battle?"

Hæthwæge shivered violently, her awareness battered and reeling beneath the onrush of vision. Ravens were fighting—not the friendly presence that was her own spirit guide, but feathered forms, huge and terrible, whose cries scored the soul.

"I see the Raven of Battle rising, men die when she screams. But Woden sends Hyge and Mynd against her; men battle as the god and the goddess strive. . . ." Her spirit soared with the battling birds.

Then with a suddenness that seared her vision, the scene was split by a Sword of Light. Hæthwæge stiffened, features contorting. For a moment she glimpsed the figure that gripped it in all His glory. "Tir comes, Tir comes! Beware the Sword of War!"

Light and darkness crashed together around her and with it vision and consciousness were swept away.

When she could hear once more, she realized that she was lying on the cold stone of the walkway, her head resting on Octha's arm.

"Hæthwæge," he said softly, "do you hear me? Come forth from the dark plain and the dark lake. Return to Middle Earth—in Woden's name I summon you! Your raven will show you the way. Come to my calling until you can feel the night air on your skin and the bench beneath you. Come then . . . come. . . ."

With a murmur of soft speech, as if he were gentling a fractious mare, Octha continued to call her. Hæthwæge forced herself to breathe, to reconstruct the image of the dark lake and to send forth the inner call that would bring her raven to her side. She wanted only to float in the friendly darkness, but Octha's voice was insistent, and so, painfully, she moved to the gate, and image by image, summoned the landmarks of the spirit that would show her the way home.

By the time she had recovered control of her limbs and was able to sit up again, her memories were fading.

"What is it?" she asked, looking at the grim faces around her. "What did I say?"

"You called out to Tir, and told us," said Baldulf, "to beware the Sword of War."

For a moment she closed her eyes. "I remember," she said finally, "it blazed in the sun."

"What does it mean?" Octha asked then.

"I give you vision," answered the wisewoman tartly. "It is for you to find the meaning." Then a fragment of memory came to her. "But in the land of the Huns, I have heard, there were once great smiths who forged seven magic swords for the god of war."

"There are no Huns here," said Colgrin.

"Perhaps not. But there are swords. Make an offering to Tir before you fight, and perhaps he will spare you."

"Tir is a god of justice, not mercy," muttered one of the men, but Hæthwæge shook her head and would say no more.

The earth trembled beneath the tread of the warriors as the Saxon army marched out to meet its foe. Their footsteps rang hollow from the great arch of the gate and pigeons fluttered screaming from the cornices. Then five hundred spear butts smote as many shields, and thunder leaped from earth to heaven. Oesc, a helm drawn down to hide his features and a tattered cloak concealing his lack of armor, felt himself become one with the men who were crowding through the gate. The driving rhythm overwhelmed thought and hearing, and with it, the fear that even now his father might somehow discover he had disobeyed and send him back.

Then they were through the gate, and the crush eased as men began to spread out into the wedge formation called the Boar's Head. Faint through the thunder he could hear the blare of British trumpets, then the irregular drumming of hoofbeats blurred the rhythm of spear and shield. In the next moment the British horsemen struck the Saxon line, and the thunder gave way to the clash of steel.

Oesc was lifted off his feet for a moment as the shock of the charge drove the man on his left against him. Then the Saxons steadied, spears bristling outwards, and began to drive forward against the foe. Oesc got his breath back just as a horseman in a scarlet cloak crashed through. He made a clumsy sweep out and heard the horse scream. Then another man thrust upward and the rider fell, blood spraying red around him.

The boy stared, but there was no time to worry about his reaction. Another enemy, dismounted, was slashing wildly with a long Roman cavalry spatha; a Saxon fell, then Oesc jabbed and caught the blade with his spear. The impact jarred down the shaft, almost knocking him over, but in the next moment two warriors speared the Briton through the body and he went down.

A figure in Roman armor loomed up before him and he thrust, then stared in horror as his point sank in and the man's face contorted in agony. Oesc jerked the spear free, shuddering. Again and again his swordmaster had told him that in battle there was no time for thinking. He had never explained that no sane man would want to think about what his blade was doing as it tore through flesh and bone.

Then another figure lurched towards him, and without his will he turned, taking the attack on his shield and jabbing back until his foe fell or the tide of battle tore him away, he never knew which, and the next enemy came on.

Some endless time later, a scream from overhead recalled him to himself. His spear had broken, and the short seax was in his hand. All around him, Saxon warriors were staring upward, their arms faltering as the raven wheeled above them, alternately black and white as the sunlight flared from its wings. He saw the litter in which the British king had been carried to the battlefield, and near it his father, staring upward with a face as anguished as his own.

But the British returned to the attack with courage renewed. "Cathubodva, Cathubodva, Raven of Battle," they cried.

Oesc yelped at the sting as a spear tip sliced across his shoulder and got his shield back up, striving to shut out that dreadful keening cry. The enemy spear struck again and he felt the wood begin to crack, then two shadows flickered past and it seemed to him he heard a deep voice crying—

"Stand fast, son of Woden, and you shall have the victory!"

Wind swirled in the dust of the battlefield; suddenly the air had a bite that tingled through the veins. Now it was his enemy who paused. Oesc glanced up and saw two smaller, darker, ravens, engaging the first one in a deadly aerial dance. *Hyge and Mynd*—he thought. *Hæthwæge has called on the god!*

The British raven screamed her fury, and the two attackers replied, and as those cries clashed in the heavens, to Oesc's blurred vision his opponent was revealed as a monster, the foulest of etin-kin. The burning in his belly erupted in a scream of fury, and casting away both seax and shield, he leaped upon his foe.

It was a Sword of Light, searing through mind and vision, that separated man from monster and mind from madness. When Oesc came to himself he was on his hands and knees, with the iron taste of blood in his mouth and his chest and arms splattered with gore. Guts roiling, he struggled to his feet. All around him those who could still stand were doing likewise. Only near Uthir's litter were men still fighting, but as Oesc stumbled towards it, an arc of brightness seared his vision once more.

For a moment he saw, red against the radiance, a figure who rose from the ruins of the horse-litter, wielding in his single hand a Sword whose stroke scythed down all foes within a radius of ten yards. Then the light flared beyond his strength to bear it. Sobbing, he sank to his knees, arm raised to shield his eyes from that deadly flame.

And then it was gone.

The plain light of day seemed dim in contrast. But there was enough of it for Oesc's recovering vision to make out the body of his father, blood still pumping from the stump of his neck. The head had fallen a few feet away; its features still bore a look of appalled surprise.

Scarcely knowing what he did, Oesc crawled forward, pulled off the remnant of his cloak, and began, fumbling, to wrap the head. As he did so, one of the stricken figures stirred. It was Baldulf. Groaning, he gained his feet, then stopped short, features contorting with grief as he saw the boy, and the headless body of his lord.

He cast a quick glance around him, then limped forward.

"Tir's judgment fell against us—" he said hoarsely, "the field is lost, but our hope lives so long as you are alive."

Oesc looked up, dimly aware that most of the figures that were beginning to move around them wore British gear. Beyond Octha's body he could see the British king sprawled among his cushions, in his hand a sword whose brightness still hurt the eye. Baldulf took a step towards it, but the British warriors were too close. Swiftly Baldulf gathered up Octha's torque and his seax. Then he hauled Oesc to his feet and hurried him away.

There was no wind.

Oesc was never able to recall much about the journey that followed. His wound went bad, and at times he was fevered, but mostly he simply did not want to remember. At some point Hæthwæge found them. He did recall the foul taste of the herbal teas she brewed to bring down his fever, as her compresses and charms fought the infection in his arm. For three nights, he was told, they had hidden in the forest, waiting for the crisis and muffling his delirious mumblings when British search parties went past.

Of that, the boy had no recollection. All he retained were visions of a dark land and a dark lake beside which he wandered, calling his father's name, until the wisewoman came walking through the shadows, her raven on her shoulder, and led him back to the light of day.

And through all his illness, and the travel that followed, the head of Octha, hid now in a leather sack and packed with leeks to preserve it, stayed by his side.

Travelling mostly by night, they fled to the East Saxon lands, where they found a boat to carry them across the broad mouth of the Tamesis. After that, they were in Hengest's country and could move openly, following the old Roman road between the sea and the North Downs. By then, of course, word of their coming had gone before them, and Hengest had sent an escort and a horse litter in which Oesc could travel like the British king.

But Uthir was dead. Even in hiding, they had heard that news. The High King of the Britons had died after the battle and left no heir. If the Saxons had lost the battle, and with it the greatest of their own leaders, at least that much had been achieved, and they, like the British, would have time to heal before the warring began once more. Better still, the rumor was that Merlin, the witega who had caused such devastation with his magic, had disappeared.

For Oesc, life began once more when they drew up in front of the meadhall Hengest had built in the ruins of Cantuware and he saw his grandfather, tall and weathered as a storm-battered oak, waiting for him there.

Oesc swung at the practice post set into the mud of the yard, wincing as the wooden blade hit the straw that had been bound around it and the impact jarred the weak muscles in his arm. In the three months since Verulamium his flesh had healed, but it still hurt at times. Since he left his bed, he had spent his days in ceaseless motion, hunting, running, even chopping wood for the fires. And whenever Byrhtwold was free, he had pestered the old warrior to give him more work with the sword.

His body was fined down to bone and sinew, and day by day he could feel his arm growing stronger. But no exercise he had tried could make his heart strong enough to deny the pain, and though each night he fell into bed, too tired to move, the hours of darkness brought dreams from which he would wake whimpering, his vision seared by a sword of fire and his cheeks wet with tears. But once awake, though his throat ached with grief, he could not cry.

Only when it grew too dark to see the post did Oesc give up. From inside the hall he could hear voices, but the yard was empty. Above the wall the first stars were glittering in the deepening blue of the sky. A bird flew towards the trees, crying, and then it was still once more. Now that he had stopped moving, fatigue dragged at back and shoulders. Sweat drying cold on his skin, he stumbled towards the hall.

After the brisk air outside, the warmth was welcome. His stomach rumbled at the scent of boiling beef and he realized that he was hungry.

His grandfather was already in the high seat, long legs stretched towards the fire, his gaunt frame as splendid in its ruin as a Roman tower. Once Hengest had fought to master all Britannia, but now he was content to cling to the corner that the Vor-Tigernus had given him. But his son would never inherit it now.

At his feet sat the shope Andulf, head bent as he tuned his harp. Firelight glistened on the silver strands threading his brown hair. As Oesc approached, the shope straightened, and the murmur of conversation began to still. Once, and then again, he struck the strings, then, in a voice with the honey of sweet mead and the bite of its fire, he began to sing.

Eormanaric, noblest of Amalings,
Great king of Goths, who got much glory,

Fought many folk and fed his people,
Lost land and life to Hunnish horse-lords.

Hengest beckoned, and Oesc joined him on the broad
bench. In a few moments one of the thralls brought him a
wooden bowl filled with savory stew, and he began to gobble
it down. The first bowl took the edge off his hunger. He held
it out to be refilled, able to listen now to the mingled honey
and gall of the tale of the great king who a century earlier
had led the Goths to create an empire, and when the Huns
invaded, lost it. From the Pontus Euxinus to the Northern Sea
he had ruled, and from the Wistla to the great steppes, con-
quering tribes whose names were lost in legend. He had defeated Alaric, king of the Heruli who had made a kingdom
north of the Maiotis, and controlled the trade routes to the
western lands.

Mightiest among his warriors, Eormanaric had been a man
of evil temper, who had the young wife of a chieftain who
had deserted him torn apart by tying her limbs to four wild
stallions. Her brothers sought to avenge her, splitting the
Gothic forces at the moment when they most needed unity.
And so the Huns had rolled over them and the Goths who
survived fled westward, some to cross the Danuvius and seek
service with Rome, and some to push all the way to Iberia,
where now they ruled.

Fierce to his foes and to the faithless,
Betrayed by trampled traitors' kin,
In old age he embraced his ending,
His blood in blessing fed the ground....

In the end, ran the tale, Eormanaric had taken his own life,
seeking by the offering of his own blood to placate the gods.
"It is said that one should not praise a day until it is
ended," said Hengest, when the last note had faded to silence.
"I suppose that the same is true of a king. He lost his empire,
but perhaps his blood bought some protection for his people,

since they have prospered in their new land. At least his death had meaning. . . ."

"That is what King Gundohar said—" answered the shope.

"You knew him?" exclaimed Oesc. He had been aware that the man was a Burgund, his accent worn smooth by years of wandering, but he had thought that everyone close to the royal clan died when the Huns attacked them a quarter-century before.

"He taught me how to play the harp," said Andulf, his voice tightening with old pain. "It is he who wrote this song."

"But you don't look old enough—" Oesc broke off, flushing, as the men began to laugh.

"I was a boy, younger than you," said Andulf smiling, "serving in his hall."

"And now the Niflungar themselves are becoming a legend," added Hengest, shaking his head. "And yet I myself saw Sigfrid when he was only a child and I scarcely older. Who, I wonder, will the heroes of this time be?"

"The deeds of your youth are meat for the bards already, lord," said Byrhtwold.

"Do you mean the fight at Finnesburgh?" growled Hengest. "To keep one oath I was forced to break another, but it is not something I remember with pride."

"You will be remembered as the leader who brought our people to this good land!" said one of the other men.

"If we can hold it . . ." someone said softly.

"Does that matter?" asked Byrhtwold. "Hunnish horses pasture now in the land where Eormanaric died, and the heirs of Gundohar have found refuge in Raetia. Sigfrid left only his name behind him. But in death they triumphed, and they are remembered."

"Do you mean that if we succeed in winning all this island it will be Uthir and Ambrosius about whom men make the stories?" Guthlaf, one of the younger warriors, laughed disbelievingly.

"It may be so," said Andulf, frowning, "for the winners will belong not to legend, but to history." He began to slide his harp into its sealskin case.

The conversation turned to other matters, and as the drinking horns were refilled, grew louder. Oesc leaned against the hard back of the high seat, exhaustion dragging like a sea-anchor at his limbs.

"Send the boy to bed, Hengest, before he falls asleep where he sits," Byrhtwold said presently.

"I'm not sleepy!" Oesc jerked upright, rubbing his eyes. "Grandfather, Octha was a hero, was he not?"

The old man nodded, his eyes dark with shared pain, and the boy knew that he too was thinking of the lonely mound just within the wall.

"Do we have to choose?" he said then. "Do we have to choose between a glorious death and living for our people?" He waited, realizing that his grandfather was taking him seriously.

"Many men fall and are not remembered . . ." Hengest said slowly. "It is because they died for a reason that we honor heroes, because they never gave up, but fought to the end. Death is not a failure, Oesc, if a man has truly lived."

"Then he didn't fail . . ." whispered the boy. "We lost the battle and they killed him, but Octha had his victory. . . ."

"Boy, is that what has troubled you?" Hengest set his gnarled hand on Oesc's shoulder. "Your father waits for us even now in Woden's hall. You must strive to live so that you will be worthy to see him again."

The ache in Oesc's throat made it hard to breathe. He sucked in air with a harsh gasp, and awkwardly, his grandfather began to pat his back, then seeing his face, gathered him against his bony breast. And there, breathing in the scents of leather and horses and the old man's flesh, Oesc found at last the release of tears.

HOLY GROUND

A·D· 475

Every fall, when the raiding season had ended and the crops were gathered in, it was Hengest's custom to travel around the territory that the Vor-Tigernus had given him. At this time of year, when the quarrels of the summer were still fresh in memory, the king heard complaints and rendered judgment, lest resentment, festering through the dark days of winter, should erupt into bloodfeud and destroy the peace of the land. In the second year after Verulamium, Hengest took his grandson Oesc with him on the journey, that he might learn the land and its law.

That fall the first of the winter storms came early, soaking the stubbled fields. But it was succeeded by a season of smiling peace, and the king and his escort rode through a landscape as rich in autumn color as heaped amber, splashed with the vivid scarlet berries of rowan and holly and the varied crimsons of the vine.

Their way first led south to the coast, where the Roman fortress of Lemanis still guarded the Saxon shore. They travelled by short stages, for the king's age would not allow him to do more. In the mornings, when he stretched stiff joints, swearing, he would say that next year, surely, he would let Oesc do it all. But by evening he was smiling, and the cold knot of anxiety in Oesc's belly would disappear.

From Lemanis, they worked their way back north and east along the shoreline to Dubris, where the high chalk cliffs looked out across the sea. Their next stop was Rutupiae, where the Vor-Tigernus's son had once driven Hengest into the sea. The fortress was in ruins now, only the great triumphal arch still proclaiming the vanished glory of Rome. Here, the rich lands by the shore were thickly settled, and the cases being brought for judgment mostly quarrels over boundaries or complaints about strayed stock.

They passed through Durovernum once more and then made their way eastward along the straight line of the Roman road that led to Londinium. To their left the land rose in gentle slopes to the North Downs, scattered with ruined villas and new Saxon farmsteads. To their right the green fields stretched down to the estuary of the Tamesis, sparkling in the sun. Where the ribbon of the road passed, habitations, or their remains, were most thickly clustered, and as they neared Durobrivae, the Roman town that guarded the crossings of the Meduwege and the western half of Cantuware, the land became more populous still.

"The British have got themselves a high king!" Red-faced and perspiring, Hrofe Guthereson shouted out the words even before he greeted his king. He had come out with his houseguard to escort them into the city, but with his news the whole party had come to a halt in the road.

"Who?" barked Hengest. "Has Leudonus finally got the southern princes to accept him?"

"No—" Hrofe shook his head, eyes sparkling. "It's a fifteen-year-old boy! Uthir had a son!"

Fifteen! thought Oesc. *My age. . . .* How strange to think that the battle in which he had lost his own father had so deprived another boy as well.

"Legitimate?" asked Byrhtwold.

Hrofe shrugged. "That's not clear, but Queen Igierne has claimed him as her child by the king."

"I remember hearing talk of a babe," Hengest said, frowning, "but I thought it died. . . ." Slowly they had begun to move forward again.

"They say he was sent away to the west country for safety, so secretly that even the folk that fostered him did not know who he really was."

Hengest smiled sourly. "Well perhaps they had some reason. When you are trying to get rid of a family of bears, you should attack the den."

"Well this one is a bear cub, right enough," said Hrofe. "Arktos, they call him, or Artor."

Artor . . . To Oesc's ears, that name rang like the clash of steel.

"And they accepted him on the queen's say-so?" Hengest said dubiously. "I know the British princes, and they would be hard put to agree that the sun sets in the west without nine days of arguing."

The walls were quite close now.

"It was not the queen's word that convinced them," said Hrofe, with the air of one who has saved the best for last. "It was because the boy could handle the Sword!"

The sword that killed Octha. . . . Oesc's stricken gaze met that of his grandfather, and he saw Hengest's face grow grim.

"I had hoped that accursed weapon would go with Uthir to his grave."

"Oh no—" Hrofe babbled on with hateful cheer.

Unable to bear it any longer, Oesc dug his heels into his mare's flank and pushed past the king and through the shadowed arch of the eastern gate into Durobrivae.

Shaded by an awning of canvas, Hengest sat in judgment in the forum for five long days. Oesc fidgeted beside him, the arguments half-heard, dreaming of the hunting he was missing while the weather held fair. His other grandfather used to spend a lot of time listening to men complain against each other too. Why, he wondered resentfully, would anyone want to be a king? But even the master of a farmstead had to settle disputes among his people, he supposed. The men the king judged were more powerful, that was all.

"And how would you decide this matter, Oesc—" Hengest said suddenly.

Blinking, the boy tried to remember what the man before

them had just said. He was a big, fair, fellow with the lines of habitual ill-temper graven deeply around his mouth and on his brow.

"He says," the king repeated, "that his neighbor deliberately burned down his woodlot, and nearly destroyed his house as well."

"It is not so!" exclaimed the accused, glaring. "I only meant to burn the stubble from my fields."

"But you burned my woods!"

"Is it my fault if Thunor turns the wind? Blame the gods, not me!"

Oesc gazed from one man to the other, frowning, as he tried to remember the law. "Was it a large wood?" he asked finally. Hengest began to smile, and the boy continued more boldly. "Were there many big trees?"

"A very fine wood," said the plaintiff, "with noble oak trees!"

"Untrue! Untrue! There was one tree of some size, and around it nought but hazels!" The accused pointed at an older man in the front row of the crowd. "Tell them! You know the place—tell them what was there!"

Oesc stood up, having remembered the relevant traditions now. He cast a quick glance at this grandfather, who nodded reassurance, then held up one hand and waited until silence fell.

"It is the law of our people that compensation shall be paid for deeds, not thoughts. It does not matter why you started the fire," he told the accused man. "If you were so foolish as to burn stubble on a day of wind, and it did damage to the property of another, you must pay for it. The fine for damage to a wood is thirty shillings, and five shillings for every great tree, and five pence for each of the smaller."

"It is his word against mine as to what was there . . ." the man said sullenly.

"Your word, and that of your witnesses," agreed the boy. "Let each of you call those who will take oath to support your assertion, and so the fine shall be set according to the decision of your peers."

"Unjust!" cried the plaintiff, but the men in the crowd were nodding and murmuring their approval of the plan. Clearly the fair-haired man's taste for contention had not endeared him to his neighbors, for only two men came to his support, while the accused could choose from a dozen or more.

"Did I do right?" asked Oesc when the oaths had been sworn and the fine paid over.

"You did very well," answered the king. "That man is a trouble-maker whom I have seen in court before. A more reasonable man might have settled the matter with his neighbor privately, and not burdened us with it, but he got his recompense, and will not, one hopes, feel compelled to get satisfaction by burning the other man's hall."

"I know it is law that the man who set the fire should be held responsible, but it does seem unfair when he intended no harm," said Oesc thoughtfully.

"Do you think our laws were made to do justice? No, child, if my decisions keep our hot-headed tribesmen from killing each other I will be satisfied. It is each man's wyrd, not I, that will give him the doom that he deserves."

Oesc was glad when they left Durobrivae behind them and took the road once more. Now they moved southward, climbing the tree-clad slopes where the valley of the Meduwege cut through the North Downs. From time to time the trees would part and he could glimpse the river below them, carrying the waters that drained from the Weald, the great forest that covered the central part of the Cantuware lands.

As the day drew to its ending, the road dropped downward into the valley, and he saw the red-tiled roofs of a cluster of Roman buildings set on an oval mound, and beyond them the thatching of a Saxon farmstead amid the water meadows by the stream. Closer still, he realized that the structures on the mound were temples, and that the farm had been built on the foundations of a Roman villa. Here the Meduwege broadened, running chuckling over the stones of a ford.

"Who holds this place?" he asked as they came to a halt in the yard.

"An Anglian called Ægele who sailed in one of the first three keels that came with me across the sea. He lost a leg in the fight at Rutupiae, and I settled him here," his grandfather answered him.

"And who lives up there?" Oesc pointed toward a small square building with a peaked roof, surrounded by a covered porch on all four sides. Some of the tiles were loose, and in places the white plaster was flaking from the stones of the wall, but someone had recently raked the path.

"Ah—that is the other reason we have stopped here. I am not the only one who will find in this place a friend."

But it was not until the following morning that Oesc found out what Hengest had meant, when together they climbed the temple hill.

She could hear them coming up the pathway, the old man's tread heavy and halting on the gravel and the boy's footsteps a quick brush against the stones, his rapid questions abruptly cut off as they paused in the shadow of the porch. A breath of air set the lamp flames to leaping, lending life to the carven eyes of the figures carved on the altar, and elongating her shadow across the wall. Oesc stopped in the doorway and she put back her shawl, smiling as his eyes adjusted to the dim light and he saw her sitting there.

"Hæthwæge!" The delight on his face was like another lamp in the room. "Where did you come from?"

"Where have I not been?" She patted the bench that ran around the wall and the boy sat down. Hengest eased down on the opposite bench and sat with his veined hands crossed on the head of his staff, watching them. "I have been going up and down, searching out the holy places of this land."

Brought back to awareness of where they were, his eyes flicked uneasily around the small room. He had grown, she thought, since she had last seen him. At fifteen he was leggy as a colt, with the promise of strength in his bony shoulders and character in the line of his jaw, where the first fuzz of manhood was beginning to appear.

"And who did the Romans worship here?"

"That is their image of them—" She gestured toward the altar.

Waist-high, the edges of its flat top were scrolled and

fluted, forming a canopy for a bas-relief that showed a seated goddess in a wide sleeved, pleated garment, and three standing figures in cloaks with hoods. The goddess held something, possibly a spindle, in her hand. Below the figures there had been a Latin inscription, but the stone was too worn to make out the words.

"But who *are* they?" he asked again.

"They are not Roman, though they are figured in the Roman style," Hæthwæge said slowly. "This is an old place, where the track that runs along the downs crosses the river. It was here before Rome, maybe even before the British came. I have sat out all night upon a barrow beside that trackway and listened to those whose bones lie there."

She shivered a little, remembering voices in the windy darkness. She still limped where her knee had stiffened after that night's out-sitting, but she did not grudge it. The Romans, she gathered, had not bothered to listen, but had fastened their own names onto the native divinities and confined them in new temples, ignoring the old powers of the hills. The ancient ones had been pleased, she thought, that someone was paying attention to them at last.

"Why?"

"To learn about the spirits of this land so that we can honor them and gain their blessing. I left an offering at the barrow before I came away. You must leave a portion, also, when you go hunting in the Weald."

Oesc took one of the lamps from its niche and squatted, holding the flame so he could see.

"Do you think the Lady could be Frige, and the hooded gods Woden and Willa and Weoh?"

"Little by little our tongue is replacing that of the Romans on the land. I do not think its gods will mind if we call them by our names," Hæthwæge answered, and heard in her head a whisper of approving laughter.

Old Man, be still, she told the god within. *It seems to me you have too many names already! Are you greedy for more?*

"But is that who they really are?"

Hæthwæge shook her head. "Child, there is no name a human tongue could master that would tell you that. In many places, the Britons called their Lady Brigantia. But perhaps these are the names they will bear for us here."

"That is why I have brought the boy," Hengest said then. "So that we may make our offerings."

The wicce nodded and got to her feet. Taking up the second lamp, she moved around the altar and held it high. Light glimmered warm on the worn grey stones of the well coping, and glittered on the dark water within. Enclosed within stone walls, this place was very different from the pool in the marshes of the Myrging lands, and yet the power of its waters was much the same.

"The shrine was built around this spring. It rises from the same waters that feed the river, coming down from the Weald and the Downs. They carry the lifeblood of the Lady of this land."

Hengest had risen as well. Now he took from his belt purse three golden coins that bore the blurred image of some long-dead emperor. Carefully he bent over the well.

"Gyden . . . Frige . . ." he said in a low voice, "I took this land by the sword. But the folk I have brought to live here will tend and till it in love and law. All my days I have been a man of blood, but I have no strength now to force men to my will. Let this land feed my people. . . ." His voice trembled. "And let me leave it in frith to the son of my son."

As he spoke the air inside the temple grew heavy, as if something very ancient and powerful had directed its attention that way. Then the coins splashed into the pool and the tension broke.

It took a few moments for the king to straighten. Then he sat down again, his old eyes moving from Hæthwæge to the boy.

The wicce felt a pang of pity for this ancient warrior who had outlived his own strength and all his companions and now, at his life's ending, sought in a new land the justification for his deeds. For a moment her memory went back to Oesc's other grandfather, Eadguth the Myrging-king, who had been so bound to his land that like an ancient oak, he could not be transplanted from his native soil.

"Now it is for the heir to make his oath and his offering," she said aloud.

Oesc set the lamp he had been holding on the rim of the well and knelt beside it, staring down into the pool. The current, welling slowly from the depths, broke the reflection into a scattering of gold, as if more wealth were breeding already from Hengest's coins.

Rather reluctantly, he unpinned the silver brooch that held his cloak, the only thing of value that he had on. Once more the atmosphere changed, this time to a kind of singing tension that lifted the hair on Hæthwæge's arms and neck. Oesc felt it too. He cast an uneasy look in her direction before turning once more to the well.

"Lady of the spring, this is for you." His voice cracked on the last word and he flushed, swallowing, and swiftly tossed the brooch in. "Let me be worthy of my grandfather's trust. Body and spirit I offer, if you will give me this land as a home for my children and my people. And please, Lady, let me one day know your true name!"

The tension built to an audible hum, like crickets on a day of summer, though the leaves were turning and the air outside had the crisp clarity of fall. It intensified to the edge of pain, then, very slowly, ebbed away, leaving behind it a great peace and the conviction that all would be well.

From Ægele's ford the road cut southward through the Weald, dwindling to a rough track by the time it reached the southern coast. There, the Jute, Hæsta, had settled his clan near the old Roman iron workings where a low ridge ran down to the sea. Just down the coast, the sea-fort of Anderida provided safe harbor, and with a good wind and a pilot who knew the shoals of the coastline, they could return to Lemanis by boat in no more than a long day's sail. Hæsta's other guests had ridden eastward from the South Downs, where Aelle had been lord of his Saxons for almost as long as Hengest had held Cantuware, though he was thirty years younger. The farmstead, where the rich fields sloped down toward the sea, lay on the border between the lands the two leaders ruled.

Hæsta himself had come down to escort his guests from the landing. As they approached his hall, more men came out of it—a thickset, muscular man with grizzled hair and a king's torque who they said was Aelle, and behind him a tall young man with red hair. The child he carried on his shoulder stared at the newcomers with bright, considering eyes.

"He has brought Ceretic, I see," said Byrhtwold, "and that must be Ceretic's young son. That's a man to watch, lad. If he fights half as well as he talks, he'll be calling himself a king too one of these days."

Oesc nodded, understanding that this was one of the men with whom he would have to deal, in friendship or without it, when his own turn came to rule. Hengest's bid to claim lordship over all the men who had come over from Germania had failed, and Aelle seemed content with his coastal hills. Despite their numbers, the Saxon settlements were scattered, each under its own chieftain—men who had never gone under the yoke of Rome and saw no reason to bow down before one of their own.

Octha might have united them, Oesc thought grimly, until his battle-luck failed. But no—it had not been bad luck that felled him, but the sorcery in Uthir's sword. *I might do it . . .* he thought grimly, *and Artor will be my opponent if I do.* Then they were dismounting, and Hæsta led them into the friendly shelter, its air blue with woodsmoke and the welcome scents of cooking food, of his hall.

That night, new clouds rolled in from the sea. For three days, rain and sleet kept the Saxons inside the hall. They scarcely noticed. Hæsta had been brewing for weeks in preparation for the feasting, and so long as the ale-vats did not run dry, no one would complain.

In a break between the discussions, Oesc sat by the long hearth, carving scraps of wood into crude figures of horses and split twig-men to ride them. As each one was finished, he gave it to the child beside him. Cynric, he was called, with hair as red as his father's, the legacy of the British grandfather who had given Ceretic his name.

"That is a mighty army—" said Ceretic, looking down at

his son. Cynric nodded, took the rider that Oesc had just finished and set it in order with the others.

"These with the bark on are Romans, because of their armor, and the peeled ones are Saxons," the child explained. Several of the figures fell over and he set them up again.

"I see you are placing your unmounted warriors in a wedge formation—" commented Ceretic.

"*He* told me—" said Cynric, pointing at Oesc.

"It was what my father used at Verulamium." Oesc swallowed, his stomach knotting as he remembered that day.

"Ah, yes." Ceretic transferred his attention from the child. "You were in that battle, I have heard."

Oesc flushed. "Against my father's orders," he said with a quelling look at Cynric. "But I brought away his head so that the British should not dishonor it. I have sworn that I will avenge him one day."

"Perhaps we will march to battle together. For now, I am in Aelle's following, but my father rules in Venta, and he refused to acknowledge Ambrosius as his master. It is certain he will not bow before this child the British are calling high king!"

"You are British?" Oesc stared at him. But of course, he thought as he looked at the milky Celtic skin and bright hair, it must be true.

"My father is—" Ceretic's lips twisted wryly. "Maglos took my mother as a second wife when he made alliance with Aelle. I grew up speaking both tongues equally. My father likes Saxons because they are good fighters, and if this new high king tries to recover the lands around Venta, Maglos will need more men to defend them. So he has sent me to Aelle."

"Does Aelle have them?"

"Not enough—hence, this meeting. Your grandfather's people have held Cantuware long enough for there to be a few younger sons who need new holdings. If they come to the Isle of Vecta, my father will make no objections. But I will need to bring more men from Germania to settle the land around Clausentum, along the estuary of the Icene. From there I can drive northward into the heart of Britannia. Maglos thinks he can defend the land with Saxon settlers and still call it British. But when I rule in Venta, I can strike northward to the British heartland!"

Listening to him talk, Oesc understood how it must have been for Hengest and Horsa when they were young. But in Durovernum the scars of warfare had been repaired, the burnt houses scavenged for building material or allowed to go back to the soil. The British who remained there were grateful for the protection of their new masters, and the Saxons were rooting themselves ever more deeply into the soil.

"And what about you?" asked Ceretic, as if Oesc had been thinking aloud. "Will you push westward as well? You are young, with your name yet to win. Have you no ambitions to take Londinium?"

"Londinium and the British lands around it divide us from the Anglians in the fen country, as Lindum divides them from the north. We would be stronger if we could take it," Oesc added thoughtfully, "but the city was more important when there was trade with the Empire. In itself, it is not so useful now."

"Go around it, then. If I push northward and you move west, our armies can join forces, and who will stop us then?" He threw his head back, laughing. In the flickering light his hair was as red as the fire.

"What armies? Are you Woden, to breathe life into these sticks your son is playing with, and make them men? Let us wait at least until the seed is planted before we sell the tree!" exclaimed Oesc. "When you have brought your warriors from Saxony and I command the men of Cantuware, we may talk of this again."

"It is so! It is so!" shaking his head, Ceretic hunkered down and began to help his son pick up his scattered men. "Always, my dreams have outstripped reality. But it will happen. Among the Saxons a second wife has equal standing, and my mother went willingly to Maglos's bed. But the Christian priests called her a Saxon whore and me a bastard. I had to fight for every scrap of food and nod of approval, but the sons of my father's Christian wife were killed in battle, while I survived and took a wife from my mother's people. Maglos has no choice now but to trust to me and my Saxon kin to defend him. I have come too far already not to believe it is my Wyrd to be a conqueror."

Oesc believed him. Ambition pulsed around Ceretic like heat from the flame. *And what is* my *Wyrd?* he wondered then. But even as he questioned, a memory came to him of lamplight on dark water, and a breath of wind.

My Wyrd is to be a king. . . .

Hæthwæge dipped up a spoonful of broth, tasted it, and decided that she could add a bit more of the infusion of galluc root and mallow without rendering it so bitter the king would refuse to drink it down. As she poured, she bent over the pot, whispering—

"Galluc, Galluc, great among herbs,
You have power against three and against thirty,
Against poison and all infection,
Against the loathsome foe that fares through the land. . . ."

In her mind's eye she saw the plant from which that root had come, its broad leaves frosted with prickles, the pale pink-purple flowers trembling like bells in the breeze. *Boneset,* they called it sometimes, but it had great power also to heal internally. The mallow would soothe and smooth it on its way.

Hengest would not admit that he was ill, though the cough he brought home from his visit to Hæsta's hall had hung on throughout the winter, and his frame grew as gaunt as the horsehide hung over the poles at the offering pool. Her more elaborate curing methods were useless if the patient would not admit he needed them. All she could do was to doctor his food and drink as unobtrusively as possible, and sing her charms over her pots as she prepared them.

Eadguth had been much the same in his old age. *Why,* she wondered, *have I spent so much of my life nursing old men?* But the god she served appeared most often in an old man's guise, so perhaps it was not so surprising.

And to balance the old man she had the young one, although these days Oesc spent most of his time outdoors, hunting, exploring the countryside, even helping the farmers with the work of each season as it came. She supposed it was inevitable, after his dedication at the sacred spring. The goddess of the land was speaking to him in each tree and hill, and as time passed, he would learn to understand her.

Oesc came to the wisewoman for liniment for sore muscles, and sometimes to dress a wound, but on the whole he was a healthy young animal, for which she thanked the gods.

She stirred the broth once more, then dipped it carefully into a carved hornbeam bowl, its wooden surface smoothed to a rich patina by the years, and carried it from the cookshed across the yard to the hall. In the years since Hengest had built it in the space adjoining two of the better preserved Roman dwellings, trees had grown up on the western side, screening the weed-covered waste where half-burned houses had been pulled down to serve as building material. Afternoon sunlight slanted through the branches, glowing in the new leaves. A pattern of shadow netted the path.

As she passed, a portion of that shadow solidified into a human shape: a tall man, wrapped in a cloak and leaning on a staff. Hæthwæge stopped, eyes narrowing. *High One*, she queried silently, *is it you?*

As if he had felt the touch of her mind, the stranger straightened, turning toward the light. The wisewoman noted the dark eyes beneath their heavy brows, the brown beard where only a few strands of silver yet showed, and let her breath out in a long sigh. It was not the god. But neither, she thought as other senses picked up the aura that surrounded him, was this entirely a man. And knowing that, she thought she could put a name to him.

"Merlin Witega, wæs hal! Be you welcome to this hall!"

His eyes widened at the greeting, and some indefinable tension in his posture ebbed away.

"A blessing on you also, woman of wisdom. I had heard there was a bean-drui in the house of the king, and I think you must be she."

Hæthwæge bowed her head, accepting the compliment.

She should have expected that he would be able to see beyond the old shawl and apron to her own aura of power.

"Come with me, then. The king has been ill, but he is well enough to speak with you. Perhaps he will be ashamed to fuss about drinking this down if you are by."

His broad nostrils flared, though it seemed unlikely he could pick up the scent from there. Then he began to ask if the king's cough had lasted for long, and she realized that he had indeed recognized the herbs.

"We were not certain whether Hengest was still living." His deep voice rumbled up from somewhere near his belly. "I knew him when I was a boy in the Vor-Tigernus's hall."

"He is old, but he still has his wits." Hæthwæge answered the unspoken question.

A swift grin of understanding split the flowing beard. "Then he will remember me. But it might be better if to the rest I were known only as a messenger." He said, and Hæthwæge, remembering how Oesc still blamed Merlin for the magic that had caused his father's death, had to agree. Then he pushed open the door and together they entered the hall.

He is an old man, Merlin told himself as they made their way past the empty feasting benches toward the high seat. *He cannot hurt you now.* Somewhere inside him there still lived a child who remembered Hengest as a towering force that could break him without even breathing hard. But in the man before him there was nothing of the Vor-Tigernus's war leader but the eagle gaze. *Who would have thought that the terrible Hengest would live to be so old?*

"Am I well?" Hengest echoed his question. "At my age it is enough to be alive. No doubt you seem ancient to Artor." He chuckled grimly. "I have outlived all my enemies, and most of my friends. But I will last until my grandson is old enough to rule. Uthir's son has the name of king already, but is it he or his council who have sent you here?"

"His council—" admitted Merlin. "But the boy is no weakling. In time he will be a powerful leader in peace or in war."

"I don't suppose you have come to say that Artor wants me to give back Cantium. Even the hotheads on his council must recognize that we have sunk our roots too deeply into this soil."

"Nor have I come to ask whether you will try to take advantage of Artor's youth to attack Londinium," Merlin answered pleasantly. "What my king and his council offer is a treaty to confirm your possession of these lands, in return for your support against any of the Saxon kings who would try to expand their territories."

Hengest gave a bark of laughter, took a sip of broth, and grimacing, set it down again. "Why come to me? I am not high king of the Saxon kind. Do you think they will listen to me?"

They may not obey you, old wolf, but they listen, thought Merlin as the old man went on. *What is it that you are not telling me?*

"While I live, the warriors of Cantuware will not march against you. I can give no surety for the others, nor even for what my grandson will do when he has drunk my funeral ale."

He looked up, a warmer light coming into his old eyes, but Merlin had already felt the stir in the air as a youth who stood, like Artor, on the threshold between boy and man, came in. He was taller than Artor, and fair where the other boy was brown, and in his gaze Merlin perceived something watchful, as if he had already learned not to trust the world, where Artor's gaze was still open and unafraid.

"Not for a long time, I hope," he said, sitting down at the old man's feet.

"This is Oesc, Octha's son," said the king. But Merlin had already recognized the set of the shoulders and something of Hengest about the line of brow and jaw. "He is the one who will have to deal with Artor, not I."

"Yes . . ." Merlin shut his eyes, shaken by a sudden inrush of images—Artor and Oesc side by side on a hill where ravens flew, at feast and at hunt, and again, older, striving to meet amid the blood and terror of a battlefield. As foes or as allies? And if they fought, which one would have the victory? That knowledge was not given.

Then the moment of vision faded. When he looked up

again, Oesc and his grandfather were still talking, but the witch-woman, Hæthwæge, was watching him with troubled eyes.

"If you wish to keep your anonymity," she told him when the interview was over, "you had better come with me. I will tell the thralls to bring food for us both."

Merlin nodded. He would lose the chance to pick up whatever revealing gossip the men might share in the hall, but it seemed to him that he knew the answer to his question already. Cantium would stay quiet, but the council had better keep a sharp eye on the South Saxons and the Anglians from now on. This wisewoman, on the other hand, clearly had considerable influence with both the old man and the boy. He could not afford to leave her a mystery.

He sensed a prickling beneath his skin as he entered Hæthwæge's house and smiled a little, recognizing in its pure form the feel of the wardings he had noted in the hall. Flame leaped as she built up the fire, and he looked around him with a fellow-professional's curiosity. Since his studies with the Vor-Tigernus's wise men when he was young he had had little to do with other workers of magic.

His nostrils flared at the mingled odors, spicy or musty or sour, that swirled around him, and with them the mingled currents of power. A witch he had called her, and the drying herbs that hung from the rafters, the sacks and baskets and packets ranked neatly on their shelves, confirmed it. What else she might be he could not yet tell.

Hæthwæge poured mead from a Roman flask into a silver-mounted drinking horn. "Do not fear," she said when for a moment he hesitated, "I know better than to set a spell upon it beyond a blessing on the yeast to make it brew, even if I thought such a thing would escape your notice."

"I did not doubt you," he said stiffly. He drank, savoring the fiery sweetness, and handed the horn back to her, then seated himself on the bench beside the fire.

The wisewoman drank in turn and took her place across from him. She was a woman who would look much the same from her middle years to extreme old age, deep-breasted and broad-hipped, with a lacing of silver in her hair—ordinary, in fact, with no claim to beauty, until you met her eyes.

Those eyes held his now, with a silvery glow that hid the depths behind them like light on a pool.

"You ask Hengest what he will do with his warriors, as if those were the only powers at war over this land. Of another messenger I would have expected that, but not of you. Have you come to spy out our defenses, as you did when you rode the body of the bird at Verulamium?"

Merlin suppressed a shudder, remembering that day. Then the sense of what she had said reached him.

"That was you, with the ravens, opposing me?"

"For a little while—until it became a battle between your goddess and my god. You should know that Woden has long been a friend to the goddesses, and he will seek to learn her wisdom. Even then, it was not she who defeated him, but the god in the Sword. Will it kill its new master as it did your king?"

"Artor is its destined master, the Defender of Britannia. When he draws it in a just cause, it will bring him the victory." Remembering the particular pulsation of power the Sword carried, he became abruptly aware that he was sensing something similar here.

He turned, attention fixing on a long shape in the corner, swathed in leather wrappings and spells. Now that it had attracted his attention, its power overwhelmed all the other magics in the room. Behind him, Hæthwæge had gone very still.

"I should have realized that against you, the magics that hide it from other men would be useless..." She spoke slowly, as if listening to some voice within. "But perhaps... it was meant that you should see it." She moved slowly to the corner and began to unfasten the wrappings, and he saw that it was a spear.

For one moment only Merlin glimpsed the physical form— the wooden, rune-carved shaft and the blade of translucent stone. Then its power swirled through his senses in an explosion of meaning; its shaft a chain of incantations, its blade piercing the heart with pure song. Altered vision perceived it

limned in light, as bright as the radiant being who was offering it to him.

"Take it by the shaft. . . ." Through his confusion he realized that Hæthwæge was speaking.

With an effort he managed to answer. "What will happen
if I do?"

"You will know the god . . ."

"Woden? He is no god of mine!"

"You may say so, but still you bear a part of his wisdom
in this world. You do not know him, but he knows you, and
he claims this holy ground. . . ."

"Is it a weapon?" He mumbled, thinking it might be his
duty to seize it. "Will your kings bear it against the Sword?"

"It is a weapon, but not for war . . ."

Sound came and went. He was not certain of her meaning,
only of his own rejection of what she was telling him. And
then the power was muted. Ordinary vision returned, and he
saw that she had replaced the wrappings around the spear.

"I have walked this land through the seasons, and Woden
went with me," said Hæthwæge. "He likes this country and
will stay here. He says to me that you will serve him also,
and it will be easier if it is with your will."

Merlin shook his head. "I serve the Lady of the Land."

"Of course," said the wicce, "but in time to come, their
purposes may prove to be the same. . . ."

†HE OS†ARA OFFERIΠG

A·D· 477

In the second year after his acclamation, the High King of Britannia kept the feast of the Resurrection at Sorviodunum on the borders of the Dumnonian lands. The Roman town had been burned during the first Saxon rebellion and only partially rebuilt afterward. Merlin, riding in behind Artor's houseguard, had thought the intervening years would have faded his memories, but instead, the ghosts of Ambrosius and Uthir now haunted it along with the shades of those who had been murdered by Hengest's men.

The little church, only lightly scorched, remained. While Artor heard the Pascal mass inside with Docomaglos of Dumnonia and his sons, the rest of the princes and notables waited with more or less patience in the open area around it, nourishing their spirits on the incense that drifted from within, and the earthier scents that drifted from the cauldrons where the feast was being prepared.

Merlin sensed the strength of the mystery that was being celebrated within those whitewashed walls, but the power that he was feeling did not come from the church, but rather flowed through it, drawing him northward through the gate to stand staring across the plain. To the north lay the Giant's Dance. He could not see it, but he could sense its presence. As the Christian ritual built to its climax the power moving along the line between them increased until he could see a pathway of light. Did Uthir's spirit ride that road from his grave by the ring of stones to the church where his son knelt in prayer?

The druid lifted his hands in salutation as the light flared and then began to fade. With its passing, he was aware of the fragile balance of light and darkness as the world stood poised for the explosion of growth that the approaching summer would bring. Always, in the old days, men had propitiated those forces at this time with an offering. The Christian priests said the death of their god was a sufficient sacrifice for all times to come, and from the point of view of the divine powers, that might be so. But it seemed to him that sometimes it was men, like Abraham in the Christians' stories, who needed to make an offering.

Light filtered coldly through the interwoven branches to illuminate the features of the British princes. Brush had been bound over a framework of beams to shelter the council, since there was no building in Sorviodunum that would hold them all. The fire that burned in the center seemed to produce more smoke than heat, which might also be said, thought Merlin, of the arguments.

Artor had a place close to the fire, with Merlin behind him. From habit, the druid cloaked his aura. The British chieftains, at first inclined to be suspicious of his motives, had become accustomed to his silent presence. They did not accept his influence on the boy so much as ignore it.

"Last year they came by the hundreds, and the year before!" exclaimed Catraut, who had fought his way through two ambushes on his way down from Verulamium. "As a dead horse breeds maggots, Germania breeds men. Who knows how many more will arrive when the sailing season begins? There are so many Anglians now they have brought over their King Icel to rule them, with his lady and his sons, while *you*—" he swept an accusatory finger towards the Dumnonian lords, "flit back and forth across the sea to Armorica like migrating birds, preparing cozy nests to which you can flee when by sheer pressure of numbers the Saxons have crowded us into the sea!"

Docomaglos, who had inherited Dumnonia after his brother Gorlosius died, bristled indignantly, while his sons, Cataur and Gerontius, looked uncomfortable. "My home is in Isca of the Dumnonii, and I will defend it to my life's end!"

"That may be so," Catraut continued implacably, "but can you deny there's scarcely one of your lords who does not have a cousin or a brother waiting to welcome him across the narrow sea? You must forgive those of us who do not have such a refuge if we say that your risks and ours are not the same!"

"My lords, my lords—" Eldaul of Glevum extended a placating hand. "We have been hearing these arguments since the days when the Vor-Tigernus strove with Aurelianus. The men of the east protest their sufferings, and those of the west, their loyalty. If we had all been willing to aid each other then, we might not face this threat today...."

There was an uncomfortable silence. Artor, whose eyes had begun to glaze, roused suddenly, looking around the circle. In the past year he had added several inches to his height, and he was beginning to learn how to manage his long limbs.

"It seems to me, my lords, that Eldaul speaks truly, and since it is so, surely we ought to be taking council on how we may meet the threat instead of wasting our energy accusing each other!"

For a moment they stared, as if one of the posts had grown a mouth to speak to them. Then Merlin saw their expressions change as they remembered that it had been their decision to make this boy their king. At this point, one might wonder if they had really meant it, or whether, to paraphrase that bishop Augustinus whose new ideas were upsetting everyone, they had prayed God to give them a king, "but not yet."

"My lord, it is clear that we must mount a campaign in the midlands," answered Catraut finally, "to destroy this Anglian kinglet before he is firmly seated in his power."

"From where you sit, that may be clear," said Matauc, who had ruled the Durotrige lands from Durnovernum on the coast for many years, "but when I look eastward, what I see is that Devil's cub Ceretic in Venta Belgarum!" His tone remained mild, and Catraut, who had begun to frown, sat back again.

"*He* has been bringing in more men from Germania as well," said Cataur, "with their families, so it is clear that these wolves are after more than plunder—they mean to plant themselves on the land."

"Leonorus Maglos has been a traitor since the time of Ambrosius," answered Eldaul, "but he is concerned only with the Belgic lands."

"He is an old man—" Docomaglos's second son, Gerontius, spoke then. "Ceretic speaks for him now in Venta, and Ceretic thinks like a Saxon, for all he bears a British name."

Artor nodded. For the past year Gerontius had captained the men who guarded the king, ate at his table and slept by his door, hunted and played at *tabula* and taught him the art of the sword. It was inevitable that the boy would end by either loving or hating him, and Gerontius was as good-hearted and fair-spoken as he was tall and dark and strong. No wonder, then, if his young king listened with admiration in his eyes.

Cataur, seizing the opening, leaned forward. "The word that we hear from Venta is that Ceretic means to expand northward. Do you want to fight the Anglians with his Jutes and Frisians snapping at your heels? Icel is not yet firmly seated in his power, and he must bring those chieftains who have grown accustomed to living without a lord into line before he can lead them against us."

One or two of those present looked embarrassed at that, for what he had said of the Anglians was surely true of the British as well. But Cataur was continuing—"Ceretic's men are sworn only to him. Your argument for fighting Icel applies to Ceretic as well—let us cut out this canker on our flank before it grows!"

There was a murmur of comment at that. Artor allowed it to continue for several minutes before lifting his hand for silence once more. In two years he had at least learned how to manage a council, even if he did not yet always have the confidence to impose his will. Silently, Merlin projected his aura towards the boy and allowed some of his own energy to flow into it. To the others, there seemed only an intensification of his presence, which focused their attention until everyone was still. At first, the fifteen-year-old king had needed such bolstering constantly, but along with his father's armor, he was growing into his power.

"I think we agree we're going to have to fight somebody—" Artor's grin was reflected in the faces of some of the younger men. "And the choice seems to be between Icel and Ceretic. They are both dangerous. Tell me what we have to fight them with, and maybe that will help us to decide."

If you want to know how the colt will run, look at his breeding, thought Merlin, hearing echoes of Uthir's easy style. It sounded ingenuous, but clearly Gerontius had been talking, for it was obvious, when you looked at the problem, where the men and resources would have to come from if the British intended a spring campaign.

"By the end of this month my people will be done with the spring planting," said Docomaglos. "I can have three thousand men on Ceretic's doorstep before he gets word we are moving. We can hit hard and fast and drive him into the sea by Pentecost."

"That reasoning seems good to me—" answered Artor. "Catraut is right—Icel is a problem, but I think we'll tackle him with more confidence without Ceretic's spears pricking between our shoulder blades."

Merlin suppressed a smile. Uthir would have said ". . . poking up our backsides." But without the crudities, the boy certainly seemed to have inherited his father's knack of putting men at ease. The northern princes not only dropped most of their objections, by the time the council ended, they had even promised to send men.

It was the sound of swordplay that led Merlin to the king. After dinner, most of the princes had gone back to sit and talk and drink by their campfires, watching the daylight fade from the sky. When the druid went to look for Artor, he found that most of the younger men had disappeared.

He hardly needed magic to find them. Just outside the

town, where the river flowed quiet through grassy meadows, two figures strove, shadow against shadow, the last of the sunset flickering from their swinging swords. After the first shock Merlin realized that they were doing slow work, bodies moving with the graceful deliberation of dream. But it was still dangerous. He drew breath to stop them, then let it slowly out again. He could not keep the boy swaddled forever; Artor was almost a man.

But it was a boy's voice that protested, laughing—"But how can I touch you, Gerontius, when I can hardly see?" He danced back out of range and stood leaning on his sword, breathing hard.

"If the enemy makes a night attack you won't be able to see, or in the dust of the battlefield, or if you take a head wound and blood blinds you." Gerontius straightened, his voice cool and unstressed.

A third figure, by his voice, Cai, spoke up—"At least in battle you don't have to worry about hurting your enemy."

"If you can see which ones *are* the enemy," said Artor. "Once battle is joined, Gerontius, how do you *know?*"

"If his spear is pointed at your belly, he's an enemy!" said one of the others.

"If he shouts at you in Saxon—"

"If he's facing the opposite direction from your line—"

"Artor is right—" Gerontius cut into the discussion. "In the confusion of battle it can be hard to tell friend from foe, especially now, when our warriors and the Saxons copy each other's gear. What I am trying to do with this exercise is to teach you to perceive your opponent with senses other than sight or even sound."

"Ah . . . Merlin has showed me something of that . . ." said Artor. "He said you have to sense your enemy's energy, to become one with him. But I'm not good enough to risk it with the blade, so—" He stooped suddenly, scooped up something from the grass and flung it.

There was a blur of movement and then a thunk as Gerontius's sword struck the incoming missile and smote it to bits.

"Wretch!" he said, over his students' laughter. "If that was a cow patty, I will make you clean this blade."

"No," Artor caught his breath on a whoop, "only a piece of sod."

"Very well." Gerontius tried to sound stern. "And now it truly *is* dark, so I suppose we must bring this practice to an end. There should be time for some more work tomorrow morning, however, before the *consilium* begins again."

"Not more meetings!" exclaimed Cai over the murmur of talk as they began to gather up their gear.

"Do you think that several thousand men and all their gear are moved into place by magic, as they say Merlin sang up the stones to make your father's monument? There is still a great deal of planning yet to do . . ."

As the group started back toward the buildings, Merlin fell into step beside them. Artor had learned enough to sense *his* presence—Gerontius started and went for his sword when the dark shape appeared at the king's elbow, but Artor only sighed.

"Your teaching is done for the evening, but there is still time for some of mine," Merlin said to the warrior. "Take the others back to camp. I have something to show the king."

"He must be guarded—" objected Gerontius.

"Do you doubt my ability to protect him?" He drew in a breath of power, holding it until even the warrior must be able to see his glow.

"Do you doubt that I will track you down and break every sorcerous bone in your body if you fail?"

"Stop it!" exclaimed Artor. "I feel like the bone, with two dogs growling over it. Go on, Gerontius. I'm sure we will be back soon."

"Yes, my lord—" Gerontius's voice was harsh with reluctance, but he obeyed.

"We *will* be back soon, won't we?" asked Artor when he had gone. "I've worked hard this evening, and I'm tired."

"No. But we will take horses, so you can at least sit down."

Artor stopped short. "Horses? Where are we going at this hour?"

Don't you trust me? thought Merlin, but trust and reason

made poor bedfellows. He remembered suddenly something that the Saxon witch had told him about her god, that he sometimes seemed treacherous, betraying men for their own good, or some purpose greater still. Maybe he himself was a little like Woden after all. *If you learn to trust me in small things, that I can explain, perhaps you will obey when the time comes to follow my lead without knowing why. . . .*

"We go to the Giant's Dance. It lies six miles hence. If we go now we can be there before the moon is high, and I do not know when we will be in this part of the country again."

There was a long silence. "My father is buried there . . ." Artor said at last. "Very well. I will come with you."

The standing stones cast long shadows, stark in the moonlight. In silence Artor and Merlin rode around the circle. The plain stretched away before them to a horizon dim with distance, its pale, moonwashed expanse broken only by the line of mounds.

"Who set up those stones? What are they for?" asked Artor, eyeing the henge circle uneasily.

His father had asked the same thing. Remembering, Merlin began to tell him of the ancient tribes and how they had watched the stars.

"The plain is so empty," Artor whispered when he had finished, "as if we were the only living beings in the world."

Merlin looked around him, seeing with spirit sight the need-fire that danced above the mounds.

"The only ones living, perhaps—but these spaces are thronging with the spirits of those who have gone before. That is what I have brought you here to learn. All things pass, but nothing is lost."

Artor swallowed. "Where is my father's grave?"

Merlin pointed toward the last of the mounds, the one they had raised next to the mound of the lords killed in the Night of the Long Knives.

"He lies there, with Ambrosius his brother."

"I never knew him . . . If I could meet him now, I wonder what wisdom he might have for me?"

"They say that if a man sits out the night on a sacred

mound, by morning he will be mad, or dead, or a poet. We must be back at the camp before dawn, but if you wish, you might sit there for a little while."

"Is it dangerous?" Artor's voice, the druid was pleased to note, held not fear, but a healthy caution.

"The dangers are those you bring with you," he answered. "Anger for anger, fear for fear. Remember what I have taught you, and you will do well."

And if he does not, I may as well go back to my northern forest and stay there, Merlin thought wryly, *for my life will not be worth a denarius here!* But his fear was not for the boy's physical safety. If Artor failed this testing, then everything for which Merlin had worked and suffered would be lost as well. And for the druid, this place held its own dangers; it would be fatally easy to come too close to the nexus of powers that met here, and be drawn through into some other world.

And so, as the young king took his place upon the mound that held his father's bones, Merlin his teacher sat down upon a boulder a little to one side of the line of power that ran from it to the henge of stones, to watch with him while the moon sailed serenely westward and the skies wheeled towards dawn.

When, in the grey hour before sunrise, the druid called his charge to come down from the mound so that they could begin the ride back to Sorviodunum, the boy's face was drawn, his eyes scarcely seeming to focus on the world. It was not until they were nearly back to the encampment and the first streaks of light were awakening the sky that Artor sighed and the bleak look began to leave his eyes.

"Did your father speak to you?"

"Don't you know?" The boy's voice held mixed wonder and bitterness.

"You are a child of prophecy, as am I, but our choices are our own. And this was *your* mystery," Merlin said gently. *I must learn . . .* he told himself, *to let him go.*

"Yes . . . I think he did . . ." Artor answered then. But he would not tell what the spirit of his father had said to him.

*   *   *

Oesc caught the blur of motion against the blue sky and dodged, thrusting up his wooden shield. The stave thwacked home with a force that nearly knocked him from his feet. He stumbled backward, shield-arm throbbing.

"You blocked well, but you were off-balance," said Byrhtwold, resting the oak stave on the ground and leaning on it.

"That hurt." Oesc let the shield slip off and rubbed his shoulder.

"No doubt. But without the shield a blow like that would have broken your arm."

"If I had a weapon I could hit you back," said Oesc. "You act as if I were still twelve winters old!"

"Maybe, but if you lose your blade in battle, only your shield will save you until you can grab another weapon," the old man replied. "Because you have been in a battle you think you are a warrior. I think you have habits which you must unlearn. So we go back to the beginning. When you can hold me off with shield alone you can practice with the blade. In the meantime, keep strengthening your sword arm."

"Chopping wood?" Oesc asked with a sigh. "That's thralls' work, I only did it before to strengthen my arm."

Byrhtwold grinned. "But good practice. And if you cannot master the skills of the folk who serve you, how will you keep them to their work?"

Oesc nodded, recognizing the futility of argument, and Byrhtwold handed him the stave.

"Tomorrow morning we will practice again." Byrhtwold turned away, then paused, relenting. "Be patient, lad—you will be chopping something more than wood soon enough. Ceretic has asked that you come with the men your grandfather is sending to Venta Belgarum. You are going to war."

Oesc stood watching as the warrior walked away, his mind in a whirl. The morning was sunny, though great puffy clouds like hanks of wool were moving in from the west, casting dappled shadows across the wall of the old theatre that dominated the remainder of the city like an old oak, after a storm has blasted all the lesser trees. No doubt there would be rain before evening. When his father first brought him to Cantuware, he had thought the buildings that still stood in

Durovernum the work of etins. Then he had seen Eburacum and Verulamium, noble still despite their battle-scars.

But Venta had never been destroyed. Venta had welcomed the Saxons as the rightful heirs to the empire, as Gallia was welcoming the Franks even now, and the Visigoths had been received in Iberia. Even Durovernum was becoming Cantuwaraburh on men's tongues. *We are the future,* he thought, and if he marched with Ceretic, his own name might live in that future as well.

Ceretic assembled his allies in the fields outside of the old naval fortress of Portus Adurni that another German, the admiral Carausius, had built long ago, and there they held the feast of Ostara. It was a tribal celebration, in the old style of Germania, meant to remind men of their common heritage. The penned animals moved anxiously, as if aware of their role in the proceedings, but the rest of the camp hummed with anticipation.

Scouts had confirmed the rumors. The British princes were advancing, led by Docomaglos of Dumnonia with his sons and the boy whom they had made their king. Leonorus Maglos had fled Venta, and Ceretic had no desire to test the enthusiasm of his allies by exposing them to a seige. It would be better to meet the foe in open battle on the flood plain across from the Isle of Vecta, where the estuary of the Icene met the sea.

In the midst of the fields was a fine grove of oak trees. Here, some Roman had set up an offering tablet to Mercurius. It had been abandoned when the Christians came and grown over with vines until Ceretic had claimed the place and raised beside it an altar of heaped stones.

Oesc stood holding the tether of the white ox that Hengest had sent for the sacrifice. Across the field he could see the fyrd of Cantuware, farmers who had left their fields at their king's command, and the professional warriors of Hengest's household who had come to guard his heir. The ox stamped, and rubbed its head against his thigh, rocking him on his feet and leaving a smear of white hairs across the crimson wool of his tunic and knocking off some of the primrose blossoms from the wreath around its horns, then bent and lipped up more of the grain that had been poured out for it. A little of Oesc's anxiety eased. It was holy corn, mixed with sacred herbs and blessed by the priests, and for the ox to eat it signified acceptance of its role as offering.

He could see Hæthwæge standing with the other god-folk who had been assembled to bless the proceedings: the ancient Godwulf, who had once served at the court of Vitalinus, and two witegas who had been brought over from Germania with the most recent shipload of warriors. From the eagerness with which they surveyed the cattle, he guessed it had been some time since they had had sufficient beasts on which to practice their craft.

In the space between the animals and the men of the army three tumblers were performing, while another beat out a cheerful rhythm on a small hand drum. As the day drew towards its nooning, the clouds began to part, and the bits of metal sewn to the players clothes flashed and glittered in the sun. Then the light broke through completely, and from within the sacred grove came the call of a horn.

The chieftains who held the nine white horses began to lead them forward, followed by the oxen. As the beast next to him moved out, Oesc jerked on the halter of his animal and joined the line. From the sound, the pigs were being brought up behind them; he pitied the men who had to keep *them* under control.

In slow procession, men and beasts moved sunwise around the grove. Aelle's son Cymen was just ahead of him, with another ox, even bigger than his own. Men of the fyrd stepped out from the encircling crowd as they passed, draping the beasts with additional garlands, or simply patting the smooth hides as they murmured their prayers—"Let me fight bravely!" "May I kill many of the enemy!" and sometimes, "May the gods bring me safely home."

As they came around for the second time, each animal was led inside the grove. The beasts were becoming more restive as the blood-scent grew stronger, but when Oesc's turn came the ox followed docilely down the well-trodden path.

The heads and skins of the earlier victims already hung

from the trees. Now the ox did plant his feet, nostrils flaring, and though the boy tugged on the rope, refused to stir. As Oesc struggled to make it move, Hæthwæge came forward, singing softly, a spray of ash leaves in her hand. He recognized "Ger" the rune of harvest, and "Sigel" for victory. At the sound, the ox calmed and stood quietly as the wicce moved around him, brushing the leaves across head and back and flanks.

Ceretic came after her, a knife in his hand. He cut a pinch of hair from the curling cowlick on the animal's forehead and stepped back, holding it high.

"Woden, to you this ox is offered, for you made holy. Accept it, War-father, and give us the victory!"

The air around the altar tingled with the energy of the blood that had been spilled already. As the war-leader spoke, wind whispered in the leaves and lifted the hair from Oesc's brow, and as Ceretic opened his fingers, the white hairs whirled away.

Hæthwæge's fingers closed over Oesc's hand on the rope, and the ox followed them to the altar, where the butcher was waiting. He was a huge man, heavily muscled, with a hammer in his hand. As the ox reached the edge of the blood pit, he swung. There was a loud thunk as the hammer hit, and the ox went to its knees.

For a moment Oesc simply stared. Then he remembered to draw his seax, and Hæthwæge guided his hand to the pulsing vein in the throat of the ox and he struck and pulled the blade through.

The animal jerked, but within seconds the gush of blood dropped its internal pressure past the point of pain and the breath sighed out through the sliced windpipe in long gasps. Like everyone, Oesc had helped with the butchering each autumn, and when he was hunting, given the mercy stroke to hares or deer. Death was always serious, but he had never before understood that it was holy.

"Make your prayer now—" whispered the wisewoman, holding a brass bowl underneath the ox and letting it fill with blood.

"Woden, receive this spirit, and fill us with your soul. Father of Victory, bring my men back home to their fields, and me to my grandfather's hall!''

The eyes of the ox were dull already, and he could feel the life of the body ebbing from the flesh beneath his hands like grain from a torn bag. But the grain still existed even when the bag was empty, and he had the sense that the life of the ox had not been extinguished so much as drawn away.

Your flesh will give us power! he thought. *May my own blood, when the time comes, be as good an offering!*

The blood was draining now in spurts. Hæthwæge took Oesc's arm and pulled him to his feet, and as the last of the flow dribbled into the pit, men looped ropes around the ox's feet and hauled it away to be skinned and butchered for the feast that would follow. The wicce dipped the spray of leaves into the blood and sprinkled Oesc, then handed it to the boy and gave him the bowl.

Still dazed, Oesc made his way out of the grove to bless the men whom he hoped to lead to victory.

The armies came to battle three days later, under weeping skies. The Saxons formed their shieldwall on the shores of one of the streams that came down to the sound, feet planted in the muddy soil, watching the British cavalry sweep towards them across the plain. Rather than creating a solid line, Ceretic had ordered each contingent to form a wedge, so that more of the spears could come into play. It was a saw-edge that would cut the British to pieces, he had told them, riding up and down along the river bank.

Now the commander stood with his hearth-companions at the center, his white horse led off by a thrall to the rear. If he turned his head, Oesc could see the gleam of the gilded boar image that crowned the steel crest of Ceretic's helmet. On the other side, Aelle waited with his sons beside him. Oesc's helm was rounded, with a nasal and side flaps, and ringmail hanging around the back and sides. Beneath tunic and mail shirt he was sweating, but most of his men would fight with no more protection than a leather cap banded in iron, bodies defended only by their shields.

Beyond the reed beds, pewter-colored waters stretched

away to a smudge of darker grey that was the island. Above the army, gulls rode the wind, crying like wælcyriges seeking out the slain. Soon they would be able to make their choices. The British were drawing steadily closer, trotting in close formation. Their shields were painted Roman-fashion, each contingent bearing its own device. He could see the glitter of their lance-heads as they came on. Perspiration made his hand slip on the shaft of his own throwing spear. Oesc leaned it against his shield, wiped his palm on the skirts of his tunic and grasped the javelin once more. Hæthwæge had a spear, he thought suddenly, as powerful as Artor's legendary sword. Why, he wondered, had Hengest not ordered her to bring it to war? When they got home he would ask her.

If he got home. . . . The British were cantering now, nearing with appalling speed. Surely the river would slow them, he thought, and then the hooves of the horses were churning the water into arcs of glittering spray. They surged up the bank like a rising wave, lancepoints dipping in deadly unison.

Oesc set his feet in the mud, lifted his left arm and felt his shield braced by those of Byrhtwold on one side and Eadric on the other, and raised his right arm, spear poised to throw. Wild-eyed horses expanded to fill his vision, the faces of the riders contorted above their shields. He felt a yell leave his throat, lost in the roar of the Saxon battle cry.

A ripple of motion swept the shield wall. Instinctively his arm swung forward, releasing the spear. Here and there the oncoming tide of horsemen faltered, but that first flight of spears was not enough to stop them. Oesc hunched behind his shield, straining to hold it in place between the others as an oncoming horseman struck the line.

The shieldwall rocked backward, and for a moment Oesc was lifted off his feet, but he did not fall. The enemy horse, pierced by spiked shield-bosses, reared, screaming. A lance thrust down at him, passing just above his shoulder. Oesc managed to get his sword free, and glimpsing a mailed body, stabbed upward. For a moment he felt as if he were supporting the entire weight of man and horse, then the foe recoiled and he caught his breath once more.

The British riders had broken the shield hedge in several

places, and were in amongst the Saxons, stabbing with lance and sword. Others had swirled off to either side in an attempt to outflank them. Over the tumult Oesc glimpsed a dragon banner that he supposed must belong to Artor. It was being carried by a big man with dark hair. Then a horse loomed suddenly above him; a sword clanged against his shield boss and he gave ground, and for a long time after that was too busy to think about anything at all.

Consciousness returned gradually on a tide of lamentation. *Why are they weeping? Am I dead?* Oesc wondered. But the dead didn't feel pain, and as awareness returned he realized he had a raging headache and was sore everywhere. For a few moments he lay still, trying to remember.

Then a flash of memory showed him Byrhtwold lying sprawled before him with a spear thrust through his chest. After that he had been seized by battle madness. That must be why he felt so awful now. *They must be wailing for Byrhtwold*, he thought then, and felt hot tears on his own cheeks. *He died saving me.*

Oesc opened his eyes. Blurred vision showed him a night sky and the shapes of men moving back and forth between him and the fires. Then he tried to sit up and discovered that his hands and feet were tied.

Alarm shocked through his body, sharpening his senses. The lamentations he heard were in the British tongue, and the faces and gear of the men around him were British as well. He had been taken by the enemy.

He knew enough of their language to make out the words—

Before Gerontius, scourge of the foe,
I saw white horses swiflty go,
After war cries, bitter the blow . . .

At least, he thought with grim satisfaction, the Saxons had accounted for one hero among their enemies. The British were not rejoicing, and yet he was a prisoner, his mail shirt enough to mark him as worth saving for ransom. Who had won the battle?

He took a deep breath and tried to break his bonds, and at the effort agony slashed through his head, dividing him from consciousness once more.

When Oesc opened his eyes again, it was morning. His other wounds had stiffened painfully, but the headache had subsided to a dull throb.

"Yes, that's him—" said a Saxon voice nearby. "Octha's whelp. I saw him in Venta."

Biting his lip to keep from groaning, Oesc rolled over. Squinting against the sunlight, he looked up at his captors. The Saxon was only a churl, of no importance. He blinked, trying to make out the features of the other two men.

"Let me kill him!" said one of them, a man of about thirty years with curling dark hair. "My brother's blood cries out for vengeance."

"Do you think I don't mourn him too?" said his companion. Oesc couldn't see him properly, but he sounded young, his voice hoarse with unshed tears. "He taught me to fight! He saved my life a dozen times yesterday ... he was my friend. ..."

"We all grieve for Gerontius, but this one is worth more to us as a hostage," said an older man.

"How so? He's no kin to Ceretic."

"True, but he is Hengest's grandson, and while we hold him, Cantium will stand surety for Ceretic's good behavior."

There was a long silence. Though his head was throbbing furiously, Oesc struggled to get up, refusing to remain bound like a thrall at his enemies' feet.

"Cut his bonds," said the young voice tiredly.

The older man sawed at the thongs with his knife and hauled Oesc to his feet, supporting him until the dizziness passed and he could stand alone.

Artor ... thought Oesc, taking in the rich embroidery on the bloodstained tunic, and the golden torque beneath the thin fringing of brown beard on the jaw. He himself was a bit taller, otherwise there was little to choose between them for size.

"Can you understand me?" Artor asked, waiting for his prisoner's nod. "We didn't win the battle, but neither did you. You will come with us, bound by iron chains in a wagon, or bound not to try escape by oath before your gods, riding free. It's up to you."

Your father killed mine . . . thought Oesc. There was a dagger at the king's belt. If he could grab it and strike, Octha would be avenged. But at this moment it was taking all his strength just to stand. Once more he met Artor's eyes, and this time he could not look away.

He saw grief in that gaze, and a weariness almost as great as his own, and something else that he did not understand. Oddly, at that moment what he remembered was the trust in the eyes of the ox he had led to sacrifice. He had heard that the Christians of Eriu called it a white martyrdom, when they were exiled from their land. He swallowed, knowing himself self-doomed.

"I swear . . . in Woden's name. I am the offering."

THE RAVEN'S HEAD

A.D. 480

WHILE CERETIC LICKED HIS WOUNDS IN THE SOUTH AND ICEL gathered strength in the midlands, Britannia lay at peace. Even the Picts and the Scotti were keeping quiet, and Artor's advisors thought the time ripe for him to take possession of his father's city of Londinium. With him went his houseguard and his servants, and Eldaul of Glevum and Catraut of Verulamium, who had become his principal ministers. And with him also went Oesc, his Saxon hostage, riding sad and sullen in the rear.

Oesc's heart ached to think of his grandfather waiting for him in that shadowed hall. Hæthwæge would take care of the old man's health, but who now would play at tabula with him in the long evenings, or bring in venison when the salt beef of winter began to pall?

And more than he could have imagined, Oesc missed Cantuware. When he closed his eyes at night he could see how the waterfowl spiraled down into the marshes, or the wind brushed gentle fingers across the growing grain. He could see sunlight falling through the forest of the Weald in showers of green and gold, and blazing with pitiless clarity on the high shoulders of the Downs.

It was that day in the temple at Ægele's ford that had made the difference, he thought, looking backward. Sometimes he

cursed Hæthwæge for having brought him there, and sometimes he took comfort in the memory. He was rooted now in
Cantuware as deeply as if he had been born there, and away
from it he would never be happy, even if he were free.

He was not badly treated. Rough repairs had made most
of the old Governor's Palace habitable, and there was room
enough for all of Artor's household there. Merlin had rooms
in an old tower, but was rarely in them, being often away to
other parts of Britannia, carrying messages, said some, while
others whispered that he went off to consort with demons.

Oesc grew accustomed to carven pillars and marble facings
and cold tiled floors. He had a whitewashed chamber to himself, with a shuttered window that opened out towards the
river. Only sometimes, wandering through an empty passage
or a courtyard where a dry fountain accused the sky, he remembered how he had felt once when he dressed up in his
father's armor. It was as if he and all the others here were
only children, playing at being kings, and soon the adults
who had built these halls would reclaim their dwellings.
Sometimes, watching Artor as he sat in splendor on the dais
of the basilica, he wondered if the high king felt that way too.

But the legions were gone. Odoacer, a warlord among the
Saxons whose father had been one of Attila's generals, ruled
now in Italia, and unlike the barbarian generals who had gone
before him, he refused to nominate a Roman as titular emperor. The Empire of the West was ended, and only in Britannia, and the parts of Gallia where Riothamus led British
warriors whose families had fled the island after the Night of
the Long Knives, did its memory live on.

On an afternoon in October, Oesc stood with the rest of the
household in the basilica, watching as Artor welcomed a delegation from Gallia. He was placed near the front, with Cunorix, the son of an Irish chieftain who had been making
trouble in Demetia. All the hostages were on display together,
he thought bitterly, like the high king's sight-hounds, who
lay panting on the mosaic floor, or the tiercel hawk on its
perch by the throne.

With nothing much else on which to spend his energy, Oesc

had found a certain interest in watching the young king grow into his power. Artor was now almost twenty, and a man's beard, clipped close, outlined the strong curve of his jaw. He had dressed for the occasion in a dalmatic of crimson silk, with twin bands of embroidery running over his shoulders and down to the hem on either side. Around his neck glinted the golden torque of a Celtic prince, but there was Byzantine enamel work on his diadem.

Oesc, who had become accustomed to seeing his captor lounging by the fire in his favorite tunic of faded green wool, suppressed a smile. But the dark-haired boy who followed the Gaullish envoy was gazing in awe at the marble facings on the walls and the gilding on the coffered beams of the distant ceiling, and most of all at the brilliant figure on the throne. To him, Artor *was* the emperor.

Eldaul stepped forward and read from a scroll, "Johannes Rutilius, Comes Lugdunensis, bears greetings from Riothamus, Dux of the Britons north of the river Liger, to Artorius, Vor-Tigernus of Greater Britannia."

"Let him approach—"

The dark-haired man with the boy bowed.

"My king, I bring the best wishes of my lord Riothamus for the continued good health of yourself and your realm." His British had an odd accent, but by this time Oesc understood the language well.

Someone in the crowd behind Oesc snorted. "About time— were they waiting to see if the lad could hold onto his crown?"

"My lord offers a treaty of trade and alliance. The Franks worry at our borders in Gallia as the Saxons trouble you here. Barbarians sit at their ease in the Holy City, and the Emperor in Constantinople is very far away. You and Riothamus, my lord, are the heirs of the Western Empire, and it is only good sense for you to work together."

"As you say," Eldaul interrupted him, "we are still fighting the Saxons. What help will Riothamus offer us?"

"Nay," growled one of the older men, "we need no help from men who fled Britannia when the Saxons first rose against us in blood and fire."

Artor frowned at both of them. "I think Gallia needs all her men for her own defense, and our own warriors can defend us here," he put in quickly.

"But the wharves of Londinium are often empty," Catraut added. "Trade has been poor while the Saxon wolves ranged the Narrow Seas. Once Britannia helped to feed the empire. Send us merchant ships, with war galleys to guard them, and we will send you corn from the rich midlands that we still hold."

The flush that had risen in Johannes's face subsided. "That is what I have come to propose, though I would add a provision that either ruler might call for aid to the other if times should change."

"That seems good to me," Artor said while his advisors were still drawing breath to answer.

"In earnest of our sincerity I have brought you my own son, the child of my wife who is sister to Riothamus, to serve you as part of your household." He set his hand on the boy's shoulder and pushed him towards the throne.

"What is your name?" asked Artor, learning forward with his elbows on his knees and the first genuine smile of the afternoon.

"I am Betiver, my lord." The boy spoke softly, but boldly enough—he must be accustomed to courts, thought Oesc.

"Then you shall be my cupbearer. Would you like that, Betiver?"

"I would like it very well—"

Betiver's eyes were shining. Oesc sighed. There was no denying that the British king had charm. All of the younger men were half in love with him. *Except for me . . .* he thought, glowering.

"Then you may stand over there, and tonight, when we feast in honor of your father, you shall serve me." Artor gestured towards the hostages.

As the business of the court continued, Betiver turned to his new companions.

"Who are you?"

"We're the king's hostages. This black-headed lad is Cunorix, an Irishman from Demetia, and I am Oesc from Cantium." Now, he thought, the boy would understand what his status truly was, despite the fine words.

"Do you dislike it?" Betiver asked with surprising perceptiveness. "They say that the great Aetius was a hostage with the Huns, and Attila himself hostage for a time in Rome. That's how we learn about other peoples and their lands."

For that to be any use, thought Oesc sourly, *you have to get home again.* But he said no more.

One evening just past Midsummer, when every window had been opened to let in whatever cooling breath of breeze might come from the river below, Artor came striding back from a meeting of the council with a face like thunder and Cai at his heels.

Oesc and Cunorix, who had been taking turns playing Round Mill with Betiver, stood up as the king appeared in the doorway. To try and get three counters in a row on the diagram was a children's game, but Oesc liked it because the pattern reminded him of a Germanic protective sigil called the "helm of awe." He made a grab for the counters as the board rocked, then straightened again.

"I've spent most of a stifling day listening to old men argue," said Artor. "They may have no blood in their veins, but mine needs cooling off. I'm going down to the river for a swim—would anyone else like to come?"

"I would!" cried Betiver, knocking the board askew as he pushed past. Cunorix rescued it this time and set it on his bed. He glanced at Oesc and then nodded.

"We'll come too."

As they trooped down the stairs towards the riverbank, it occurred to Oesc that Artor, surrounded by old men who all thought they knew what should be done better than he did, was in a sense a prisoner too. There was something sad in the thought that he had to turn to his own captives for company. It made Oesc uncomfortable to feel sorry for Artor, and he thrust the thought away, but as the evening continued, it kept coming back again.

The palace lay close to the river, but they had to follow the path along the banks for a little ways before they came to a landing where the bottom was shallow and firm enough to wade in. Some of the men from the town were already splashing happily, accompanied by shouting children. Someone looked up as they approached, saw they were strangers, and looked away.

Artor turned, his eyes alight, and held up one finger for silence. Oesc realized then that stripped down to thin tunics or breeches, with no mark of rank or royalty, they looked like any other group of young men out for a swim. He stepped out of his sandals, pulled off his tunic and laid it over a bush; in another moment his breechcloth had followed. Like all the children of the marshlands, he had learned to swim when he was small. He entered the water in a long, low dive that took him far out from shore. The current was stronger than he had expected, and cold. He had to swim hard to get back to the shallows once more.

Artor reached out and Oesc grasped his hand, a little surprised at the strength with which he pulled him in. Then he got his feet under him and stood, gasping.

"Don't go out too far—current will take you away," Oesc said in warning.

"I know . . . sometimes I wish it would. . . ."

There was a moment of strained silence. Then Artor saw Oesc staring at him, gave his head a little shake, and smiled. In the next moment he was splashing Betiver, and in the water-fight that followed the moment of understanding was gone.

But when the light of the long summer day faded at last and they reluctantly pulled on their clothing once more, Oesc still remembered that odd sense of equality.

The day might be ended, but they were young, and so was the night. A century earlier, Londinium had been the metropolis of Britannia, and for every one of the more utilitarian businesses there had been a wine shop or taberna. Most of them had disappeared with the Legions, but now that the high king was in residence, they seemed to be sprouting on every street corner once more.

Betiver, who was the sort of child who never forgot his hat or broke his shoe latchets, was the only one of them who had brought his belt-pouch. It held enough coins for them all to drink at the first taberna they stopped at, and the second. By the time they got to the third wine shop, Cunorix had won more money dicing with an Armorican sailor. At the fifth, Artor himself won them a round of drinks at ring-toss.

By this time, all of them were exceedingly merry. Oesc, a veteran of serious Saxon drinking bouts with ale and mead, discovered that he had no head for wine. But it didn't matter. Artor was a good fellow—Cai was a good fellow—and so were Cunorix and the boy. The serving girls with whom they flirted were all beautiful. The carters and tradesmen with whom they were drinking were good fellows too, seen through a vinous, rose-pink, haze.

"Got an idea—" He draped an arm across Artor's shoulder. "Take your people, my people, get 'em to drink together. Make 'em be friends!"

"You're drunk, Oesc." Artor hiccoughed, then laughed. "Guess I am too. Sounds good to me. Maybe that's how the Romans . . . got their empire!" They all laughed.

It was very late by the time they ran out of money again, and by then the tabernas were beginning to close. Betiver had fallen asleep with his head on the table, and Cai hoisted him over one shoulder as they staggered out the door. The damp night air was bracing after the boozy warmth of the wine shop, but their steps were still a little unsteady when they heard the first light footfalls behind them.

Oesc shook his head in an attempt to clear it, and saw the stars spin. If this was an ambush, he was going to have to fight drunk or not at all.

"My lord—" came Cai's voice from the darkness, the first time he had used the title all evening.

"I heard. Take the boy on ahead."

How, Oesc wondered, could he sound so cool?

"Artor! My place is here—"

"Get Betiver to safety. That's a command! Cunorix, Oesc, stand back to back with me!"

"I'll go for help!" Cai salved his conscience. He started to run, and at the sound of his footsteps, their attackers came out from the alleyway.

At least, thought Oesc as he braced himself against the others' shoulders, *this way I won't fall down.*

"We've drunk up all our money," Artor said clearly. "You'll get nothing but blows for your trouble."

"Yon black-headed lad has a silver buckle, and you are wearing a ring. That's worth food and drink to starving men."

Oesc squinted at the approaching shadows. They didn't move like starving men.

"Go to the palace if you are hungry, and they will give you food. You are breaking the king's peace and will be punished if you harm us here."

As Artor was speaking, Cunorix whispered in Oesc's ear to watch out for the man on the right, who had a knife, while the others were armed with clubs or staves.

"Why should the king care what happens in the streets?"

"Believe me, he cares!" answered Artor. His laughter ceased as their assailants came on.

The robbers were five to three, and sober. Oesc drew a deep breath. "Woden!" he cried, as the first blow hit, and heard Artor calling out to Brigantia. The wine had blunted their reactions, but all three were warriors, trained to fight even when they could not see. With fists and feet they deflected the first rush and the second. When the third came they were gasping, but alarm and exertion had burned most of the alcohol away. What remained dulled the pain of the blows.

There were a few moments of furious action, followed by a pause while everyone stood gasping. One of their opponents lay on the ground, while another was holding his belly where Cunorix had kicked him. Oesc felt Artor straighten.

"Well, my friends, we have cleared the board a little. I think it is time for the king-piece to break out of the fortress!" Before they could object, Artor had sprung forward and scooped up a fallen club and was swinging it at the nearest foe.

Cunorix shrieked something in Irish, lowered his head and charged, and Oesc headed towards the third man. At last he was free to fight! The rage he had repressed during his captivity filled him with a new intoxication. He saw a stave whirr towards him, lifted his left arm to protect his head and heard a crack as it hit. The impact whirled him around, inside his opponent's guard, and his right fist drove towards the other man's throat. Something gave way with a sickening crunch and the man fell, gurgling.

Artor had felled his man, and Cunorix was grappling with the other one. Oesc drew breath to speak and gasped as the numbness in his arm began to give way to a throbbing agony. Artor held up one hand, listening.

More men were coming. But what they were hearing now was the ring of hob-nailed sandals and the jingle of military harness, not a footpad's stealthy tread. Cai had rousted out the city guard at last.

Oesc's broken arm healed slowly, though the tongue-lashing Artor received from his advisors when they returned to the palace no doubt left deeper wounds. Only Merlin, who had returned from one of his journeys shortly after, seemed to understand. Rumor had it that the reaction of Artor's mother, arriving for one of her periodic visitations, was more vigorous.

To occupy Oesc's mind during his convalescence, a priest called Fastidius was sent to teach him the language of the Romans, and the others involved in their escapade were encouraged to study with him, whether as a punishment or to keep him company was not clear.

"*Arma virumque cano . . .* " The words were intoned with the sonority of a man who loved the language and a clarity of accent that Oesc was already learning to recognize as being of another order entirely than the camp Latin many of the soldiers used. "And what, my child, do those words say?"

"*Arma*—that means weapons," answered Oesc. This sounded much more interesting than the grammar the old man had been teaching them before. "Does *virumque* have anything to do with men?"

Through the open window he could hear the sounds of men and horses, and from farther off, a distant mutter of thunder. The heat wave had broken, and the air was cool and moist with the promise of rain.

"A man," Fastidius corrected. "The object of the verb. And the *que* at the end of it—what does that mean?" His watery gaze fixed on Cunorix, who stared as if an armed man had sprung from the ground before him. In fact, thought Oesc, he would probably have faced a warrior with less fear.

Artor took pity on him. "It means *and*, does it not? 'Of arms and the man I sing.'"

"Hmm," said the priest, "you have studied the language before."

"It was spoken in the home of Caius Turpilius, who fostered me," answered the king. "But I have not had much practice in reading."

"Ah . . . you will want to understand the messages you receive from foreign kings without depending on a scribe, and to make sure the messages written for you express what you want to say."

It had never occurred to Oesc that a king could be his own interpreter, but he could see now that it would be useful. Certainly the priest seemed to understand. Fastidius was an old man, trained in the golden days before the Saxon Revolt when his namesake the bishop wrote letters of civilized amusement at the idea that sensible men could ever accept Augustinus's harsh doctrine. Their sufferings at the hands of the Saxons had made a belief in predestination more credible, but the old priest still behaved as if the purity of one's Latin were as important as the purity of one's soul.

Cunorix cleared his throat. "But what does it mean?"

Fastidius smiled, and without looking at the scroll, began to chant once more—"*Troiae ui primus ab oris Italiam fato profugus Lavinaque venit litora* . . . Who from Troy by fate caused to flee came first to the shores of Italia and Lavinium . . . It is the story of Aeneas, who escaped the fall of the great city of Troy and became the founder of Rome."

"I have heard of him," Artor said slowly. "They say that the ancestors of the Britons came from there with Brutus, his great-grandson."

But to Oesc it seemed that the story of this Aeneas must be very much like that of his own people, driven by need to seek a new home on a foreign shore. He pointed to the scroll.

"How did this Aeneas get to Italia, and what happened to him there?"

Fastidius smiled. "I thought that you might like the story. It is full of battles. Some of my brethren would say that you should study texts of the Holy Fathers. But it seems to me that you will learn better with something you find interesting, and also, Vergilius wrote much better Latin."

"Even Cai, here, might learn something if it is about battles—" Artor punched his foster-brother playfully. "He was a very poor pupil to our housepriest at home!"

It did seem that with the *Aenied* for their text they made better progress, following the adventures of the Trojan hero around the Mediterranean in his search for a home. And when the frustration of untangling Latin declensions became too much for their patience, Fastidius could be tempted into regaling them with tales of British heroes, for he came from the isle of Mona, where memories were long.

When autumn arrived, the whole court followed the Tamesis upriver to the hills for a few weeks of hunting, and came back brown from sun and wind and pleasantly fatigued by hard riding, with enough wild meat to vary the menu for some time. It had been good to get out, but in some ways the city seemed even more stifling afterward, especially when the weather changed and the early winter rains set in.

"Do you know any stories about Londinium?" asked Betiver one day when the leaden skies wept steadily and damp draughts crept in under every door.

Fastidius set down the tablet on which he had been checking Betiver's lists of Latin verbs and smiled. "I have told you already how Brutus founded the city and called it Troia Nova, which was in the British tongue, Trinovantum, because the Trinovante tribe came to dwell there. They say that his descendent, Lud, built walls and towers and renamed the city after himself. But that was just before the great Julius Ceasar brought the Romans to these shores. The Latin histories tell us that Londinium was only a small river town which the Romans rebuilt in stone, so I do not know what the truth may be."

"Buildings are not very exciting," said Cunorix. "Are there no other tales?"

Fastidius's brows, which were white like his hair, and

rather bushy, bent. "There is another story, that ends here. If you will take up your tablets and write out all the forms of *placare*, 'to soothe or calm,' *conloquor*, 'to negotiate,' and *agere*, 'to make a treaty,' then I will tell you a story from Pagensis, where the Ordovici ruled, about a king who was so great in stature that no building could hold him."

"You think that we are so averse to using words of peace that we must be bribed to learn them?" asked Artor, laughing.

"I think that you are all young men, who believe that glory can only be won in war . . ."

Betiver had already picked up his stylus and tablet and was busily making marks in the wax. Grinning, the others began to work as well.

When they had finished and been corrected, Fastidius kept his promise.

"A long time ago there was a ruler of the Britons called Brannos, so great a king that men called him Blessed, and that became part of his name—in British, Bendeigid Brannos. He gave his sister Branuen in marriage to the king of Hibernia, but one of her half-brothers was angry because he had not been consulted, and he disfigured the horses of the Hibernian king, which was a great insult. Brannos paid compensation, and the girl went over the sea with her new husband, but the Hibernians still brooded on the insult, and presently they forced the king to punish his wife by making her a servant at his court. But Branuen had some magic of her own, and she trained a starling to carry the news of her torment to her brother in Britannia."

Nobody looked at Cunorix, who had gotten rather red in the face, but Artor motioned to Fastidius to go on.

"So the princes of Britannia went to war, the warriors in ships, and Bendeigid Brannos wading across the water, and there were great battles, and greater treacheries, and in the end, the Hibernians were defeated, but of the Britons only seven remained beside the king, who had been wounded by a poisoned lance in the heel. When Brannos saw that the poison would overcome him, he gave certain orders. And then, as he had commanded, they struck the head from his body, and took it back with them to Britannia."

"What were his orders?" asked Artor.

"What happened to Branven?" asked Betiver. Cunorix only glowered.

"The princess, remembering that because of her, two great peoples had been destroyed, died of sorrow. But the seven companions feasted for seven years in one habitation, forgetting their sorrows, and in another for seven again, listening to the birds from the Otherworld, and the head of Brannos was with them, uncorrupted. And when that time was done, they opened the door that looked towards the south, and then, as he had prophesied, they remembered everything."

It was a strange tale indeed, as Fastidius had promised them. To Oesc it seemed as if for him and Cunorix it had more meaning, for their people still lived as the Britons had lived before the Romans came. Cai was staring out the window, bored, as usual, by anything that was not about fighting, and Betiver listened with a child's wonder. But what did Artor make of this story of an ancient king?

He was already taller than Oesc, who overtopped most men. But in the past year Artor's body had thickened to match the promise of the strong bones. *This is no longer a boy to be led about by old men,* thought Oesc, *I wonder when his advisors will realize that their bear cub has become a bear?* The cold illumination from the window lit one side of the king's face and left the other in darkness, eyelids half closed to hide his thoughts, mouth grim. *His father killed mine . . .* Oesc told himself, but some other part of his being wished only that Artor would smile.

He cleared his throat. "What did they do then?"

"They followed Brannos's orders. They carried the head to the White Mount, the sacred hill by the river in Londinium, and there they buried it, face set towards Gallia. The word of Bendeigid Brannos was this, that while his head remained there, so also would his spirit and his power, to ward Britannia from plague and destruction."

"So, even in death a king may still watch over his people . . ." said Artor. His mouth was still grim, but there was a light in his eyes.

"It is so in the old Jutish lands," said Oesc. "There, when a king's reign has been peaceful, with good harvests, they build a great mound over his bones and set out offerings, so that his name is remembered and he becomes one with the gods."

"It is the bones of the saints and the blood of the martyrs that protect Christian lands!" said Betiver.

"Neither saints' relics nor a severed head seem to have protected the empire from the heathens," growled Cai. "I prefer to trust to stout hearts and strong arms."

"Perhaps Brannos's protection depended on a different kind of power," said Fastidius placatingly, and unrolled the scroll containing his grammatical notations once more.

The winter drew on, cold and wet. In the north and the midlands, it was a cruel season, with storms in which both men and cattle froze. But in Londinium, the sleet never quite seemed to turn into snow. The high king's household struggled with the old hypocaust system, but even when they got it working, the warmth that came up through the floors was never quite enough to offset the cold drafts that came in around the doors. There were many times when Oesc missed Saxon farmhouses. Dark and odorous though they might be, they were warm.

But presently the days began to lengthen, and occasionally they saw the sun. The skies echoed with the bitter music of the wild geese as they winged northward. Messengers went out to call the princes of Britannia to council. In the midlands, the snow that had fallen on hill and dale was melting, and the Tamesis began to rise.

"Am I or am I not the king?"

Oesc, who had been repairing his bow in hopes that they might soon get some hunting, opened his door and peered out. That had sounded like Artor's voice, but he had never heard it so angry.

Now he could hear a murmur of other voices, soothing or remonstrating.

"Be still—you prattle at me as if I were a fractious child!"

It *was* Artor. Oesc set down the bow and went out to see what was going on. He found Cai leaning against a pillar, watching the king stride back and forth across the cracked stones of the courtyard.

"He's always been like this, even when we were boys," said Cai. "He doesn't get mad often, but when he does, it's bad. He broke my nose and left me bruised for a week once when he thought I'd mistreated a horse, back when I was twelve and he was nine and I was a head taller than he."

Oesc didn't ask whether it was true. Cai was heavy handed with most things; he broke weapons and wore out his mounts faster than other men.

"He needs to crack someone's head or take a woman," Cai added, "but I don't suppose he will."

Oesc nodded. He knew that Cai sometimes went to the whores who served the soldiers, and Cunorix found comfort with the Irish serving girls. Oesc himself had always feared to be rejected because he was a Saxon. What Artor's reasons for continence might be he did not know.

"What's set him off now?" He asked.

"The old men on the council. They want someone to sit on the throne and look handsome, not a king. Artor got mad when they voted to exempt all Church lands from taxation."

"Does he want money?"

"Not for himself—for the troops up on the Wall. Your people have been quiet, but the Picts and the Scotti are always a threat, and all the regular army Britannia still has is up there. The landowners at least send men and supplies, but the Church expects to be protected for nothing."

Artor's long stride had slowed, and the high color was beginning to leave his cheeks. "Can't they understand? The time to build up your dikes is before it floods. We need to maintain a fighting force that can deter invasion, and that means money."

The placating murmur continued.

"I think God hears soldiers as well as priests. I have no

quarrel with the Church, but its business is prayer, not politics, and not all in this land are Christian. Anyhow, that isn't the problem now. They wouldn't even listen to my reasoning! They as much as told me to run away and play, and I didn't—I couldn't—answer them!"

Oesc hid a smile. That's how it was for Saxon war-leaders most of the time. Except for the sword-thanes, vowed to stand by their chieftains till death, warriors served voluntarily, and felt free to argue. It amazed him sometimes that the Germans had been able to conquer as much as they had. But hunger was a powerful motivator. These Britons were too accustomed to safety. They had received a sharp lesson, but clearly it was easily forgotten. If they had been willing to pay the troops who protected them, Hengest would never have asked for land.

"If you could—if they would listen to you—how would you order Britannia?" he asked.

"With a strong government. Rome succeeded because there was strength at the center to make all the provinces help and defend each other. It failed because it got too big. Britannia is a good size for communications, with defined borders."

"You mean to rule all the island?" asked Betiver.

"What about the Picts? asked Cai.

"What about the Saxons?" Oesc echoed.

"It seems to me," Artor said slowly, "that when tribes or regions think too much about their own rights and practices and needs they fight their neighbors, and then they are easy prey for any better organized enemy who moves in. Julius Caesar conquered the British tribes because they could not work together. Your grandfather overran half the island because Vitalinus and Ambrosius would not make an alliance, and failed to keep it because your Saxon tribes would not accept a single high king. I know that rival emperors fought each other, but for most people, most of the time, within the empire there was peace."

"But at what price?" asked Cunorix. "Your Romans leveled peoples as they leveled the ground for their fortresses. Is peace worth losing everything that makes you who you are?"

"Did I say I thought it would be easy?" Artor said ruefully.

"I would be king for the Romans and the British, the men of Eriu who have settled on these shores and the Picts and even the Saxons, if they would accept me, each with their own customs, living in peace with their neighbors."

"Foster-brother, you are crazy," Cai shook his head pityingly. "Even the Lord Jesus could not make them all agree."

"Jesus himself said his kingdom was not of this world, though some of our bishops seem to have trouble remembering it. What I am talking about requires an earthly king."

"You certainly seem to have spent some time thinking about it—" Betiver said admiringly.

Artor shrugged. "Sitting through all those meetings, what else do I have to do? I know that the king has to be strong enough to defend the borders and keep people within them from killing each other as well. He should encourage trade and sponsor public works. All this requires taxes, which people do not want to pay. He must keep local chieftains from oppressing their own people, but give them enough freedom so they will support him. Maybe it *is* impossible—but if they would stop treating me like a child, I would try!"

"You have a magic sword. Does not that give you the authority?" asked Oesc.

"That's an *old* miracle," Artor answered bitterly. "I need a new one to impress the princes—or maybe I am the one who needs a sign that this is what I am supposed to do. . . ."

Artor was still muttering when a workman appeared in the doorway, eyes bulging and muddy to the thighs.

"My lord, come quickly! They've found a head—some say it's a demon and some say it's a god. It was walled up, my lord, like a thing of power. They want to throw it into the river. I tried to tell them not to, but they wouldn't listen!"

"I know how you feel—" said the king. "Very well, I'll come. Perhaps the *people* will be willing to listen to me!"

"They call it the White Mount, my lord, but it's only just a little hill beside the water—"

Oesc saw Artor's step falter for a moment, and remembered suddenly where he had heard that name before. He hastened his own steps to catch up with them as the workman chattered on.

"The river's been rising, you see, and we was trying to drive in a few stakes to help hold the bank. And we hit something hard, though of course we didn't know that's what it was, and Marcellus says, 'That's funny—' and then the ground just sort of fell away and we could see the big slabs of stone with the water gurgling round."

Ahead a knot of people had gathered by the waterside. Someone saw the king coming, still dressed in the finery he had worn to the council, and shouted, and the crowd began to swirl towards them.

"I told them to leave it be, but Marcellus said that's good building stone, and he got a hook down the crack and pulled, and the whole slab came over, and then—"

But by then they were at the riverside, and Artor gestured for silence. As the workman had said, it was only a small hill, but it was crowned by three fine oak trees. Several ravens were sitting there, and as they approached, more came flying, calling as they circled the hill. Oesc felt a prickle of unease, and seeing Artor frown, knew that he too had felt the breath of the Otherworld. Cai stood with his arms folded, glaring back at the crowd.

People gave way before them. At the edge of the water the hill gaped open, the slab that had fallen revealing a small, square chamber, walled and roofed with stone. This was no Roman construction—the size of the stones reminded Oesc of etin-work he had seen. Water had seeped across the stone floor and around the stone block that stood in the midst of the chamber. On top of it was what appeared to be the head of a man of giant size, frozen in stone. Blank, almond, eyes stared out from either side of a long straight nose, the whole surrounded by masses of undulant hair.

Artor gazed at it for a moment, then bent to peer in. "Look, Cai—" he called. "It's pottery, not stone at all."

"Don't touch it—" Cai began, but Artor was already entering the chamber.

"Nonsense," he said over his shoulder. "If we leave it here

it will be destroyed." There was a general gasp as the king grasped the pot in both arms and turned to carry it outside.

As he brought it into the sunlight, the shouting subsided. "Bendeigid Brannos . . ." said someone, and the whispers became a murmur of awe.

Seen full on, the features reminded Oesc a little of Merlin, and yet, though the druid's brown mane had the same wildness, Oesc had never seen on his face such a look of majesty. But he did not have long to compare them. As the light fell full on the surface of the pot, a fine network of cracks began to ray out across it.

Artor fell to his knees in the mud, cradling the pot against his chest, but in moments the clay was crumbling. As it fell away, they saw that it held neither ashes nor treasure, but a single human skull. For a moment only they looked upon the great empty eye-sockets and the mighty jaws, and then the skull also began to crumble. Clay and bone fell in fragments through Artor's fingers into the water, and the current whirled them away.

The ravens came skirling down from the trees after them, lamenting, but above their cacophony rose a woman's scream—

"The Raven of Britannia is gone! Brannos the Blessed has abandoned us and we are lost!" Now there was an edge of hysteria in the hubbub of the crowd.

Artor looked down at his hands, still white with clay and bone, then he stood up again, and there was something in his face that made Oesc go cold inside, for in that moment it held the same look he had seen in the statue's eyes. With a single easy movement Artor leaped up onto the grass.

"People of Britannia, do not despair . . ." The king's voice was not loud, but it carried. "The ancient king protected you for many years, but his task is done. His remains have been released to find rest with the sea, his father, but his spirit remains with me." He held out his arm, and the largest of the ravens, circling, alighted upon it.

"Do you see—the ravens recognize my right! Now it is I who shall be Brannos, and take upon me his duty. To the end of my life and beyond I will be your protector!"

"You are only a man, and one day your bones will be dust!" came a hoarse voice from the crowd.

Artor turned, and the people grew silent. "Keep this place holy, a sanctuary for the ravens, for I tell you now—so long as the ravens dwell on this hill, my spirit will ward Britannia!"

"Artor Brannos!" came the cry, "Artor the Blessed! Artor! Artor!" The echoes rang.

The people were all around Artor now, asking for his blessing, touching his hand. Oesc watched with wonder and pity in his heart. When he made his own dedication at the shrine it had only been for one lifetime. He sensed in this spontaneous avowal a commitment far more binding than whatever oath Artor had given to the Christian god when he was made king.

Eventually the people dispersed and the king was able to return to the palace. The raven flew back to the oak tree, but it was a long time before the strangeness left Artor's eyes.

"It was only a skull," said Cai very softly as they passed through the gates. "And Brannos was only a legend."

Oesc nodded. That might be true, but the moment during which that skull, whoever it belonged to, had been visible had been long enough for him to see that it was larger than the head of any ordinary man.

VI

THE FEAST OF LUGUS

A·D· 486

JUST AFTER BELTAIN, IN THE ELEVENTH YEAR OF ARTOR'S KING-
ship, Naitan Morbet, King of all the Provinces of the Picts,
broke the peace that Leudonus had imposed upon him and
came south in force. It was a year of barbarian victories. In
Gallia, the new king, Chlodovechus, had led his Franks
against Syagrius and defeated this last Roman at Augusta
Suessionum. In Italia, the Ostrogoth, Theodoric, ruled as *mag-
ister militum* in the puppet emperor Zeno's name. And in Britannia, it seemed as if the time of the wild tribes had returned.

Before Leudonus could gather men to stop them, the Picts
had swept around his eastern flank, across the tumbled stones
where once the Romans had sought to establish a far northern
frontier, and were swarming up the vale of the Cluta, burning
everything in their path. King Ridarchus had warning enough
to marshal his warband, but they were powerless against
such a host and barely made it back to the safety of the Rock
of Alta Cluta, where they took refuge, cursing. For this was
no raid, but a carefully planned campaign. Leaving a swathe
of destruction behind them, the Picts rolled up the old Roman
road and through the passes, heading for the rich Selgovae
lands and Luguvalium.

In Londinium, their first news came from a dust-covered
courier whose horse fell dead beneath him as he pulled up

before the palace. The scroll he bore was as clear a cry for help as anyone had ever heard from Leudonus. Indeed, commented Cai when he heard of it, ever since the British princes had chosen Artor over him as high king, the king of the Votadini had sent very few communications of any kind.

"Maybe so," Artor had replied, "but he has been sending his taxes, and even if he had not, this challenges the whole of Britannia."

Since the episode of Brannos's head, Artor had begun to assert himself. His counsellors protested, but they could not stop him from sending out messengers to speed past the fields of young grain, calling on the men of Eburacum and Deva and Bremetennacum and all the forts that were still manned along the Wall to gather to his banner at Luguvalium by Midsummer Day.

Oesc listened to the hubbub of preparation with mounting frustration. In the past, he had tried not to mind when Artor rode out against the Angles or the Saxons. But Artor and Cai and even young Betiver were already making names for themselves as fighters, while he, as young and strong as they were, practiced his Latin and his archery. Even if he were freed, why should his own people accept a man with no experience in war?

He was in the library of the palace, helping Fastidius to sort scrolls, when a sudden draft set the lamp flames to flickering and he turned and saw it was the king.

"It is your arms you should be sorting through, not these scrolls," said Artor, standing with arms folded in the doorway.

Oesc felt his cheeks grow red. He had never quite dared to think of the British king as his friend, but surely too much respect had grown between them for the other man to mock him.

"My lord, don't tease him—" said Betiver, appearing next to him. "Oesc, go get your gear—Artor wants you in his warband when we go against Naitan!"

From red, Oesc knew he was becoming pale. Artor came forward and grasped his arm. "I could not ask you to fight your own folk, but the Picts are no kin to you, and I will need every man. And indeed, I would be honored to have the grandson of Hengest at my side. . . ."

Oesc found his voice at last. "I have fought beside you once already, my lord." He rubbed the arm that had been broken in the fight, which still gave a twinge now and again when it was about to rain. "I will be glad to come."

Betiver looked up at the red sandstone walls of the great fortress called the Petriana with a grin of sheer pleasure. *This* was Rome, whose mighty works none of the new tribes would ever equal. The Petriana was still the headquarters for the senior officer of the Wall command, and it was better cared for than most of the forts the Legions had left behind them. When he surveyed the massive gatehouse and the strong walls that protected the city of Luguvalium, a few miles to the south, he was certain that the Empire of the West would be restored, with Artor as Imperator.

First, of course, they would have to do something about this troublesome Pictish king. But Betiver had grown from spindly youth to warrior in Artor's service, and it never really occurred to him that his king could fail.

Certainly, with the army that was gathering here to support him, Artor must have the victory. They had filled up all the empty barracks within the fortress, and more were camped along the banks of the river. And even as Betiver turned back towards the Principia, where Artor, following tradition, had made his headquarters, he heard a horn call from the eastern tower. Another band of warriors was coming in.

By the time Betiver reached the king, they all knew who it was. Leudonus of the Votadini, having come south by the eastern route and then along the Wall, was bringing all the men he could spare from the defense of his own lands to fight with them. Gualchmai, the eldest of his four sons and Artor's nephew, rode at his side.

That evening they feasted in the great hall of the Praetorium, where once Artor's grandfather had ruled with Caidiau, commander of the troops at the western end of the Wall. If there were a few more cracks in the tiled floor and a few more nicks in the pillars, still, it was a noble room, especially when the flower of Britannia filled it, glowing in their tunics of crimson and ochre and green, with gold at their necks and wrists and gleaming on the hilts of their swords. Artor himself had honored the occasion by putting on the Chalybe sword. It made some people uneasy, but there was no doubt it added to his majesty.

Artor had suggested that Betiver and Cunorix sit beside Leudonus's son, reasoning that he was the most likely to understand how a youngster new to the court might feel. Not that young Gualchmai had any problem with self-confidence—he was big for his age, with sandy hair and the promise of his father's burly build. One saw the resemblance to Artor only in the set of his eyes.

"My father is the greatest king in the north," he stated as the platters of boiled meat were being brought in. "Naitan Morbet is a sneak and a coward. If he had attacked Dun Eidyn instead of running around us, we would ourselves alone have been beating him already—"

"And saved the rest of us a very long ride," Cunorix responded pleasantly. "It was kind of you to let us share in the fun."

Gualchmai frowned, as if not quite sure how to take that. "I am hearing that my uncle Artor is a great warrior too," he said a little more politely. "It will be fine to see him fight."

"There are many fine warriors in your uncle's army," Betiver continued in the same tone. "There is Cai, who was his foster-brother, and Cyniarcus, son of the prince of Durnovaria. Beside them sits Cataur of Dumnonia, who is a very mighty man." He saw Oesc grimace at the name. Cataur had never ceased to hate the Saxons for killing his brother at Portus Adurni, and had made no secret of his opposition to Oesc's presence on the campaign.

"The men of the north are mighty too," Gualchmai said stoutly. "There is Peretur son of Eleutherius, come in from Eburacum, and Dumnoval of the southern Votadini over there by his side. But when myself and my brothers are grown we will be the greatest warriors in Britannia."

Betiver took a drink of ale to cover his smile. "How many

brothers do you have?" he asked when he could control his face again.

"Gwyhir has thirteen winters, a year less than me, and wild he was that he could not come with us. But my mother would not allow it. If she could, I think she would keep all of us by her, but my father insisted, which he does not do often anymore. Aggarban is only ten, which is far too young for war, and Goriat is four and just a baby. But they are all big and strong for the years they have, and I have given my promise that the first of them who can knock me down shall have my dagger!" He patted the weapon that hung at his belt, a handsome piece of work with a cairngorm set in the hilt.

Later that evening, when Leudonus had taken his heir off to bed, Betiver found himself with Oesc by the fire.

"I am sure that Artor set me there so that the boy might have a friend among all these warriors, but believe me, that young man needs no reassurance." He proceeded to summarize their conversation, hoping to get a smile. Oesc was a good fellow, but too often one saw sadness in his eyes.

"Where does it come from?" asked the Saxon. "Leudonus does not seem so overbearing a man."

"Not now, I suppose, though I hear he was very ambitious when he was younger. And then there is their mother, who was trained on the Holy Isle. If we get to Dun Eidyn, maybe we'll meet her."

Oesc nodded. "If we get that far."

"You will get there—" rumbled a deep voice behind them.

There's no reason to be nervous, Betiver told himself as he turned to face Merlin. But he came from a land where druids, if indeed Merlin was not something worse, were only a memory, and he never knew quite how he ought to react to the man. Oesc had stiffened, his face showing no expression at all, but then where *he* came from, every chieftain had a witch or wise man at his left hand.

"My lord Merlin—" he said politely. "Have you seen this in the stars?"

"I have dreamed of Artor standing on the Rock as the sun sets behind him." The druid leaned on his staff, frowning. "You will fight Naitan Morbet, and pursue him." The great beard, streaked with silver now, twitched as he smiled. "But I do not think I will ride with you. My bones grow too old for long marches with armies. Perhaps I will walk in the forest of Caledonia for a time, and refresh my soul."

Merlin trying to be pleasant was even more unnerving than Merlin being grim, thought Betiver.

"Do you wish me to tell you if you will survive the battle? That is what all the other warriors wish to know."

Betiver shook his head, suppressing a shiver. For a moment Merlin's eyes were unfocused, looking through him. Then the old man blinked, and that dark gaze fixed Betiver once more.

"What you do not ask, the spirits have answered," he gave a bark of harsh laughter. "You will live long, and serve your lord to the end." For a moment he looked at Oesc, frowning, then without another word turned and moved away through the crowd.

"How very odd!" said Betiver, trying to laugh.

"He is a dangerous man," answered Oesc, but he would say no more.

With the Votadini, Artor's muster was complete. They moved out in good order past the fields of ripening grain, fording the rivers that emptied into the Salmaes firth until they came to the Stone of Mabon, a finger of rock set there by men of a time so ancient no one remembered their names, and honored ever since as the phallus of the god. In happier times it had marked the border between the Novantae and Selgovae lands, and the tribes had met on the flats beyond it for trade and festival.

Betiver took a deep breath of the brisk air, rich with the scents of grass and tidal mud and the salt tang of the sea. He had fought with Artor before, but this was different. They were beyond the Wall, now, in a land which had only intermittently accepted the yoke of Rome. He tried to pray, but the Christian god seemed irrelevant in this wilderness; he understood why someone had cast a garland of flowers around the Mabon stone.

He wondered how long it would take for the enemy to get there.

Any force moving down from the north with designs on Luguvalium must pass this way or take to the water, and the Picts had never been seamen. To the north, smoke hung like a dark smudge across the sky. The enemy was coming, and Artor's army took position to meet them—in the center nearly a thousand light infantry who had ridden to the battle and left their horses in the rear, and almost as many cavalry, armed with lance and sword, arranged in two wings to either side.

Betiver's mare stamped nervously and he patted her neck beneath the mane. His sword was loose in the sheath, his shield slung across his shoulder. He unfastened the straps of his round topped helmet to cool his head, then tightened them once more and changed his grip on the lance that lay along his thigh.

When were the Picts going to come?

Artor had taken command of the right wing, spreading his horsemen out in a curve across the rising heathland above the meadows. The warriors of his household were with him, except for Oesc and Cunorix, who had never learned to fight on horseback and were stationed among the foot fighters, mostly men of the hill country to the south of Luguvalium. Cador of Dumnonia and his seasoned troops held the left, on horses accustomed to the ocean, who would not panic if the battle pushed them into the shallows of the firth. And in the middle, Peretur of Eburacum commanded, backed by the band of Alamanni warriors who formed his personal guard.

Betiver had been in battle against Saxons, using the weight of the cavalry charge to break their line. He had never fought other cavalry before. Neither had Artor, he thought unhappily. They had all done practice fighting, but it was never the same.

Every time he waited for the fighting to start he hoped that this would be the time he learned how not to be afraid. The child Gualchmai, sitting his horse behind his father, was watching the road with barely concealed impatience. But he didn't know how it was going to be. Artor's face, as always, was a little pale, his eyes intent and grim. Betiver had never yet dared to ask him if he felt fear.

Would the Picts never come?

And then between one moment and the next, the skyline changed. Suddenly, not only the road, but the meadows and the farther hillsides were covered with moving dots. Metal flashed and flickered in the watery sunlight. They didn't seem surprised to see the British force awaiting them, but then they must have had scouts out, and he had heard that a Pictish scout could lie concealed in a clump of heather, and track a gull upon the breeze.

He felt hot and then cold. The dots were becoming tiny men on shaggy ponies. Most of the British had some kind of body armor—mail or scales of leather or metal or horn, as well as helms. The Pictish warriors rode with cinctured saddle cloths and only a few of them had helms. Many bore no more than a cloak or a sheepskin over their breeches; from a distance the tattooed beasts that spiraled all over their bodies made their skins look blue. But they carried stout shields, round or square and covered with bull hide, and long spears, and wicked looking swords. They seemed to be coming without order, but here and there a rider bore a wooden standard with a painted fish or bull or some other beast, so they must be riding in clan groups or bands.

Horns blared mockingly, answered by the bitter music of Artor's clarions. A shiver ran along the British line. Betiver picked up his reins and the mare bobbed her head, pulling at the bit. The clarions called again, and suddenly Artor's cavalry wing was moving, its line extending outward to hit the enemy on the flank and force them down upon the infantry's waiting spears. Ahead, he saw a larger standard with the elegantly executed image of a red stallion.

"Artor and Britannia!" cried the men. "Ar . . . tor . . ."

The shout tore through Betiver's throat. He dropped the rein on the mare's neck and shrugged his round shield down onto his arm; racing alongside the other horses, she needed little guidance. Without his will his arm lifted, lance poised.

And then the enemy horsemen were before him. A lance flew towards him and he knocked it aside with his shield, he stabbed, struck something and gripped the mare's barrel hard with his knees as he pulled it free.

"Ar . . . tor . . ."

Thought fled, and with it, fear, as Betiver was engulfed by the fray.

By afternoon, the battle was over. Oesc was glad to mount again, for what had been a fair meadow that morning was now a trampled wasteland, and blood ran in streams to redden the sea. He had come through the fight without much harm, though there was a slash on his thigh that made walking painful. The pony whuffed uneasily as he guided it back over the battlefield, calling the wagons to pick up British survivors and dispatching the more badly wounded of the enemy with a merciful thrust of his spear.

The fleeing survivors of Naitan Morbet's army were out of sight by now, closely pursued by Artor's cavalry. Perhaps he should learn to fight astride, Oesc thought grimly, so he could go with them. It was bad enough to fight a battle, but in the grisly work that came after there was neither excitement nor glory.

Where the land began to rise there was a heap of bodies, as if some desperate band of warriors had chosen it for their last stand. Most of them were Pictish, and all were quite dead. Among the corpses lay a wooden standard, carved and painted in the shape of a red stallion. Oesc frowned, remembering how it had threatened them in the morning light. He dismounted then, and began to pull aside the sprawled limbs of the warriors. Beneath them, as by now he was expecting, lay the body of a thick-bodied man with grizzled hair. Under the jutting beard a golden torque gleamed, and across the broad, naked chest was tattooed a horse and the double disc symbol of a king.

Oesc could see no mark upon him; perhaps the gods had struck him down in the midst of the battle. That happened sometimes with old men. But there was little doubt that this was Naitan Morbet, the lord of Pictland, who had set the lands from the Tava to the Salmaes ablaze. Oesc lifted his horn to his lips and blew, summoning the British captains to come and see.

*   *   *

Leaderless, the Picts fled northward like fallen leaves before the wind. Artor released his infantry and the men who lived farthest away to go home to their harvests while the British cavalry sped after the enemy, disposing of stragglers in a series of brief, bitter engagements that left the enemy dead, or less often, captive. The Picts were not destroyed entirely. Small groups of riders who knew the land could go where the larger, more heavily armed pursuers would never find them. Nonetheless, only a tithe of the great army that Naitan Morbet had led southward at Beltain ever returned to celebrate the feast of Lugus in the Caledonian hills and glens, and an unhappy line of prisoners followed when Artor's army at last reached Dun Eidyn.

From the high ridge of rock and the dun that crowned it to the flat meadow in the cleft below, the air pulsed with the sound of the drumming. From time to time a bitter skirling of pipes would gather the rhythm into their music, but when it ceased, the drums continued, the audible heartbeat of the land. The noise had continued since the beginning of the festival. By now, Betiver was aware of it only intermittently, when some shift in the wind amplified the volume, or when, for no reason that he understood, for a few moments it would stop. Sometimes, when the drums beat softly, he thought that pulsing might be the mead pounding in his brain, for during the past three days food and drink had flowed freely.

Those of Artor's men who had not gone home to help with the grain harvest camped in the meadow; it was a welcome opportunity to relax and recuperate from the long days on the trail. The hay had been cut, and the cattle brought down from the hills. The first fields of grain to ripen had been ceremonially harvested, and the clans of the Votadini, with the cattle they wanted to sell and the daughters they wanted to marry off, had come in. For the princes and lords of the king's household, it was a visit to a more ancient world that had never gone under the yoke of Rome.

"Is it so different?" asked Oesc, leaning back on the spread hides beside him. "My own people also make offerings at harvest time." Light from the bonfire reddened his fair hair.

Betiver shrugged. "At home in Gallia the priest offers prayers for the success of the harvest and the laborers feast when it is done. Maybe the country folk do other things, but I lived in towns and never saw them. There was never this great gathering." He sunk his teeth into the flesh that clung to the beef rib he was holding and worried it free.

"That is true. Among the Saxons, the next great feast will not be until autumn's ending, but that is for the family, like Yule. It is at Ostara and sometimes Midsummer that our tribes come together for the sacrifices."

"In Eriu, Lugos of the Long Arm is still honored," said Cunorix. "We hold a great festival for him at Taltiu, with a cattle fair."

Betiver nodded. For a moment it had seemed to him that the three of them, all born elsewhere and brought to Britannia, were equally foreigners. But he came from a land and a way of life long Christian, whereas Oesc and Cunorix were still as pagan as these Celts in their multicolored garments, dancing around the fires.

"Look there—" Oesc pointed. Gualchmai was moving among the feasters, his upper body swathed in a mantle of gold and brown and black checkered wool fastened with a silver penannular brooch. The skirts of a short saffron tunic showed beneath it, with black banding woven into the hem. In his hand he gripped a silver-mounted drinking horn.

He caught sight of the three Companions and made his way towards them, grinning widely.

"See—my father has given me this new horn! Tonight I have leave to stay and drink with the men."

"I am glad to see that you came through the battle unhurt," said Betiver. "Will you sit and drink with us, then, and tell us what is going on?"

"I will that—" Gualchmai said something in a dialect too thick for Betiver to follow to the wiry, red-headed tribesman who had been escorting him, and joined them on the cowhide. "Even my mother is agreeing that I am a warrior now I've seen battle. My brothers have to be staying up there with the women—" He pointed at the enclosure of loosely woven brush where the wives of the chieftains were holding their own festival. It was a flimsy barrier, but even a drunken man would not breach that sanctuary.

Not that the rest of them were without female companionship. The tribesmen had brought their families, and many of the girls had volunteered to help serve out the ale and mead. And when one of them, liking the looks of a southern warrior, settled down on the grass with him instead, no one seemed to think the worse of her. Betiver had noticed already that the women of the northern tribes had a freedom that would never have been permitted in a Christian land.

Gualchmai's red-headed servant returned with a pitcher full of mead and refilled their horns.

"Tell me, what is that platform with the fenced space in front of it?" asked Oesc.

"Oh, that is for the ceremony. Do you not have it in the south?" he asked as the men looked inquiring. "When Lugus kills the Black Bull who has carried off the Goddess and is holding back the harvest."

"Nay," Betiver said gravely, "I have never seen such a thing."

"Well, the sun has set," answered Gualchmai. "You will see something soon."

Westward, the sky blazed with banners of gold, as if to honor the vanished sun. The last light glowed soft on the rough rock of the cliff and the timbers of the palisade above them, and the thatched roof of Leudonus's high hall. Even as they watched, a spark appeared on the ridge below the eastern gate; in the next moment there were more, a line of torches winding like a fiery serpent down from the dun.

Closer, one saw the white robes of the men who led the procession, ghostly in the half-light.

"Druids!" exclaimed Betiver. "I did not know so many of them remained."

"in the north they do—" Gualchmai said smugly.

"And in Eriu," added Cunorix.

"They call Merlin a druid," observed Oesc.

"Merlin . . ." Betiver shook his head, thinking of the stories. "He has the druid knowledge, but he is something different. Some say the Devil fathered him and gave him his powers."

"If I believed in your Devil I could believe that was so," said Oesc somberly. "But my grandfather's wisewoman calls him witega, which means an oracle."

"My father's druids prophesy, and read omens," put in Gualchmai. "But they also conduct sacrifices and ceremonies."

Betiver twitched. He had been raised a Christian and held to that faith. But so had Artor. Whatever was going to happen, they could not insult their hosts by refusing to participate. If there was sin in it, he would simply have to ask Father Fastidius to give him a penance once they were home again.

The druids drew closer, men of middle-age or older, with flowing hair and beards. Upon the breast of their leader gleamed a golden crescent, and he leaned on a staff. Then Oesc drew his breath in sharply, and Betiver saw that behind the druids walked a group of dark-clad women.

"Those are the she-druids, the priestesses—" said Gualchmai. "And my mother . . ."

But Betiver had already noticed that one of the women had covered her dark robe with a mantle of crimson. As she moved towards them, her ornaments cast back the torchlight in running sparks and flickers of red gold. He did not need to be told that this was the queen.

Margause walked as a woman certain of her beauty and secure in her power, shoulders braced against the drag of her trailing mantle, head high. Her hair fell in waves of dark fire across back and shoulders, bound with a golden band. More gold swung from her ears and lay across her breast and weighted her wrists. Men fell silent at her coming; some bent, foreheads touching the earth in reverence.

It seemed irrelevant to call her beautiful. Deep-breasted and wide-hipped, her body was made for bearing. But from her face all the girlish softness had been fined away to reveal the faultless sculpting of bone at cheek and brow. At the entrance to the women's enclosure she paused, gazing across the assembly beneath painted eyelids. Then she disappeared into the shadows within.

Only then did Betiver realize that behind the women marched the warriors escorting Leudonus and the high king.

Leudonus wore a plaid of the same hues as his son's; Artor
a linen robe the color of the ripening fields. It was the first
time since he had first set eyes on Artor as a child of thirteen
that he had not been immediately aware when his lord drew
near. He blinked, wondering if it was the mead that had dizzied him. Artor and his host were still talking. While the
chieftains feasted, the kings had spent the afternoon hearing
reports from the couriers sent to Caledonia to arrange for the
ransom of prisoners. Men said that Drest Guithinmoch was
the Picts' new king.

"And there is my father," said Gualchmai. "With the lord
Artor. When you ride south again, I will be going with you.
My mother was against it, but my father thinks it will be good
for me to learn about the southern lands."

Betiver and Oesc exchanged glances, but managed not to
smile. Until Artor married and begot a son, this boy had a
good claim to be considered his heir.

The royal party ascended the platform and took their places
on the benches there. The druids formed a line across the
front and one of them lifted a bronze horn with a curious
long shaft and blew. The sound did not seem loud, but it
echoed from cliff to cliff and vibrated in the bones. When it
finished, Betiver realized that every drum in the valley had
stilled.

> *"The host of heaven, the summer stars,*
> *Upon the sky fields they are gathered,*
> *Upon the earth, fair Alba's children . . ."*

The voice of the druid was thin and clear; Oesc felt the fine
hairs on his neck and arms lifting at the sound. The northern
intonation made it hard for him to understand some of the
words, but it hardly mattered. The dark earth was sown with
fire, and the cliffs framed a sky of luminous dark blue, blazing
with a harvest of stars. The meaning of the words blossomed
in his awareness without need for understanding as the ceremony went on. Woden had given the god-men of the Saxons

this power, but until now he had not found its like in the British lands.

"Behold, Midsummer has passed,
the moon's sickle harvests summer stars;
The womb of the Mother swells:
Cattle grow fat, grain grows high.
Her children arise and flourish in the land.

The line of druids divided, revealing a throne set at the back of the stage, and upon it the shape of a woman, swathed in dark veils.

"The Mother has given birth, and her Son is grown;
Lord of the Spear of Light, the god of the clever hands,
Let the Son of the Mother arise and come forth to bless his
people—"

The hides nailed across the base of the platform shivered, and a new figure emerged, costumed in golden straw. Plaited and sewn, it formed a helm that covered head and face. Two tiers of straw flared out in a cape and a skirt below it. But his shield was of new wood with a gilded boss, and the head of his spear flashed gold.

For a moment he stood, staring around the circle, then, his voice slightly muffled through the mask, he began to sing.

"Well have you worked and long have you labored,
Now comes the time to receive your reward.
Rest and rejoice now, all uncertainty ended;
Laugh, make music, feast and frolic—
My love is the heat that warms you;
My light is the radiance that shows you the world."

"That is Lugus," said Gualchmai. "He is the bright god who can do everything. The ravens teach him wisdom."

"In my country they say that his spear is so powerful its

head must be kept in a cauldron full of water or it would burn up the world," Cunorix said then.

Startled from his trance, Oesc stared at him.

"The god of my people, Woden, sends his ravens out to bring him knowledge, and claims the battle-doomed with his spear . . ." he whispered.

"My old tutor once told me that the mother of Apollo came from the land of the Hyperboreans in the far north, and that once he guided the people of Thera in the form of a raven," said Betiver. For a moment his eyes met Oesc's, then he crossed himself and looked away.

The god is here, thought Oesc. *Maybe this is the name he bears in the British lands*. After being for so long cut off from his own rites and his own people, he trembled, opened suddenly to awareness that the mummery before him was raising and focusing power. And even as this thought came to him he realized that the energy was shifting. The hides moved once more as a huge, dark figure shouldered between them, swathed in a cloak of some black stuff, helmed in leather that supported a pair of bull's horns.

"*Lord of the Lightning, canst Thou deny me?*" His voice was a deep rasp that raised the hackles. He lumbered back and forth, head lowered, while the bright god turned continually to face him. The druids moved back, and torchlight glittered from brooch and torque as the princes seated on the benches leaned forward to see. Artor's eyes followed the mock-combat, bright with interest.

> "*I am the Shadow at Thy shoulder,*
> *The darkness Thy light casts.*
> *I come from the depths of earth*
> *To devour the children of the day.*
> *All that the Mother bears is meat for me—*
> *The harvest and the cattle that eat it*
> *And the men whose life the cattle are.*
> *The Lady of Life I will hold prisoner—*"

He made a rush towards the platform, feinting with his club, and the veiled woman who sat there flinched. He stopped then, club upraised, and the valley rumbled with his deep laughter.

> "I am the Black Bull.
> I am the plague that kills your young men,
> the flood that drowns your fields,
> the fire that burns your homes.
> I am the Destroyer
> Who shall trample your lives to dust!"

At the words, Lugus straightened, brandishing his spear.

> "And I am the Defender!
> I fight for all that the Mother has made!
> I will stop the floods and free the Lady,
> I will bring back the sunshine and win the harvest."

The veiled Goddess rose and came to watch from the front of the platform as weapon poised, he advanced upon his foe.

Once, twice, thrice, they circled, feinting back and forth in mimetic combat. But though their movements were stylized, the energy they were raising was real. With the third exchange, the Black God struck, and a sudden billowing of dust obscured the scene. When it thinned, in place of the human opponent stood a black bull.

It was, Oesc realized in astonishment, quite real. Like the men, it must have come from beneath the platform, but how they had kept it quiet there he could not imagine, for the beast was clearly in good health and full possession of its senses. Its dark gaze fixed on the glittering figure and it snorted, head lowering. A little shiver of tension ran through the crowd; there was hardly a man among them who had not at some point in his life been chased by a bull, and they recognized the warning signs.

The priest of Lugus shook his spear and began to sidestep around the bull, getting into position for a fatal blow. But the bull, shaking its head, turned with him. The priest extended his shield arm, shaking it a little to get the beast's attention.

The massive head lowered, and suddenly the animal was in motion. If the priest had intended to strike as the bull went by, the beast was too fast for him. Even as his arm moved the bull was passing; the spearhead scored a long gouge in the animal's flank just as it hooked one horn into the shield and jerked it away.

The shield soared like a sunwheel, slapped against the fence and fell to the ground. The priest's gaze followed it, but the bull, with a better sense of priorities, was already wheeling towards the brightness of his cape and helm. The man was brave enough. He stood his ground as the bull surged forward, leaping aside at the last moment to stab.

But his courage was better than his timing. As he leaped, the bull swerved with a vicious sidewise swipe of the horns that hooked through straw and leather and grazed the priest's side. As the impact knocked him backward, the spear flew from his hand and slid rattling across the ground.

The torches flickered as a collective gasp of horror passed through the crowd. There was always this chance, that the Black Bull might win, and a murrain on the cattle and storms that spoiled the remainder of the harvest, would bring them a starving winter and death in the spring.

The bull, turned, pawing, as the priest struggled to his feet, eyeing the distance between himself, the bull, and his spear. At almost the same moment it became clear to both the man and the beast that he could not reach it in time. With preternatural intelligence, the bull moved, tail twitching, not towards the man, but towards the weapon that lay on the ground.

And then there was another movement, another figure that dropped, as if from the heavens, into the ring. For a moment Oesc thought it was one of the druids; then he recognized the barley-gold tunic and his blood chilled.

"Sacrilege!" cried someone. "He must not interfere!"

"Nay—he has the right," said another, "he is the king!"

A memory of his grandfather filled Oesc's vision, the body swinging from the old oak tree. *It is the right of the king to give his life for the people . . .* he told himself. Without willing it he leaped to his feet; his muscles locked with the effort it took to keep from rushing to Artor's aid. Betiver stood swaying beside him. Others had risen as well. But for each British warrior there were two Votadini, ready to seize him if he should try to intervene.

The bull hesitated, for a moment uncertain as to what this new foe might be. It was long enough for Artor to pick up the spear. Muscles rippled along the dark flanks as the black bull charged. The king made no attempt to evade him. Still on one knee, he braced the spear and held it steady as the bull came on.

"Sweet Jesus," exclaimed Betiver, "does he think he's facing a boar?"

But a boar-spear had a cross piece to prevent the animal from running all the way up the shaft, and hunters could be killed trying that trick even so.

Then the bull was upon him. Dust swirled madly as the bull's own weight impaled him upon the spear. The wicked horns jerked savagely—was the man under them?

The thrashing figure changed shape suddenly; somehow Artor had evaded horns and hoofs and got astride the bull's massive shoulders. One hand gripped a horn; a dagger flashed in the other as Artor bent, reached, and ripped the sharp steel through the throat of the bull.

One last time the mighty body convulsed, nearly unseating him. Then the black bull collapsed, blood pumping onto the ground.

For a long moment nobody moved. Then Artor freed himself from the body and the druids, frantic lest the sacrifice be wasted, rushed forward with bronze basins in which to catch the blood.

Oesc remembered how the life of the bull he offered before the battle of Portus Adurni had ebbed away beneath his hands. But it seemed to him that the energy that flowed out of this bull was pouring into Artor, who stood wide-eyed in the torchlight, with a crimson stain across his golden robe.

Drums began to pound, a soft insistent rhythm that transformed shock and confusion into a mounting excitement. "Behold!" cried the chief of the druids, his voice steadying as he went on—

". . . the Goddess is freed and the monster is slain.
Now shall the sun return to those lands that need it.
To each power there is a proper season—
A time for the light to shine and a time for darkness,
A time for death and a time for life to flourish.
But now it is the time for harvest!
Therefore let there be no shadow on our celebration;
The Bull's blood buys your lives!"

The druids moved among the people with their blessing bowls, and Oesc pressed forward with the others, and felt, for a little while, as if he were no longer a stranger.

The priestess of the Goddess still stood on the platform, swaying to the drum beat. As she moved, her draperies swirled around her, and it became clear that, although she was masked, beneath the veils she wore nothing at all.

The druids finished cutting off the head of the bull and hoisted it onto a pole. On the platform before the Goddess they placed some of its flesh, along with bread baked from the first grain of the harvest. Some of the others pulled Artor back up onto the platform and set his hand in that of the priestess.

Lifting their linked hands, she cried out in a great voice—

"The grain feeds on the earth,
The folk feed on the grain,
Earth feeds on the folk;
So it is, so it was, so it will be—
Eater and eaten, feeder and fed,
All that dwell on earth must become.
Receive now the blessing of the harvest
the grain that is cut down,
the blood that is shed.
From these things, my children, your life shall spring."

Men moved through the crowd carrying platters of meat and bread. Girls followed them with skins of mead and ale. The drums grew louder and the pipes began to skirl above their beat in ecstatic melody. The rhythm pulsed through Oesc's veins like fire.

On the platform, the priestess had begun to dance—if it was the priestess, for to Oesc's altered vision she seemed suddenly taller. Beneath the half-revealing veils, her pale flesh glowed. Someone handed him a horn of mead and he swallowed. He heard laughter, saw a red-haired girl grab Betiver around the neck to kiss him. For a moment he resisted, then his arms went around her. After a moment she pulled back, laughing, took his hand and drew him after her. Vaguely he remembered Cunorix following another girl a little earlier; Gualchmai had disappeared as well.

Oesc looked back at the platform. Some of the priestess's veils had come off; he glimpsed bobbing breasts, a long, rounded thigh, and felt his flesh spring to agonized attention. *Frige* . . . he thought, *Desired One* . . . then he remembered that the Lady was called Brigantia here. But whoever She was, she had the kind of beauty a man sees in dreams. Artor still stood before her, swaying in a tranced echo of her movements, his eyes wide and dazed.

A soft hand closed on his and Oesc looked down, glimpsed dark eyes and a merry grin and wildly springing black hair. But it hardly mattered what the girl looked like. He grabbed for her, groaning as soft breasts were crushed against him, a supple waist flexed beneath his hands. Over her head he saw the veiled Goddess take Artor's hand and lead him towards the back of the platform. In another moment they had disappeared into the darkness.

Then the girl's arms locked around his neck. Groaning, he let her draw him down to the hide, and after a brief struggle with their clothing sank between her welcoming thighs and came home.

VII

†HE HiGH SEA† OF HEΠGES†

A·D· 488

†HE HIGH KING RETURNED SOUTH BY EASY STAGES. BY NOW only the core of his army remained with him, the others having gone home directly to help with the harvest. The feast of Lugus remained enshrined in their thoughts, but the men did not speak of it, neither to boast of their conquests, nor to wonder if some of the laughing girls with whom they had lain that night might come away from the festival with something more than a memory.

That winter they stayed with Peretur in Eburacum. The Saxons of the north remained quiet, for which Oesc was grateful. He was finding it hard enough to remember the brief time he had spent in this country with his father, without having to face in battle men who had given him his first lessons with the sword.

For he knew that if Artor asked, he would ride with him. The other men had accepted him as one of the high king's chosen Companions. At night he dreamed in the British tongue and by day found his memories of Cantuware growing dim. Even if he returned there, would the people accept him? He had become some curious hybrid, neither fully British nor truly Saxon anymore.

From Eburacum they moved south and west. For a time they stayed with Bishop Dubricius in Isca. There was some fighting as well, for Cunorix's kin in Demetia had been re-inforced from Eriu, and were seeking to extend their territory. They proved more troublesome than expected, and the campaign lasted through the summer. And so it was not until early in the following year that the high king returned to Londinium.

Just after the feast of Candlemas, a rumor came to them that Hengest had died. Oesc knew of it first when men began to look at him oddly, whispering. An overheard remark revealed the cause, but he continued to behave as if he had not heard, grateful for time to try to understand his own feelings before he was forced to some public acknowledgment.

Oesc had at that time been among the Britons for nearly nine years. If this had come in the first years of his captivity, he thought, his grief would have been overwhelming. But for too long his memories of Cantuware had brought only pain, and so he had walled them away where even he could not reach them anymore. And that, he told himself, was probably for the best. No doubt Hengest's empty high seat would soon be filled by some ambitious Jute, or perhaps it would be seized by one of Aelle's sons.

By the time a month had passed, he had well-nigh persuaded himself that he believed this. And so when Artor summoned him it was, at least to his conscious mind, a surprise.

"Let us walk along the river—it is too fine a day to stay indoors." Artor reached for the crimson cloak that lay across the chair.

Oesc raised one eyebrow, for the wind had been brisk as he crossed the courtyard, and Artor flushed.

"Well, maybe it is a bit chilly, but I refuse to stay cooped up here. You can wear a cloak of mine—"

And so they fared out, wrapped alike in royal crimson and very much of a height. From a distance, the only difference between them would be his fair hair against Artor's brown. But Artor was lord of most of Britannia, and Oesc was, despite all the marks of consideration, his prisoner.

A brisk wind was blowing up the Tamesis, ruffling the ripples into little wavelets as it scoured the smoke of Londinium's hearthfires from the sky. They had both been right, thought Oesc, wrapping the crimson mantle more securely. It was cold, and it was a beautiful day. With the air so clear, he felt he ought to be able to see downriver all the way to the sea. A sudden memory came to him of sunlight on the water of the estuary below Durobrivae, and he turned swiftly away.

"Was there no one else to keep you company, or did you have something to say to me?" He realized too late how ungracious that had sounded and tried to soften it with a smile.

Artor, who had been gazing southward at the scattering of farms and fields and the distant blue line of the downs, turned back to him, frowning. Oesc felt himself being assessed and examined; it was a look he had learned to recognize when they were on campaign. Then the king released his gaze with a little smile. But there was still trouble in his eyes.

"What is it, my lord?"

"A messenger has come from Cantium. Your grandfather is dead."

Oesc felt a muscle jump in his cheek, but he kept his gaze steady. "He was very old. Many people think he died years ago." *When the Britons captured me. . . .*

Artor cleared his throat. "The message is from your witenagemot, a formal request from the elders of your people to send you back to them to be their king."

Oesc felt all the blood leave his face and then flood back again. For a moment, staying on his feet took all his strength of will. Then he felt Artor's hand on his arm and his vision cleared.

"And what . . ." he swallowed and tried again, "what was your reply?"

"I have not yet given it. I have to ask you—do you want to go?"

Oesc stared at him. "I have a *choice?*"

"I cannot hold prisoner a man who has guarded my back and fought at my side," said Artor impatiently. "I blame myself now for keeping you by me. It was selfishness on my part. I should have given you this choice a year ago. I suppose it's time to let Cunorix go as well."

Thoughts and emotions suppressed so long Oesc had forgotten them battered against his awareness. Seeing his trouble, Artor went on—

"Oesc, you have earned a place among my Companions. You would be accepted. My own grandfather was a German in the service of Rome. As a man I would ask you to stay—there are many who fight for me because it is their duty, but few who do so because, if I dare assume so much, they are my friends."

There was a short silence. Oesc watched a gull soar towards the sun, then swoop earthward once more. He cleared his throat.

"And what do you ask . . . as a king?"

"If you stay with me, someone else will seize power in Cantium. I cannot afford to have an active enemy on my doorstep. As a king, I want a man in Durovernum who will at worst be neutral, and at best, perhaps, a friend." It was his turn, now to look away.

Gazing at that bent head, Oesc understood two things. The first was that what he felt for Artor was a love which he could never give to any other overlord, and the second was that he had to go home.

"Your grandfather was a Germanic Roman officer. Mine was the man who killed him, as your father killed mine," he said painfully. "If I were not who I am, I would serve you my life long. But if I were not Hengest's grandchild I would not be here at all. And there is another thing. Before ever I saw you I had made my dedication to the goddess who rules the land of Cantuware. I must go back to be her king."

"The Lady . . ." Artor turned back to him, his eyes clouded by memory. "I understand. I will miss you—" He reached out to grip Oesc's hand. "Because of you, even those Saxons whom I must fight will never be a faceless enemy, and to those who live in the lands I hold I will be a fair and honest lord."

Oesc nodded. Surely it was the wind that was making his eyes sting with tears.

"And one more thing, in thanks for the service you have done me. I will have a treaty drawn up between us, confirming you in the rights granted to Hengest by the Vor-Tigernus. It has been three generations since Cantium became Cantuware—even if we were to take it back tomorrow, the Britons who used to live there are scattered and gone. To you and your heirs I grant it, Oesc; it is Saxon soil."

The night of Oesc's farewell feast Artor got drunk for the first time since the rite to Lugus at Dun Eidyn. At least Betiver believed that the king had been drunk that night, certainly everyone else had been, and he did remember that Artor had been as red-eyed and dazed the next morning as the rest of them.

The feast was formal, the menu heavy on the Roman side, with spiced beets and wild spring greens dressed with oils, boiled grains with sauces, and chickens delicately seasoned as well as a suckling pig stewed in wine. For certain Oesc was not going to get a meal like this in his Saxon hut, thought Betiver, trying to decide whether he had room for just one more morsel of elderberry pie. But though his mouth still watered, his belly had another opinion, and he had let his belt out one notch already. With a sigh he pushed his plate away.

"Are you not wanting that?" Gualchmai reached across the table and scraped the remains from Betiver's plate to his own. Gualchmai had grown at least a foot since coming south with Artor, and was always hungry. He was going to be a big man.

Servants cleared the plates away and began to serve more wine. Oesc proposed a toast to the king; the king responded in kind, his cropped brown hair rumpled and his eyes very bright. Cai toasted the armies of Brittania; Artor drank to their commanders. It should have been Cataur, but the Dumnnonian, who had barely tolerated Oesc's presence with the army, had refused to attend. No one missed him. Indeed, by this time everyone was beginning to feel quite mellow, though Oesc looked depressed, except when he was forcing a smile.

The gifts that Artor was sending with his former hostage were brought in. Oesc went red and pale again as he accepted them. There was a lorica hamata of mail with punched and riveted rings and an officer's helmet with decorations in gold.

But except for their quality, they would not make him stand out at home—half the Saxon fighting force was outfitted in looted Roman gear. Betiver did wonder, though, where Artor expected the Saxon to wear them. Perhaps he intended to raise auxiliaries from Cantium when the Picts made trouble again.

There were tunics of Byzantine silk, an officer's belt with gold fittings, a pair of arm rings, and a fine woolen cloak of deep blue that was the mate of Artor's crimson, with a great round brooch of gold. There was a table service of figured red ceramic ware and a silver ewer with goblets. Taken together with Oesc's share of the loot from the Pictish campaign, it was an impressive dowry to be taking home to Cantium.

Then the gifts were carried away again and the king called for more wine. Artor stood up and began to make a speech about how brave they had all been during the Pictish war. Betiver felt his eyes closing and surrendered to a dream in which he was dancing around the festival fire with a girl whose body he could still picture in arousing detail, though he had never learned her name.

He came abruptly awake again to find Gualchmai poking him.

"There's a man come from home to bring me messages, and he's asking for you as well. He has a young woman with him who says she's brought your child. . . ."

He had not spoken softly, and Betiver's progress towards the door was followed by a chorus of advice and comment that made him redden, though he pretended not to hear.

He went, determined to see the girl off in short order. There was a widow in the city whom he visited sometimes, but he knew that she was not with child. He was not like Gualchmai, who had progressed from kitchen maids to married ladies and was reputed to have one bastard already, though he was barely sixteen.

He was starting to question the messenger, a ginger-haired fellow wrapped in the yellowish checkered stuff Leudonus' people wore, when he heard a cry. A red-headed woman came forward into the light with a yearling child in her arms, and it was the girl he had just seen in his dream.

For a long moment Betiver stared at her. "What is your name?"

"Roud—" She took a deep breath. "Do you know me, then? I was fearing you might not remember after all."

"I remember."

"Well, that's a start—" Her words tumbled out as if she were afraid that she might not have the courage to say them all. "I know you are great among the princes of the south, and I don't ask you to marry me. But the boy deserves better than I can give him, out in the hills. There was no other man for a moon before or after the festival, my lord, so I am certain he's yours. If you will swear to do right by him, I'll trouble you no more."

Betiver lifted the blanket and saw a frowning, pug-nosed face topped by a tangle of dark hair that looked so much like his own father's that he blinked in surprise. *A boy child . . . I have a son. . . .*

"A child needs his mother," he said softly. "It would be better if you stayed."

Roud stared at him, then her eyes filled with tears. "We'll be no trouble to you, I promise—"

"Nay—you had the trouble of bearing him. If I had known of this, I would have provided for you before. Tonight you may sleep in my rooms here, and tomorrow we'll see about finding a house for you in the town."

By the time Betiver had settled Roud and the boy in his own bed and returned to the feasting hall, everyone had gone but Cai and young Gualchmai, who was pouring more wine for the king.

"You never knew you were planting a field, but it seems you got a fine crop all the same!" commented Gualchmai with rude good humor.

"I remember the girl," said Betiver, "and I'm satisfied that the boy is mine."

"You have a son?" asked Artor, his eyes dark with the wine.

"It would seem so. He wrinkles his forehead just the way my father does when he's annoyed. My memory of the festival in Dun Eidyn is somewhat confused, but I would guess mine was not the only seed to sprout from that sowing."

"Ah, indeed," said Gualchmai, "it was generous of you to replace the men we lost on that campaign."

"You are an unregenerate heathen!" exclaimed Cai.

"Maybe so, but in the north, festival babes are held to be a blessing from the gods."

"A man needs to know that his son is his own," Cai replied.

"Then get married and breed them!" exclaimed Gualchmai. "When will you be taking a wife, uncle? I'm heir to my father's lands already—I've no need for yours!"

His mother would be irritated to hear him say it, thought Betiver. By all accounts Morgause was ambitious for her sons. She had a fifth boy now to follow the others, he had heard.

Artor shook his head. "Kings don't make marriages, they make alliances. So long as I'm unmarried, any man of good blood can hope to make his daughter queen."

"I suppose that Oesc will settle down now and raise a troop of flaxen-haired brats," said Betiver.

"I suppose he will—" Artor sighed. Clearly the wine was wearing off. The sadness had returned to his eyes.

"Are you so sorry to lose him?" asked Cai gruffly. "Oesc is a good fellow, for all his moody ways, and I suppose we'll miss him. But *we're* still here!"

"That's true—" Artor reached out to grip their hands. "But I value each one of you in a different way. I'm afraid that when I see Oesc again he'll be a stranger, and then he might as well be dead to me—"

Betiver felt the king's hand strong and warm in his own, but in spirit Artor was far away. He tightened his grip, trying to draw him back again. *My dear lord, are we not enough for you?*

Oesc rode across the bridge into Durovernum on a fine spring evening just before Ostara, wearing a British tunic and riding a fine British horse that Artor had given him, and still thinking, despite a week of journeying with his Saxon escort, in the British tongue. The remains of the theatre still stood like a monument in the center of the walled town, but the walls themselves seemed lower, and several of the other Roman buildings he remembered had been scavenged for building stone. The long Saxon houses huddled under their weight of thatching like sheep in fleece, and everything he looked on seemed small, and poor, and old.

As they reined in before the hall, a figure appeared in the doorway, shading his eyes with his hand against the westering light. He shouted something, and in another moment Hæthwæge appeared, Hengest's silver-mounted meadhorn in her hands. There was more silver in her hair than he remembered, but otherwise she hadn't changed.

"Oesc son of Octha, waes hal—be welcome to your hall!" She came down the steps, and he took the horn. The mead was yeasty and dry, with an aftertaste of sweetness and fire. The taste of it brought a sudden flood of memories. He drank again, dizzied by the conflict of old knowledge and new, uncertain for a moment who he was or where.

"Thank you . . ." he mumbled, clinging to the formalities. A thrall came up to take the horse's head and he swung a leg across the high front of the saddle and slid to the ground. His escort were dismounting behind him. More thralls led their horses away. A horn blew and he heard people shouting.

For so long, he thought, he had dreamed of this moment, longed for it. And now, it seemed the capacity to respond was dead in him. *What am I doing here? How can I be a king to these people? Would Artor take me back again?*

Hæthwæge was saying something. He forced himself to attend.

"You are tired. Come into the hall."

He nodded gratefully and followed her.

Inside it was cool and dim. As his vision adjusted, light from the opened smoke vents beneath the eaves at either end of the hall showed him the carved and painted pillars that upheld the peaked roof and the curtained compartments to either side. But he had become accustomed to separate sleeping chambers and columns of stone. Then the scent, composite of woodsmoke and ale, dog and old leather and the sweat of men, caught at his throat, and for a moment he was thirteen years old once more. Someone opened a side door, and a rush of fresh air brought him back to the present.

"There are only half a dozen men now in the houseguard, and most of those are old," Hæthwæge was saying. "He gave the younger men land to farm. And there is only one cook and three kitchen thralls, but I have asked some of the women to come and help us."

Oesc nodded, thinking he would have to use much of the treasure Artor had given him just to set things in order here. Compared to the crowded, noisy place he remembered, this was like a hall of ghosts.

His footsteps echoed on the planking as he passed the boards and trestles for the tables that leaned in stacks against the walls, and he thought of colored mosaic floors. The raised stone hearth nearer the doorway was cold, but a little blue smoke rose from smoldering coals in the one before the high seat at the end of the hall. He remembered the clear light that fell through windows of nubbled glass, and Artor's marble throne.

The wisewoman paused as if she expected him to sit there. Oesc looked up at the serpentine carving on the posts, worn where Hengest had leaned against them, and at the cushion that still bore the impress of his body, and shook his head.

"Not yet. It has been a long time, and my soul is still stretched like a drying hide between here and Londinium. Build up the fire and let me sit on a bench beside it. I'll take the high seat when we drink Hengest's funeral ale."

She frowned at him thoughtfully and handed him the meadhorn once more. From outside came the sound of many voices. The light from the door flickered as if someone were hovering there.

"The people are gathering, wanting to see you. Two lambs are already roasting, and tonight you will feast. When you are ready, come to me and I will tell you how your grandfather died."

It was late before the shouting and the singing died away in the hall. But when the last of the revelers set off for his home or rolled up in his cloak beside the hearth, as Hæthwæge had known he would, Oesc came to her.

He had still been a boy when he left them, with the soft flesh of youth covering his bones. Now the strong structure of his face made the resemblance to his grandfather clear, all the more so because he looked so tired.

"Was it too bad?" He would have had more than enough ale in the hall. She dipped some of the mint tea that had been steeping on the hearth into a beaker and offered it.

Oesc sighed. "The skin of the boy who lived here nine years ago no longer fits, and the man he became is some sort of Saxon-British hybrid who doesn't fit anywhere. I told them I was tired from the journey, and they made allowances, but I am afraid my grandfather's thanes will think they have got a bad bargain in me."

"You have half a moon until the feast of Ostara when the æthelings and freemen will gather to drink Hengest's funeral ale. It will be better by then."

"I hope so! Otherwise I might as well lay myself in his mound . . ." He took a long drink of the tea and settled back on his stool. "This place is as I remember, and so are you. Talk to me, bind me back into this world again. . . ."

At least he knew what he needed, she thought, watching him. She would have to shape the man as she had shaped the boy, but it would be harder now because he was not so much scarred as armored by his time in the British lands.

"When one has a slow illness, or is very old, there comes a time when the spirit turns inward. Mostly our folk go quickly, in battle or sudden sickness, but I have seen this often enough so that when Hengest began to drift away from us I understood what it was. His health was no worse, nor was he in pain. He ate less and slept more, and delegated most of the household decisions to Guthlaf or to me. When he sat in his high seat he spoke of the battles of his youth sometimes, or of you, but as time went on, he mostly stayed in his bed."

Oesc frowned unhappily. "I should have been here for him. I knew how old he was—I should have begged Artor to let me visit him."

"It would have made no difference. It was that boy whose skin is too small for you that he remembered, not the man you are now."

"Whoever *he* is ..." muttered Oesc, and refilled his cup. Then he straightened, obviously trying to lift himself out of the mood. "It is hard to picture Hengest, the conqueror of Britannia, dying in his bed like a woman or a thrall."

Hæthwæge shook her head. "He did not. There came a day when the hills echoed with the cries of new lambs, and the sky with the calls of returning waterfowl. There was a wind, and we opened all the doors to air out the hall." She shut her eyes for a moment, remembering the brilliance of the sky, and how life had tingled in that air. "The kitchen thrall who used to bring Hengest his porridge called me. The king was sitting up, asking for a basin to wash in and the Frankish lapped tunic with the gold borders to wear. The folk here rejoiced, thinking that he was getting well at last."

"Where did he want to go?"

"He asked me to take him to the god-grove, and to bring the Spear."

Oesc's eyes widened, and his gaze went to the shrouded shape by the door. Hæthwæge knew he was remembering how his other grandfather had died. In the same, measured tone, she went on.

They had brought a lamb, and the old king cut its throat and splashed its blood on the god-posts and the stones. She remembered how the air around them grew heavy, as if something had awakened and was watching as Hengest set his back against the ash tree and pulled open his tunic to bare his breast. The green shadows had given his old skin a sickly pallor, as if he were dead already.

And then, as he had commanded, she scratched Woden's knot into his belly just below the ribs, and tied the rags with which she stanched the bleeding onto the branches of the ash tree. And at that a great wind had shivered the new leaves.

"The god was there," she said softly. "The offering was accepted. But Hengest said that as the god had made him live so long already he would let him choose his own moment to claim him. And so he closed up his tunic and we went back to the hall.

"He sat down in his high seat and told them to build up the fire, but he would take neither food nor drink. Some of the men wanted me to force him to lie down, but the warriors of the houseguard backed me. They understood very well."

"How long did it take him to die?" asked Oesc in a still voice.

Hæthwæge drew a deep breath, remembering the old king sitting like a carven image in his bloodstained tunic, listening to Andulf sing of Sigfrid and Hagano, of Offa of Angeln and Scyld Sceafing, one of the few heroes who lived to be old. He had sung of Eormanaric. He sang until even his trained voice grew hoarse and Hengest told him to be still. That was the sixth night. Three days longer the king stayed, without eating or sleeping. By then he had stopped speaking as well, and only the occasional movement of his breast told them that he lived still.

"Nine days and nights altogether Hengest sat there, and when the tenth morning dawned, although he had not moved, we saw that his breath no longer stirred his beard. The god had come for him at last."

"And *that* is the high seat you want me to sit in?" Oesc said unsteadily.

"You will sit there, and Hengest's spirit will guide you," said Hæthwæge with the certainty of prophecy.

"I drink to Hengest, wisest of warriors, first to be king in the British lands—" Aelle lifted his drinking horn, and the others followed his example with a roar of approval.

Oesc, sitting on a bench before the high seat, gazed around him at the men crammed into the hall. They had begun to arrive just after the Ostara offerings, when by custom kings feasted with their chieftains, to celebrate Hengest's funeral ale.

He had expected Aelle to bring his son Cymen, and Ceretic to come over from Venta, and he knew that Hengest's thanes, Hrofe Guthereson and Hæsta and the others, would be there. But he was surprised by how many others made the journey—old men who had fought in Hengest's battles, and young men to whom they were legends. There was even a small party from Gallia, bearing the condolences of Chlodovechus, the Frankish king.

Each day more tents went up in the field beyond the hall as new groups settled in. It was just as well that Artor had gifted him with so much treasure, he thought ruefully, for this feast would exhaust their stores. He did not delude himself that all these folk had come for his sake. Hengest had been the father of the Saxon migration. With his death an era was ended.

Many times that night the meadhorn had gone round. Men laughed and said it was time the hall had a queen to honor the warriors. Hengest had been an old wolf, who had rather embrace his sword than a woman, but Oesc still had juice in his loins. He should take a wife—the talk grew ribald with speculation. Aelle had granddaughters, girls of good Saxon stock who would give him strong sons. Ceretic had a little daughter, but it would be a dozen winters before she was husband-high. The lords from the Anglian lands suggested that one of the Icelinga girls could bring him a useful alliance. Even Chlodovechus's representative joined the discussion, pointing out that his master also had marriageable daughters, and Cantuware possessed fine harbors that could benefit from Frankish trade.

Oesc shook his head, laughing. "Nay, I must see how my grandfather's high seat fits me before I seek someone to share it. Give me a year or three to settle into my kingship. I promise you I will consider an alliance then."

Hrofe began to talk of how Hengest had married his daughter Reginwynna to the Vor-Tigernus, and Oesc sat back with a sigh. For so long, even the idea of marriage had been out of the question; the thought of a connection more meaningful than his brief encounters with whores or serving-maids took some getting used to. More important still, any marriage he made would commit him to an alliance. If Artor had had another sister—his lips twitched as he remembered the overwhelming beauty of Leudonus's queen. Even if Morgause had been free, it would take a brave man to husband her. She was fertile, though. It was said that nine months after the feast of Lugus she too had been brought to bed of a fine boy that her husband accepted as his own.

Lost in his own thoughts, he did not realize that Andulf had begun to sing

> "... Where once he had held
> most bliss in the world, war swept away
> all Finn's thanes, save few alone
> that he might not at that meeting place
> with war against Hengest finish the fight
> nor the survivors with warfare wrest free
> from the king's thane...."

It was the tale of the fight at Finnesburgh, the first of Hengest's great deeds, though Hengest himself had never boasted about it. That was a hard and bitter story, of the time when Hengest had led the warband of the Dane-king Hnaef on visit to his brother-in-law the Frisian Finn, and when enmity between Finn's men and Hnaef's had become warfare, first forced the Frisian king to divide the steading between the two sides and keep them through the winter, and when the Danes insisted on revenge, broken the peace-troth pledged with Finn in order to avenge his lord.

> "... But they bid him take terms,
> that the king another hall should clear,
> hall and high seat, that they half would hold
> of all the Jutes' sons might possess,
> and at wealth-giving, Folkwalda's son
> every day the Danes would honor,
> and Hengest's riders, with rings as was right
> even as well with treasured wealth
> and golden cups, the Frisian kin
> in the beer-hall he bolstered in spirit."

Hengest had done the same thing again, he thought, when for the sake of his people he turned against the Vor-Tigernus and attacked the British princes. Oesc looked up at the empty high seat, contemplating once more the stature of the man who had occupied it. *What would I do, faced with such a decision?* he wondered then. *If I am ever forced to choose between my own folk and Artor, what will I do?*

Andulf ended the story of the slaying of the Frisians, and once more the meadhorn went round. The tales of Hengest's deeds had inspired his mourners to vows of emulation, most of them, as might have been expected, at the expense of their British neighbors.

"This is my oath, in Woden's name—" Ceretic lifted the horn. "To push the borders of the West Saxon lands outward until Dumnonia is ours, to found a line of kings who shall rule in this island for a hundred generations, to leave a name that shall be remembered as that of the father of this island's kings!"

That did not leave much scope for the other dynasties, and there were a few raised eyebrows, but neither was it much of a threat to the present balance of power. Oesc waited with growing apprehension for the horn to come round to him. Even when he took it in his hand he did not know what he was going to say.

For a long moment he stared at the empty high seat, then he turned to face his guests once more.

"I have fought in battles and killed enemies," he said slowly, "but all my great deeds are still in the future. I am too new in my lordship to make great boasts for my people. I was not here at Hengest's death to take his blessing. To sit in his seat without having performed some great exploit would be overweening pride. This therefore, is my boast. I will go from this place now, at night's high noon, and sit out upon my grandfather's grave mound. If I can sit in that high seat without scathe until dawn, I will claim his place as king."

As he finished, men began to nod and pound the tables in approval. Oesc's vow was unexpected, but not unworthy. It was true that Hengest had met his death in good heart as befitted a warrior and had no reason to hate the living, but the ghosts of the mighty dead could be unchancy, especially when disturbed in their howes.

*   *   *

At first the chill of the night air was welcome after the heat of the hall. But as Oesc approached the mound that had been raised for Hengest just inside the southeastern wall he began to feel the cold, and was glad of the heavy cloak he had brought along. Mist lay heavy on the fields, beyond the tumbled stones, luminous in the light of the waning moon. A dog howled in the town behind him and he suppressed a shiver, hoping that the two warriors who were escorting him had not seen. His shadow lengthened before him in the light of their torches, as if his fetch were hastening towards the mound.

The hill they had raised above the box containing his father's head was as he remembered, flattened a little by time and covered with green grass. Hengest's mound rose stark and black beside it, the colors of the white stallion carved on his grave-post still bright.

"Hengest son of Wihtgils, it is I, Oesc, blood of your blood, who come to your howe seeking counsel. Accept this food and drink, grandfather, and allow me to sit with you in safety until dawn." He unstoppered the flask of mead and poured its contents into the ditch that surrounded the grave mound, then crumbled the barley cake between his fingers and scattered it there.

He waited in silence, and presently it seemed to him that the night had grown a little warmer. "Woden, lord of the slain, be with me now . . ." he whispered, then he gathered up the folds of his cloak and leaped across the ditch onto the mound. He lifted one hand in salute to his men. Then they turned and left him alone.

Oesc's first awareness was of stillness without silence. From the woods beyond the fields he heard the bark of a fox and from the town a dog answering it. From time to time some unusually exuberant burst of shouting echoed faint from the hall.

He patted the earth beside him. "I am glad that you can hear the celebration, grandfather, and that you are not completely alone out here in your mound . . ."

The Christian priests would say that Hengest burned now

in their Gehenna, and that it was superstition to talk to him as if he were alive in the mound. But that did not stop them from praying at the graves of their saints, who were said to dwell with their god in bliss. Hæthwæge had always taught him that a man was a vastly more complex creation than the Christian duality of body and soul, and that while part of the being that had been Hengest feasted in Woden's hall, another part might still cling to the ashes buried in this mound, while the clan-soul which he had inherited from his forebears waited to take flesh again in some future child of his line.

He had seen how they buried Octha's head, and he supposed that after they burned Hengest's body, the bronze urn containing his ashes had been treated likewise, set within a wooden chamber with his shield and seax and spear, his helmet and arm rings, bronze-bound buckets and bowls with food and drink and all such other gear as he might need. Oesc tried to imagine what it was like down there in the heart of the mound.

"I have no wish to disturb your rest, grandfather, but I need your wisdom," Oesc said softly. "Give me your mind, teach me what you have learned from your deeds; and give me your luck, the might and main that carried you across the sea to claim this land, and that will help me to hold it. It is not your treasure that I need from you, Hengest, but this ghostly inheritance."

Once more the wind blew, ruffling the guard-hairs on the fur that lined his cloak. Oesc pulled it more tightly around him and settled himself to wait, breathing in and out in a steady rhythm as Hæthwæge had taught him. Time seemed to move slowly, but when a night bird's cry brought him briefly to awareness, he saw that the moon had moved a quarter of the way across the sky.

It was in the dead of the out-tide, when even the singing from the mead-hall had stilled, that Oesc became conscious in a way that was different from before. He saw the moon low in the west, but he saw also the grey shape that sat beside him on the mound. It was Hengest, the metal-woven braid on his Frankish tunic glinting in the moonlight, but though the wind bent the grass, it did not stir a hair of his flowing beard.

His lips did not move, and yet Oesc felt knowledge precipitating in his awareness like the dew on the grass. He knew the snarling faces of men now fifty years in their graves, the white cliffs of Dubris above the heaving grey waves of the sea, the clamor of a thousand fights, and the long slow years in Cantuware, growing into the land. Everything that had made Hengest a king was now his, if he had the might to use it.

"I see now what you have done . . ." he sent his own thought to that powerful presence, *"but not what I must do . . ."*

There was amusement in the answer that returned to him. *"That is your Wyrd, not mine. But this I will say—land-right belongs to those who give themselves to the land. Seek the Lady, and offer Her your seed and your soul. . . ."*

In the sky the stars were fading. Hengest's form dimmed— for a moment Oesc could see the shapes of field and tree through it, then it was gone.

He took a deep breath, returning sensation rushing tingling through hands and feet. Stiffened muscles did not want to move, but he got upright, and going carefully, for his balance was still unsure, descended the mound. On the other side of the ditch he fell to his knees and plunged his fingers through the new grass and into the soil.

"Earth, my mother, my life is yours. In return I take this kingdom into my hand."

As the first light of the new day scattered gold across the softly flowing waters of the Stur and glowed on the grass, Oesc son of Octha son of Hengest returned to his grandfather's mead-hall and ascended the high seat that was waiting for him there.

VIII

BATTLES IN THE MIST

A.D. 493

"Can there be any Angles left in Germania?" Artor
slapped the table so hard that the map shivered and the ink-
well skipped dangerously. "For fifteen years every spring has
brought more of them flocking northward like wild geese
across the sea. But these geese don't fly home again. The Iceni
and Trinovante lands have long been lost to us, and now the
Angles are spreading into the Coritani country. If they link
up with their countrymen above the Abus, King Icel will have
a stranglehold on half the island!"

The flicker of a hanging lamp added an uncertain illumination to the grey light coming in through the thick panes of
the window, further distorted by the rain that was streaming
down them. It had been raining for some time.

"To answer your first question," answered Betiver, "in Gallia they say that the Anglian homeland has become a wilderness. There are no more reinforcements left to come. To
answer your second question, the last messengers we had say
that Lindum is surrounded. Even if he does not take it, eastern Britannia already lies in Icel's grasp. . . ."

"You are such a comforter," commented Gualchmai, loung-
ing against the doorframe. He had grown taller even than
Artor, and had to duck these days to go through. His brother
Gwyhir, who had joined Artor's household two years after

his brother, was almost as tall, and no doubt young Aggar-ban, the third of Artor's nephews to come to them, would be a big man too.

"Lindum was badly hit last time the Saxons attacked, and the walls were never repaired." Betiver traced the line of the Roman road northward. "By now it may have fallen. We should have reinforced it long ago."

"Gualchmai is right," muttered the king. "You *are* depressing."

"You would not thank me for lying to you . . ."

Artor looked up with that quick smile that took the sting from his words. "You are right, of course, but this is horrible weather for doing anything with cavalry. Do the Angles have webbed feet? I'm told that Anglia is all fenland—they must feel right at home."

Gualchmai guffawed. "I'll wager they do! I ought to have looked at old Oesc's feet when he was here. But he is a Jute of some kind, is he not?"

"His mother was Myrging, but Hengest was Anglian. Fortunately Oesc is rooted in Cantium, and content to keep to his own borders, thank God," added Betiver.

"But he is oathed to Artor—surely you could call—"

The king shook his head. "I raised a wild gosling once that followed me as if I were its mother. All through one summer it fed with the white farm geese and seemed content. But when the wild geese passed overhead in the autumn, my gosling opened her wings and flew away. I tried to call her back, and she circled thrice, but she could not deny her nature and so I lost her."

Gualchmai met his gaze blankly.

"I believe I have won Oesc's friendship, and I have his word," Artor said then, "but even though Hengest's line and Icel's were rivals, I know better than to overstrain Oesc's loyalty. There is more to kingship than giving orders—you must understand the nature of those you rule."

Gualchmai's ruddy skin grew redder. "Your orders are enough for me . . ."

"Because that is *your* nature," answered Artor softly.

"No doubt Cataur will send men, but it will take some time

for them to get here," Betiver said into the silence that followed. "He loves killing Saxons, whoever they may be. There will be a troop from Glevum, and one from Deva—" He began to reckon the forces at their command.

"And we'll need some infantry. I wonder . . ." Suddenly Artor smiled. "Perhaps Cunorix would like to bring me a band of his wild Irishmen. They should have no objection to fighting Icel if they get a good share of the spoils."

Outside, it continued to rain.

It was raining in Cantuware as well. Oesc made passing travelers welcome in his hall and listened to their news. Sitting snug by his fire, he told himself that he pitied men who had to march across the soggy soil of the Coritani lands, that there was no glory in that kind of fighting anyway.

The weather that had delayed the royal messengers also slowed the men who were responding to Artor's call. But the Angles, accustomed to muddy footing, pushed onward, and shortly after Beltain, word came that Lindum had fallen. Icel now possessed a base, if he could keep it, from which he might control everything between Eburacum and Durolipons.

Oesc tossed a coin to the pack-man who had brought the news and strode out of the hall. The fine drizzle beaded the blue wool of his cloak with tiny crystals, but he scarcely noticed the damp. He was seeing not the mud of the yard, but the bloody earth of a battlefield, and instead of Wulfhere and Guthlac and the other men of his household, Betiver and Gualchmai and Artor himself, riding against the foe. He should have been with them—but he understood why the king had not called him. Did Artor really fear that Oesc would have been tempted to fight on the other side?

He had faced Artor in battle once before, when he did not know him. His gut twisted unpleasantly at the thought of doing so again. But his body cried out for action, he wanted to fight. At that moment he scarcely cared who, and the folk of the steading scattered before him.

Presently he found himself in front of the barn.

He called for his horse. Someone asked a question about hunting, and he nodded, and a few minutes later he was trotting towards the southeastern gate of the town. The road cut straight across the flats to the east of the river for several miles. To their right the river gleamed among marshy islets. Beyond it the skirts of the North Downs were clad in forest. But Oesc made no move to get to the other side—these woods, so close to the town, held no game capable of challenging him now.

It was nightfall before they crossed the river and came to the ancient trackway that climbed to the tops of the Downs. There they made camp, and before the sun was high they were taking the path into the hills. A night in the open had muted Oesc's sense of urgency. As riding warmed him, stiff muscles began to ease. He drew a deep breath of the morning air, heavy with the scents of leaf mold and new grass, and felt something that had been drawn tight within him grow easier as well. He actually *saw* the scenery he was looking at for the first time since leaving his hall. And when, just after noon, they crossed the track of a stag, awareness of all else fell away and he gave himself entirely to the joy of the chase.

By the depth of the prints, the stag was old enough to have learned all the tricks by which a hunted beast can elude its foes. But Oesc's tracker was a lad whose folk had lived on the Downs since before the Romans came, and he knew the beasts of his native woods as well as his own kin. A little past noon, they caught sight of the quarry and kicked their horses into all-out pursuit. Oesc's mount was the swiftest, and so he was out of sight of the others when, swinging wide to avoid a fallen tree, his horse put a foot into a hole. Oesc felt the beast lurch beneath him, but before he could get clear the horse went down. He was aware of trees blurring past, and then a resounding impact, and then, for quite some time, of nothing at all.

When Oesc came to himself again the clouds had wrapped the hillside in a damp embrace; everything beyond a few feet was dissolving into featureless grey. His horse stood a few feet away, one foreleg barely touching the ground. With a groan Oesc got upright, made his way over to the animal and gently felt the limb. It did not seem to be broken, thank the gods, though it was clearly a bad sprain. When he tugged on the rein, the horse followed, on three legs only, after him.

Their progress was painfully slow. It hardly mattered, thought Oesc grimly, since it was becoming increasingly apparent that he was lost. Even if he had known this countryside, the mists would have made everything seem strange. And yet to keep moving, even with no goal, was better than bleating like a lost sheep in hopes that someone would find him.

He could see nothing but the shadows of tree trunks in the mist, but downhill, he knew, the forest grew thicker still. His only hope was to struggle up to the bare open slopes that crowned the Downs, where he might strike the ancient track that crossed them. Local legend held that these hills had been well-peopled in ancient days, when the world was warmer and there were no iron ploughs to turn the heavier lowland soils. One still sometimes found the marks of ancient round houses in the soil. Even today, Oesc might hope to encounter a shepherd, or a pack-man trudging across the hills.

Once he found the track he could follow it back to the river, and have a good laugh at his escort, who must be quite frantic by now. But he had his bow, and had learned which of the spring greens could be eaten. He might be separated from his friends, but at least there were no foes hunting him. He was still better off than he would have been in Artor's army.

The same storms that pounded Cantuware had drenched the north as well, saturating the soil and exposing Artor's army to attack by the elements as well as the enemy. Rising waters lapped the raised Roman causeways, wagons bogged down in the sticky mud and animals went lame. Rain spoiled the rations they carried, and though water surrounded them, it was thick and foul. The fact that these hazards had been anticipated did not make them easier to bear. More than once men wished for Merlin to magic the clouds away, but the sorcerer was in the north on some errand of his own.

The Anglians, well aware of their danger, made good use of the country's natural defenses. And yet, though bowstrings stretched and leather rotted, still the Britons came on. In a battle near the ruins of Lactodorum they faced the Eslinga Saxons and had their first victory. Artor took oaths and hostages from their leaders and sent them eastward to Durolipons to garrison the fens against their former allies. Two more muddy skirmishes, hardly worth dignifying with the name of battle, could be counted as victories, since it was the Anglians who retreated when they were done.

Artor led his army along the old legionary road beside the Blackwater. By the feast of Pentecost the royal forces could see the smoke of Anglian cookfires in Lindum across the marshes to the northwest, where the Blackwater, curving into the lowlands, had breached its banks and made a lake of the land. Even in high summer the country of the Lindenses was largely water meadow and marsh. In a wet spring, it seemed an inland sea, in which the scattered bits of higher ground stood like islands. To beseige the city, surrounded by marsh in the midst of hostile territory, was not an attractive prospect, given the problems the Britons had already experienced with supply. But perhaps Icel, unfamiliar with both cities and seiges, would not be aware of Artor's difficulties.

Two days after Pentecost, the king sent one of his captured Saxon chieftains with a challenge. If the Anglians would wager all upon one battle, the Britons would abide by its outcome—to take back all the Lindenses lands if they won, and to abandon the campaign and cede the territory to Icel if their foes had the victory. When the delegation had gone, Artor ordered his army to make camp. The cooks began preparing the first hot meal they had had for a fortnight, and every warrior was set to repairing and preparing weapons and gear.

For three days they remained in camp, waiting for an answer. Then, leaving the baggage train on the high ground, they set out once more upon the road to Lindum.

"Be thankful, man—it could still be raining!" Gualchmai's beard and mustache glittered with fine droplets as he grinned. The clouds still hung low, but the weather had warmed, and the earth was giving back its excess moisture in the form of patchy mists that drifted among the trees.

"What's this, then? Liquid sunshine?" growled Betiver,

shifting uncomfortably in the saddle. His thighs were chafed from riding in wet breeches and his nose was stuffy. But he was luckier than some, for the flux, plague of armies, was beginning to thin their line.

"Man, it would be counted a fine day in my own country!"

Betiver shook his head, wishing they had stayed in camp a day longer. But they might stay for a week and still be plagued by bad weather, while in the meantime the Anglians could be filling Lindum with supplies and men. Here, the Blackwater ran to their right, more or less paralleling the road. But soon, as he recalled, it would make a bend to the westward, where it flowed through the marshy valley. The Romans had made a ford there, so that the road could continue straight along the narrow neck of higher ground that led towards the town.

"Soon we'll be over the river, and then a straight march to Lindum it will be!" said Gwyhir, peering ahead. The mist had thickened. Only the ring of hooves on stone assured them they were still on the road.

"If the floods haven't washed the ford away," grumbled Betiver. Artor's companions headed the column, though the king himself had stayed near the middle to hearten the men. There were scouts out ahead somewhere. He hoped they hadn't gotten lost in this gloom. His stuffed nose was turning into a headache, and his back and shoulders hurt as well.

"Nay, they went out to look last night, remember, and reported that it was still whole," Gwyhir replied. He was, like his brother, exasperatingly cheerful in weather that made everyone else complain.

"If I were Icel, I would set stakes in it, or tear out the stones. He knows we must pass this way . . ."

"What's that?" Gualchmai checked his mount, peering ahead. Betiver strained to see, wishing he were taller. A touch of damp air on one cheek was echoed by a shift in the intensity of the greyness before them.

"The fog is lifting—" he began. A flicker of light rippled through the mist. He stiffened as the wind strengthened, rolling back the mist to unveil the road before them, where morning sunlight gleamed from the well-honed points of a host of spears. With each moment the size of the army that faced them grew clearer. A British horn bugled alarm.

Betiver let out his breath on a long sigh. "It would seem that Icel has given us his answer, after all."

Hooves clattered, and Artor pulled his big black horse to a halt beside them.

"Well. Now I know why our scouts did not return." He was scanning the foe, calculating numbers and dispositions. The Anglians had formed up on the other side of the ford, on the last broad piece of solid ground before the land narrowed. "They've chosen well. The ground's too soft for our heavy cavalry to flank them. Icel wants to force us into a slugging match. . . . we need some way to improve the odds."

The king's tone was detached, as if he were considering a board game. Could he really be that calm?

"Use your archers to soften them up, then," suggested Gualchmai. "They're mostly unarmored."

"Not yet—" Artor frowned. "First, let's try a parley."

"Do you think it will do any good?" Gwyhir asked.

"No, but I need a better estimate of their numbers, and a check on the state of the ford."

"I'll go—" offered Gwyhir.

"Nay, that you will not! You've not the experience—" retorted his brother. The king shook his head.

"The task is for neither. Your eloquence is all in your sword arm, Gualchmai—" Artor grinned. "This requires sweet talk and flattery, so Icel won't realize I'm playing for time." He looked at Betiver, who sighed.

"I understand. Let me wear that white cloak of yours with all the gold embroidery and I'll flatter him like an emperor."

It was amazing, thought Betiver as he splashed through the ford, how the imminent expectation of a spear in the gut put other pains in perspective. He could hardly feel the aches with which he had begun the day.

At least the ford had not been damaged. Perhaps, he thought as he looked around him, the Anglians had considered that precaution superfluous. There were certainly a lot of them, drawn up in groups surrounding their chieftains. Icel sat his white stallion in the middle of the line. He was a big man with a fair mustache, glittering in a shirt of ringmail and a spangenhelm inlaid with figures of gods and heroes in gold.

Meeting that cold grey gaze, Betiver found that respect came easily. Icel's homeland might be small compared to the empire, and poor, but he traced his descent, father to son, through a line of kings that went back to the god Woden, and that was an older lineage than either Artor or the emperor in Byzantium could claim.

"The king of the Britons has good warriors, but they are wet and weary. My men are fresh and strong," said the Anglian king when Betiver had stated Artor's terms. "It is not for him to demand surrender. This is our land now, and we will defend it. Eight hundred spears stand ready to prove my words—" He gestured. "We have heard much of Artor's battles and are eager to fight him. Go tell him so—"

As Betiver rode back towards the British lines it occurred to him that the Eslingas and Middle Saxons had been eager too, and Artor had beaten them, but Icel had spoken truly, and his own side, battered and muddy, seemed a rag-tag excuse for an army next to the barbaric splendor of the warriors surrounding the Anglian king.

But though Betiver's embassy had been fruitless, Artor had made good use of the delay. The British were armed and ready, their heavy cavalry in the middle, the archers positioned in the wings. The king was cantering along the lines, his red cloak bright against the black horse's flanks, his armor gleaming dully in the sun. He listened to Betiver's report with a smile that did not reach his eyes.

Then he wheeled the horse and came to a halt before the first line.

"Men of Britannia—" His voice was pitched to carry. "You have marched a weary way. But Lindum is in sight, and the Anglians have come out to make us welcome!" He waited for their answering laughter. "We have faced their kin three times already and beaten them. But Icel's own warriors have not encountered our like before. We are the heirs of Rome and the children of this island. Draw up strength from this sacred soil, and we will prevail. One more battle, lads, and we will break them. The way to Lindum lies before us—win this one, and tonight we'll lie in soft beds with roofs to keep out the rain!"

After the past few weeks, thought Betiver, dry beds sounded better than gold. He jerked the chin-strap of his helmet tight, wondering wistfully if the baths of Lindum were still usable. Artor was right. He would kill for the chance at a hot soak at the end of the day.

Artor lifted his hand and the air rang to the bitter calling of the horns. The enemy ran to meet them, intending to close the distance so there would be no room for a charge. A ripple of movement swept through the ranks of mounted men, and then the column was moving forward and Betiver's awareness narrowed to the area above his horse's ears through which he could see a glittering line of spearpoints that grew more distinct with every stride.

The air darkened as the archers let fly. The riders splashed through the ford. A horse went down on the right, where the bottom was treacherous, but the others kept their feet and labored up the far bank. An Anglian, outstripping his companions, cast a spear that sped past Artor's shoulder and gashed the flank of the horse behind him. The animal squealed and lurched, but its rider kept it going. Gualchmai plucked a javelin from its loop and cast, and the Anglian went down.

First blood to us— thought Betiver, but now all his vision was filled with grimacing enemy faces. He dug his heels into the horse's sides, striving for the momentum they would need to smash the Anglian line. More spears flew and he heard cries. One after another he reached for his own lances and threw. Then they were crashing into the first group of enemy warriors; for a moment the charge faltered, then they drove onward.

A spear jabbed up at him. Betiver swung his shield around to deflect it and pulled his sword from the sheath. It was all blade-work now, as their pace was slowed by crowding foes. But still they pushed onward, and then they were through. Artor called to them to form up again and hit the enemy from the rear. Light flared from his sword. In that moment of freedom Betiver heard shouting from the flanks. He blinked in confusion as figures rose up like ghosts from the misty waters. Then a familiar war cry shrilled above the clamor of battle and he laughed as Cunorix and his wild Irishmen emerged from the marshes and fell upon the foe.

Artor yelled again, and Betiver's mount, catching the excitement, lurched into motion after the others. His sword arm swung up, and screaming, he charged back into the fray.

The bay horse lifted its head, ears flicking nervously, and Oesc stilled, listening. In another moment his duller ears caught the bleating of sheep. He let out his breath in a long sigh, only then admitting his fear that he might have wandered somehow into Nebhelheim, and would never find his way back to Middle-Earth again. Through the thinning mists a ewe gazed at him with a flat, disapproving stare that could only belong to the sheep kept by humankind. Then the herd dog caught his scent and dashed forward, barking.

"There, boy, down—I mean no harm—"

The dog, a brisk black-and-white beast with a plume of a tail, did not seem convinced. It continued to advance, growling, and he looked around for the shepherd.

He was waving his hands to repel the dog when something moved on the hill. He looked up, saw a blur in the air, and threw up his arm. There was a crack. He reeled, then gasped as pain flared through his arm like white fire. Someone was running towards him, whirling a slingshot in one hand and brandishing a staff in the other; Oesc stepped back, caught his heel in a root and went down.

The stick whistled through the air where his head had been. He rolled as it thwacked downward, and made a grab for his assailant. His good hand closed on a slim ankle and he pulled. The staff went flying and they grappled, rolling over and over in the wet grass.

His foe was wiry as a wildcat, but Oesc was a trained fighting man, and despite his useless arm, in a few moments his size and strength began to tell. It was only when he had got his opponent's arm in a twist and the thrashing legs locked between his own long limbs that he realized his attacker was a girl.

For several moments neither could do more than gasp. He stared down into a heart-shaped face, flushed now with fury and surrounded by a Medusa-tangle of nut-brown hair. Her eyes were a gold-flecked brown, like amber, he thought, gazing into them, or honey-mead.

"A fine welcome you give to strangers here on the Downs," he said finally.

"I thought you were a robber." Her gaze fixed on the fine embroidery at the neck of his tunic, and the golden arm ring. "They've taken two sheep in the past week. I thought they'd come back again." She tensed, trying to free herself, and he was abruptly aware that it was a female body that lay crushed beneath his own.

"It's not mutton I would have from you—" He muttered, and kissed her, at first a light brush of the lips that held her still with surprise, and then hungrily, until she began to struggle once more beneath him and he came up for air, his heart beating hard in his breast.

"How *dare* you!" She got a hand free and tried to box his ear. He pinned her with his body, since he could not use his arm.

"You owe me some weregild—I think you've broken my arm—" he began, and felt her stiffen.

"You're a Saxon!"

He stared at her, and realized they had been speaking in the British tongue.

"A Myrging, to be more precise, and your master—" he said then.

"Then you *are* a robber, after all! My grandfather was lord of this land!"

"You're Prince Gorangonus's kin? We're well matched then, for *my* grandfather took Cantium away from him." He grinned down as her face flushed with angry color once more. His body was urging him to take her, but this was no thrall to be tumbled on a hillside, even if at the moment she looked more like a troll-maid than the daughter of a royal house.

"Hengest's brat—" On her lips it was a curse.

"Hengest's heir," he corrected softly, "and Cantium's king . . ."

"How can you be the king, when you were born across the sea?" She had stopped struggling, and sorrow was extinguishing the fire in her eyes.

"So were the Romans, when they came here—" He released her and sat up, wincing as the movement jarred his arm. "And it was they who put your father's fathers on that throne."

"Perhaps, but it was my mother's mothers who gave them the right to rule. That's why I came back—" She gestured towards the misty sweep of the Downs. "Folk of my blood have dwelt here since before the Romans, even before the Cantiaci came. This land belongs to me!"

For a moment Oesc felt the moist chill of the shrine on the Meduwege once more and remembered how its spirit had spoken to him there. There was a sense in which her claim was true. Men ruled by right of conquest, but sovereignty came from the Goddess and the queens who were her priestesses. Still, he knew better than to admit that, or to point out that without the power to defend it, she might as well have been the wild child she appeared.

"What is your name, granddaughter of Gorangonus?" He winced as an unwary movement jarred his arm, the same that had been broken in Londinium.

"I am called Rigana, for my mother said I should have the name of a queen even if I spent my days keeping sheep upon the hills."

"Very well, then," said Oesc. "I will treat with you as a king does with a queen. Give me shelter. Bind up my arm and tend my horse, which has gone lame, and when my men come to find me you shall have gold."

In a single supple movement she was on her feet, looking down at him.

"That is not the way you treat a queen, but an inn-wife. It is as a queen I will shelter you, for you are the suppliant. But the boy who helps us will go for your men as fast as he may, for I would not have the sight and smell of you in my house for one hour longer than hospitality compels."

*   *   *

Clean, warm, and dry at last, Betiver considered the captive Anglian lords. It made him shiver even now to remember what a near thing the battle had been. A score of times during that dreadful morning he had been sure they were beaten. But whenever he could stop to draw breath long enough to consider surrender he had seen that Artor was still fighting, and gritted his teeth, and kept on. He was not ashamed at his own grim satisfaction—now it was he who was dressed like a prince, and the Anglians who were gashed and grimy. However the reversal of fortune did not seem to have daunted their pride.

"Look at Icel!" exclaimed Gualchmai. "Lounging at his ease, as if he still held this hall! You would think he'd be showing a wee bit of apprehension. Did he never hear about the Night of the Long Knives?"

"He trusts to Artor's honor, and besides, that atrocity was the work of Hengest's Saxons. They may all look like the same kind of barbarian to us, but to Icel, his folk are as different from the other tribes as, say, your Votadini are from the Picts who are their neighbors."

"Hmph. Well, I won't deny the Picts have come to us at times for husbands for their princesses. But their sons are raised by their uncles, and mother's milk is stronger than father's blood."

Betiver lifted a hand to silence him. Artor stood in the doorway, drawing men's eyes and stilling their tongues. He too had taken advantage of Lindum's baths, and had dressed in a Roman tunic of saffron-dyed linen with bands of purple silk coming down over the shoulders to the hem and patches bearing eagles worked in gold. His mantle, also edged in goldwork, was of a red so deep it was almost purple, and he wore a Roman diadem upon his brow. Cai, behind him, was actually wearing a toga. Gualchmai whistled softly and grinned.

"Is it the emperor himself who's come to call on us? I hope Icel is impressed."

There had been a flicker of appreciation in Icel's grey eyes, but his face showed no emotion at all. That clothing had certainly never made the muddy journey from Londinium. Betiver, wondering which rich merchant had provided it, fought to keep his own face still. Icel had sought to impress them as a folk-king, lord of a mighty people, but Artor was meeting him as the heir of Rome.

Moving with conscious dignity, Artor seated himself on the carved chair on the dais, and Betiver and Gualchmai took their places with Cai behind him. Icel and two of his surviving chieftains, still in the grubby tunics they had worn beneath their mail, had been given low benches on the floor.

"You fought well, " said Artor, "but your gods have given you into my hand."

"Woden betrayed us," muttered one of the chieftains. "Nine stallions we gave him, and yet he did not give victory."

"But many of your warriors earned a place in his houseguard," said Artor, who had learned something of the German religion when Oesc was his captive. Icel responded with a rather wintry smile.

"Woden will take care of his own. My care is for the living. What is your will for those who are your prisoners?"

"Kill them," muttered Cataur, "as they slaughtered our men."

Most of those who had survived the battle, thought Betiver, belonged to Icel's houseguard, who had made a fortress of flesh around their king. If he had fallen, they would not have survived him, and only Icel's order could have made them lay down their arms. He leaned close to Gualchmai. "He doesn't ask about himself—"

Gualchmai snorted derisively. "He knows the high king cannot afford to let him go."

But Artor was leaning on the acanthus-carved arm of his chair, resting his chin on his hand, and frowning.

"What would you have me do?"

The question disturbed Icel's composure at last. "What do you mean?"

"You are their king—what did your people seek on these shores?"

"Land! Land that will not wash away in the winter rains!"

Artor raised one eyebrow, indicating with a turn of the

head the flooded wastes outside the town, and someone laughed. But Icel was shaking his head.

"Oh yes, this land floods, but the water will go away again and leave it all the richer. We can ditch and dam and make good fields. The river is not so greedy as the sea."

"The Romans did not have that craft—"

Icel's lips twitched again. "The Romans built like etins, great works of pride and power that forced earth to their will. Our farmers are content to work with willow wands and mud and coax our Mother to be kind."

Artor's gaze moved slowly around the faded frescoes of the old basilica, and the worn mosaics on the floor, and he sighed.

"The Romans were mighty indeed, but they are gone, and the land remains," he said then. "And save for your folk, there are now none left to till that soil."

Something flickered in Icel's gaze at the words, but he kept his features still. Cataur's face began to darken dangerously.

"Many men of my blood have died," Artor went on, "but my duty is to the living also. To leave this place a wasteland and its shores desolate will serve no one. But I *am* high king, and any who would dwell here must go under my yoke." He frowned at Icel. "If I give you your lives, will you and your folk take oath to me, to hold these coasts and defend them in my name? As the Romans gave districts to the Franks and Burgunds and Visigoths, I will give the Lindenses lands to you, saving only Lindum itself, which I judge my own people better able to garrison."

As the Vor-Tigernus gave land to Hengest . . . thought Betiver grimly, *and look what that led to!* But Hengest's men had been a rag-tag of mercenaries and masterless men, not a nation. It was the same agreement Artor had made with Oesc, in the end, and that seemed to be working well.

There was a short silence. "What guarantees . . . would you require?" the Anglian king said then.

"That you shall swear never again to take arms against me or my heirs, to defend these lands against all others, and to send a levy of warriors at my call. You shall pay a yearly tribute, its size contingent upon the size of your harvest, and in cases affecting men not of your people, be judged by my laws. I further require that you give up all looted goods and treasure, that one son from each of your noble families shall be sent as hostage to dwell among the youths of my household, and that all warriors who are not of your tribe shall remain my prisoners."

Cataur surged forward, and Gualchmai moved to stand between him and the dais. "My lord, you cannot do this! He's a *Saxon . . .*"

"An Anglian," Artor corrected coldly, "and I am your king—"

"Not if you betray us!" Cataur exclaimed, his hands twitching as if he reached for someone's throat. But Gwyhir and Aggarban had come to stand beside their brother, and Morgause's three sons made a formidable barrier. "You'll regret this day!" Still sputtering, Cataur whirled and strode from the room. Gualchmai started after him, but Artor waved him back.

It took a few minutes for the murmur of comment to die down. But despite the fact that there were those on both sides who like Cataur would obviously rather have kept on fighting, it was a fair offer. Indeed, it was more than generous, especially when the alternative was to be slaughtered like a sheep, without even a sword in one's hand. Icel must have hoped for something like this, even if he had not dared to expect it.

Icel got to his feet, his eyes still fixed on Artor. "I am the folk-lord, and I stand for my people before the gods. But for all things that belong to this land and the Britons I will give my oath to you."

Artor gestured to one of the guards. "Unloose his bonds." He looked back at Icel. "As you keep faith with me, so shall I with you, for the sake of Britannia."

A little past sunset three weeks after Oesc returned from his ill-fated hunting trip, the hounds who ran loose around his hall began barking furiously. Oesc, who had been drinking to ease the ache in his arm and trying not to think about Rigana, sat up, and Wulfhere rose to his feet, reaching for the spear that leaned against the door.

"Who comes to the hall of Oesc the king?"

"One who carried him on his saddlebow when he was a boy, came the gruff answer, "and I have not made my way across half Britannia, beset by enemies, to be challenged in Hengest's hall!" Taking advantage of Wulfhere's astonishment, the newcomer shouldered past him and into the light of the fire. Two other men came after him, looking about them nervously.

Oesc leaned forward, striving to see behind the dirt and the dried blood and the wild grey-streaked hair.

"Is it Baldulf?" he asked, coming down from his high seat and opening his arms. "It must be! You stink too badly to be aught but a mortal man! Old friend, what has happened to bring you to my door like—" He shook his head, seeking words.

"Like a fugitive?" Baldulf sank down upon a bench, took the horn of ale the thrall-woman offered and drank it down. "That's what I am, boy—fleeing a lost battlefield and the wrath of your young high king."

"You were in the north—" Oesc said, "were you with Icel?"

Baldulf grunted. "I was safe enough in my dale, until that smooth-talking Anglian sent messages around seeking allies in his campaign against Lindum. All went well for a time, but Artor came at last, and brought Icel to battle. Lad, I was lucky to survive that day, and luckier still not to be captured. The Anglians have taken oath to Artor, but the other prisoners were killed. If I never see another marsh I shall count myself happy!" He shuddered reminiscently and held out his horn to be refilled with ale.

"I won't give you up to him, if that's what you were wondering," said Oesc, "but I can't keep you here."

"Nor would I stay—help me to a ship and I'll be over the water to the Frisian lands." He took another drink and reached out for a hunk of the bread which had been set before him. "There may be no Anglians left to replace those Icel lost, but there are still fighters on the coast who might be willing to try their luck in Britannia. Two men only survived from my warband—" He gestured towards his followers, who were being fed at a table by the door. "But I'll soon raise another. The Britons have not heard the last of me!"

Oesc nodded bemusedly. Listening to Baldulf was like stepping back into another time, to the days when Hengest and his father tore at Britannia like wolves. Things were different now. He understood why Icel had accepted Artor's peace. Now Britannia was his land, too. After a moment he realized that Baldulf had asked him a question.

"Come with you? No—all that I want is here—" He shook his head, smiling.

"All? What about a plump wife to warm your bed, and fair-haired children about your knee? Shall I look for the daughter of a Frisian chieftain, or maybe a Frankish princess, to be your queen?"

Oesc stared at him, all his frustration focusing suddenly into a single need. "I do need a wife," he said then, "but not a woman from across the sea. I must marry into this land if my heirs are to hold it. . . ."

Suddenly Rigana's face filled his vision. Tomorrow, he thought, he would ride to the hut on the Downs. After that first encounter he had not touched her, but one way or another, he knew that she would be his queen.

ALLIANCES

A·D· 494

Torches had been set into the crumbling city wall and upon the green height of Hengest's mound. They flickered with pale fire in the last light of the soft summer day. The space before the mound had been cleared and spread with rushes to accommodate the tables for the wedding feast. The King's Hall had not room enough for so many, and in any case, this close to Midsummer it was far too warm to huddle indoors.

The sound of Andulf's chanting floated on the wind. He was old now, and his voice no longer as resonant as it once had been, but he still had the trick of pitching it to carry across the field.

> *"Hail the heir of high-born heroes—*
> *Son of the Saxons who first to these shores;*
> *West over whale-road, borne by the wind,*
> *The old land left, new lives to fashion—"*

Oesc, who had gone to consult with his steward about serving more mead, surveyed the scene and smiled. Two dozen tables rayed out in a semicircle from his own, where Rigana, draped in crimson silk and hung with gold, awaited him. Her features were half-hidden by the fall of her veil, but his pulse leaped at the sight of her all the same. In the month since he had brought her home to Cantuwaraburh, he had discovered that he could always sense her presence, and his pulse quickened at the mere brush of her hand.

But he had, in addition, a very different reason for feeling satisfaction. The Cantuware chieftains, nodding approvingly as Andulf began to recite Oesc's ancestry, had all turned out with their sworn men, but that, he had expected. It was their duty to witness the wedding of their lord to the woman who would give him his heir. But Ceretic had brought his West Saxons, and Aelle, his hair now entirely white but his frame still well-muscled, had journeyed up from the south coast to attend the celebration, and that was an honor on which Oesc had not dared to depend.

And beside Rigana, where her father, had he been living, would have had his place, sat Artor the High King, who had made time between campaigning against the Anglians and dealing with the new threat from Irish raiders in Demetia to come. He almost looked the part of a father, thought Oesc, watching them. In the past year or so Artor had broadened out—not with fat, but with the muscle that comes from wearing armor for long hours over an extended campaign. In Artor's eyes Oesc could still recognize the boy he had first faced across a battlefield sixteen years before, but the body was now emphatically that of a man, and a king.

It was with enthusiasm that Artor had accepted Oesc's invitation to stand for the family of the bride at the wedding. More eagerness, to tell the truth, than Rigana had shown when she heard about it. To be sure, it was Vitalinus the Vor-Tigernus who had given away her grandfather's princedom, not Uthir, but even though there was now no man of that line fit to hold Cantium, Rigana blamed the House of Ambrosius for not having won it back to British rule, and Artor for confirming Oesc as its lord.

It was no use to point out that if the Saxons had never come, she would most likely have been married off young to some lord living elsewhere in Britannia, whereas now she would be queen in her own country. Oesc was coming to understand the bride he had brought home from the hills. Courageous she was, as well as passionate, but logic was not one of her virtues.

> *"In wisdom he weds a noble woman,"* sang Andulf.
> *"Daughter of drightens, radiant as day.*
> *Bold is her heart, as bright her beauty,*
> *Lady who links the lord to the land."*

Surely that must please her, thought Oesc. Artor had signed the marriage contract on her behalf, and now he was slicing meat from the joint that had been set before them, and as he transferred slices to her platter, she smiled. Should that make him uneasy, wondered Oesc?

Watching them, he saw in Rigana's face no coquetry, but it seemed to him that there was something wistful in Artor's eyes. The question of the high king's marriage had been often discussed, but although many maidens had been proposed for the honor, there had never been time, it seemed, for him to court one of them. But if Artor had found love of a more casual kind, no one had heard about it.

Oesc did not think the high king could have had a mistress in secret, but he was not a cold man. When he came to love, it would be deeply.

It is not my bride I should fear for, Oesc thought then, *but my king.*

He saw Ceretic's daughter Alfgifu approaching, bearing the great silver-mounted aurochs horn filled with mead. Andulf struck a last chord and finished his song.

Oesc strode quickly back to take his place at Rigana's side as Artor accepted the horn.

"It is my honor to be the first to offer a toast for the couple who sit before you. Any marriage is a harbinger of hope, for thus the race is renewed. But this wedding, more than most, gives me hope for the future, for the groom, who was once my enemy, has become a friend and ally, and the bride, a woman of my own people, is a living link between the old royal line and the new. It is always something of a miracle that two creatures so different as male and female can live in harmony—" He paused for the murmur of laughter. "But if Oesc and Rigana can do so, then there is hope that Britons and Saxons can live in peace as well.

"This, then, is my wish for the bridal couple—that as they join their lives, our peoples may be linked as well, and if they do not always manage to live in perfect accord—" again, he waited for the laughter "—then I wish that their differences may be quickly resolved, and that from their union new life shall spring!"

He turned the horn carefully so that its tip pointed down, and raised it to his lips, taking a long draught without spilling a drop. Then he handed it back to Alfgifu, who bore it to Aelle, and then to Ceretic and the other chieftains.

The other blessings were more conventional, with a heavy emphasis on the breeding of strong sons. Oesc scarcely heard them. His beating pulse reminded him that soon the feast would be finished, and it would be time to make Rigana his wife in fact as well as name.

When the toasts were completed, the women led Rigana off to the hall to be prepared for bed. As their singing faded, the sound of men's laughter grew louder as the male guests were released from such bonds of propriety as they had observed so far.

"Drink deep, my lord," said Wulfhere, refilling his horn.

Oesc took it and drank, fighting not to cough as he realized that this was not the mild ale mead they had been drinking, but a brew whose heavy sweetness did not quite hide its strength. He swallowed, feeling his head swim as the fire began to burn in his belly, and handed the horn back to the other man.

"That's fine stuff, but I'd best go easy or I'll be no use to my bride—"

"You'll be no use either if you cannot relax," said Ceretic with a grin, offering his own horn. "Drink up, man!"

"That's true," answered Oesc. He reached for the horn.

Ceretic moved closer, bending as if to continue his teasing. "At your wedding feast, the high king of Britannia himself sits down with his Saxon enemies. Are you not honored?" He was still smiling, but there was something unexpectedly sardonic in his tone.

Oesc raised an eyebrow. "Shouldn't I be?"

Ceretic shrugged. "Artor sings a sweet song about peace between Briton and Saxon, but it is like trying to build an alliance between dogs and wolves."

"You yourself are half Briton—" Oesc began.

Ceretic grunted. "But my heart is Saxon. The blood may mix, but the spirit must be singular. The Britons lick their wounds now, but they hate us still, especially Cataur, who has never forgiven us his brother's death at Portus Adurni. They say he protested making peace with Icel and left the army immediately afterward with all his men, nor will he take them to Artor's aid in Demetia. That man wants blood, and he'll not care where he gets it. I would put a guard upon your borders if I were you."

"Artor will keep him leashed—"

Ceretic shook his head. "Artor may desire peace, but one day his princes will force him to turn against us. When he summons you to war against your own people, which will you choose?"

For a long moment Oesc frowned back at him, the mead growing cold in his belly. "I will choose my own land," he said finally. "I will fight for Cantuware."

Ceretic opened his mouth as if he would say more, then closed it without speaking. The torches flared suddenly in a gust of wind, and Oesc turned. Hæthwæge had come into the circle of light. Silence spread as men saw her standing there, and one or two made a surreptitious gesture of warding where they thought no one could see. It occurred to Oesc that Hæthwæge must be in her sixth decade by now, but as always when she put on the regalia of a priestess, she seemed beyond age.

The wisewoman looked around the circle, smiling slightly, then turned to Oesc. "This is a time of change, when the spindle twirls and new strands are woven into the web of Wyrd. Would you know, my king, what fates shall fall as a result of this marriage of yours?"

The men who stood nearest backed away uneasily. Oesc found himself abruptly sober once more.

"Are you afraid?" she asked then.

He shook his head. This was Hæthwæge, who had guided and guarded him since he was a child.

"I fear neither my fate nor you. Whether my Wyrd be good or bad, foreknowledge will enable me to face it well."

The guests drew back to leave a space around them. Hæthwæge spread a square of linen on the ground and drew the bundle of runestaves from her pouch.

"Say, then, what it is you wish to know—"

For a moment Oesc stood in thought, choosing his words. "Tell me if this marriage will prosper, and whether my queen will bear a son to follow me in this land."

Hæthwæge nodded. Her eyes closed, and she whispered a prayer he could not hear. Then she bent, and with a practiced flick of the wrist, scattered the runestaves across the cloth.

The yew wood sticks rattled faintly as they fell, bounced against one another, and then lay still. Oesc leaned forward, trying to make out the symbols incised and painted where the sides of the sticks had been planed smooth. It was quite dark now. In the flicker of torchlight the rune signs seemed to twist and bend.

Like any man of good blood he knew something of the runes, but their deeper meanings, especially in combination, were a mystery. The sticks the old woman had cast lay scattered across the cloth. Most of them had fallen near the edges; it was the ones that lay within the circle painted in the center that would provide the prophecy.

"*Ing*, the rune of the king who comes over the sea, the god in the royal mound—" Hæthwæge pointed to a rune of crossed angles that lay in the middle of the cloth. "Your seed will take root in the ground." There was a murmur of appreciation from the other men.

"And there, near to it, are *Ethel*, for heritage and homeland, and *Ger*, the rune of good harvests. It means that you will bring luck to your land. But *Hægl*, the hailstone, lies close by them. Some violent upset threatens as well."

"What is the rune that lies across the other, just to the right of the middle of the cloth?" asked Oesc.

For a moment Hæthwæge stared at them, swaying back and forth and muttering softly. Then she sighed.

"*Gyfu* is crossed by *Nyd*—the rune of gifts and exchange cut by Necessity. You see how similar they are—one equal-armed, the other showing the firedrill crossed by its bow. *Gyfu* is a rune that wins great gains, but it is also a sign of self-sacrifice. Some say that *Nyd* represents the slash of a sword, or the spindle of the Norns. Whichever is true, these two crossed runes intersect." The wisewoman looked up at Oesc, and his heart chilled at the sorrow he saw in her eyes.

The wisewoman sighed, then spoke again. "This is the Wyrd that these runes show to me. Your reign will be fruitful, my king, and your son will rule long in this land. But there is a price to pay. Always. Only if you are willing to give all will all you have wished for come to pass."

"All?" he echoed softly, remembering how his grandfather's body had swung from the tree. Since childhood he had understood what might be required of a king. "I made that offering before I ever ascended Hengest's high seat, when I sat out upon his mound."

"You have answered well." Leaning on her staff, the wicce straightened. "Your bride awaits you. Go now, and fulfill your destiny."

The light around them brightened. Oesc turned and saw that four of the women who had escorted Rigana to the hall had returned, bearing fresh torches whose flames were whipped out into ribbons of fire by the rising wind.

"To your destiny!" echoed Ceretic, grinning, "and a fair one it is!" He gave Oesc a push, and fell in with the other men behind him, cheering, as the women lit his way towards the bridal bower.

To satisfy his bride's Roman preference for privacy, Oesc had built a partition to wall off the end of the hall that held the king's boxbed from the rest. Four pillars still supported the framework, stuffed with straw and featherbeds. But instead of closing the space between them with wooden slats, it now was hung with lengths of heavy woolen woven in bands of crimson and gold. A wooden floor had been laid and a wolfskin rug cast over it. Terracotta lamps hung from brackets on the wall, and the women had garlanded the bed with greenery and early summer flowers.

More important still, the bower had a door. As he shut it firmly behind him, Oesc was suddenly extremely glad he had taken the trouble to build it. This moment would have been even more difficult if there had been no more than a single bedcurtain between him and the raucous encouragement he was being given by the men outside. He cleared his throat.

"Rigana?"

From the other side of the curtain came a noise that sounded suspiciously like laughter.

She answered, "The sooner you come to bed, the sooner those louts outside will shut up and go away."

Oesc fumbled with the clasp of his belt, dragged his tunic over his head and dropped it, and pulled off his breeches. As he pulled aside the curtain and climbed into the bed he could feel his heart beating as it did when he was going to war.

Light filtered through the rough weave of the curtains, glowing on the pale flesh of the woman who sat cross-legged on the coverlet. Oesc's breath caught as he looked at her small, uptilted breasts and rounded thighs, confirming with his eyes what his hands had learned about her body when they struggled on the grass. Since that day, she had scarcely let him touch her. But she did not seem to be afraid.

"Are you drunk?" she asked suddenly.

He blinked, then shook his head. "Did you think I would have to be drunk to lie with you?"

"I only wondered what was keeping you so long." She settled back among the pillows, looking at him with the same frank interest with which he had eyed her.

Hoping that the dim light would not show his blush, Oesc climbed the rest of the way into the bed.

"Hæthwæge read the runes. She says we will have a fine son to be king of this land."

"Does she? Then we had better get started on making him—"

Oesc could not decide whether her smile held eagerness or defiance.

He had meant to be tender, to take her slowly. He had dreamed of this moment in exquisite detail—how he would stroke first her cheek, and then work his way carefully down until her breast lay like a tender fruit in his hand. He had not anticipated the way that lust would flame in his blood in response to the challenge in her smile. *Frige be with me!* he thought desperately as he pulled Rigana into his arms.

The wiry, whipcord strength was as he remembered, but the feel of her smooth skin against his own as they wrestled together made his mind reel. His fingers tightened in her hair as he kissed her, his body straining against hers until she lay still. She cried out as he thrust through her maidenhead, and began to fight him again, but imperceptibly their struggles became harmony, their breath coming together in harsh gasps as they rode the storm. He felt her convulse in his arms, and her final frenzy swept his own awareness away.

An eternity later, they became aware of each other as separate beings again. Wind was whispering in the thatching, and from the feasting ground they could hear men's voices lifted in song. Oesc raised himself up on one elbow, looking down at his bride.

"Don't think it will be this easy every time..." she said shakily.

"Easy?" Oesc winced as bites and scratches began to sting. "I feel like a ship that has barely survived the storm. If this coupling has made a son, he will be a warrior!"

"A typical Saxon!"

"As fierce as his mother!" Oesc replied. He shook his head in exasperation. "If you hate us so, why did you marry me?"

"You carried me off—" she retorted, "what choice did I have?"

"You know very well I would not have forced you. And at the end there, your body seemed very eager for mine! Rigana—the same wind buffeted us both, and brought us in the end to safe harbor. Even now will you not give truth to me?"

"The truth is ... that my body may have surrendered, but my mind still tells me that you are my enemy."

"And your heart?" he asked softly.

Rigana sighed. "My heart is a slow learner—you must give it time to understand."

In the weeks that followed, Oesc remembered those words. Marriage with Rigana was like sailing the sea at the mercy of conflicting winds. At times they blew as balmy as some fabled southern isle, and Oesc, half-drunk on his new wife's kisses, would swear that he had won her at last. But then some clash of culture or concept, or even the sight of the ruins over which her grandfather had ruled, would set the wind wheeling round to the north again, with a chill that could freeze his soul. But the body had its own imperatives. Their lovemaking, when Rigana would submit to it, was a force that shook them both to the core. And soon it became apparent that Oesc's seed had taken root in fertile ground.

Pregnancy, of course, gave the queen a whole new source of invective, especially during the early months, when she was often ill. Nonetheless, as the result of their lovemaking became increasingly apparent, Rigana began to turn to her husband more and more. It was a golden year, with a bountiful harvest and a mild winter, and Oesc tasted his new happiness with astonished joy.

Just after the spring equinox, when the rain storms followed each other in stately succession across the land, Rigana's pangs came upon her. The bed in the bower was spread with clean cloths and fresh straw for her lying in, and Oesc was banished from the room to wait beside the fire in the hall with the other men.

"Women!" exclaimed Wulfhere, "they act as if all men were monsters when one of them is in the straw!"

"Not all men—" said Oesc, wincing as he heard Rigana swearing from the other side of the wall. "Just me. . . ." He rubbed his left arm, where Rigana's slingstone had cracked the old break in the bone. He had still not gotten back full use of that hand.

"She has a good vocabulary," observed Wulfhere, running a hand through his thinning ash-brown hair.

Oesc managed to smile back at him. Wulfhere was a good

friend, he thought, straightforward and steady, as good a man as one might find in the Saxon lands. But he had been born in Cantium, son to a man who had come over in Hengest's first warband. He understood Oesc's love for this land. More to the point, he was also the father of four children, and understood what his lord was going through.

Oesc looked up suddenly, realizing that he could hear nothing from the bower. He started to get to his feet, but Wulfhere shook his head.

"Someone will come out if there's news." He pushed the beer jug across the table.

"No. I don't want to be drunk when—if—she's been at it since morning and it is past midnight! I'd rather fight a battle than wait here. At least I could *do* something there!"

"This is a woman's battlefield. But life, not death, is the victory."

"I hope so—" Oesc sat down once more.

From the bower came a grunt, and then something very like a battle cry. The two men stared, scarcely daring to breathe, until they heard, like an echo, a thin, protesting wail.

Women's voices murmured busily as the door opened and Hæthwæge beckoned. Two steps brought Oesc to her side.

"Is Rigana—is the baby—" He could not find words. Beyond the wicce he saw his wife lying in the bed in which the child had been begotten. A pile of bloodstained cloths lay on the floor. She looked pale, but her eyes were very bright. Walking carefully, as if his footfalls might break something, he came to her side and took her hand.

"My dear, I'm so sorry—" he stammered, "I didn't know!"

"Sorry! When I've given you a fine son? Look at him!" She flipped back a piece of linen and he realized that what he had taken for tumbled bedclothes beside her were the cloths that swaddled a tiny being who mewed at the disturbance and rooted against his mother's breast.

"You're all right?" he asked.

"Of course. I've helped too many ewes bring their lambs into the world to make a fuss—though I must say the sheep seem to have an easier time! Pick him up—is he not beautiful?"

Oesc realized that the women were all watching him ex-
pectantly, and someone had summoned his sword-thanes,
who were crowding into the room.

"Beautiful—" he muttered, although the crumpled red features looked more like those of a tiny troll than of a man.
Carefully he got his hands under the small bundle and lifted
it, and caught his breath as the slitted eyes opened and for a
moment he saw his grandfather Eadguth's face overlaid on
that of the child.

"Beautiful—" he said again, knowing what they were waiting for. "And I claim him as my son! Is there water?" He
looked at Hæthwæge.

"Here—I brought it from the sacred spring . . ." She held
out a bowl of dark brown earthenware incised with a zigzag
design around the rim.

Oesc dipped his fingers into the water and sprinkled the
cool droplets on the baby's brow. "Eormenric son of Oesc I
name you, grandson of Octha and Gorangonus of Cantium,
great grandson of Hengest of the royal Anglians, and Eadguth
the Myrging king. I dedicate you to Woden, who has given
you breath, and to the Lady of this land, who has given you
flesh. Live long, my son, for Cantuware is your heritage!"

"I think I never knew what it was to simply feel happy
before . . ." said Oesc. Wulfhere, who was riding beside him,
laughed.

"Well, lord, you have reason."

Oesc found that he was grinning. The movement of the
horse beneath him, the way the summer sunlight glowed
through the whispering leaves above the track that led north
through the Weald towards Aegelesford, even the sweetness
of the air he drew in—today, everything gave him joy. But
he had ridden through fine summer days before and never
noticed their beauty. It was the happiness he had found in
the great things of his life that allowed him to value the little
ones as well.

"To the fortunate man, all things are golden—" he repeated
the old saying. "It is true, I have been greatly blessed."

Still smiling, he silently enumerated the gifts that the gods had given him: Rigana had recovered well from the birthing, and Eormenric had outgrown the first fragility of babyhood and was now as fine and lusty a child as any man might wish for. The first, disturbing resemblance to his grandfathers had faded as he put on flesh. At three months, he was all plump cheeks and bright eyes, reaching out to grasp the world with chubby pink hands.

In his delight with the baby, Oesc did not forget the wife who had produced him. Rigana would never be an easy woman to live with, but after a year of marriage, she had lost the abrasive edge that had at first turned every conversation into a battle. Now they only fought once or twice a week, and since their battles more often than not ended in bed, Oesc could hardly regret them.

And Hengest's old hall had never been so bright. Rigana had the manner of a princess, but her life on the farm in the hills had given her a realistic understanding of the labor needed to maintain a hall. She asked nothing of her maids that she could not do better, and though at times they felt the lash of her tongue, they respected her.

His marriage had won him new respect among the men of Cantuware as well, especially the eorls and elders. *They no longer have to fear I will lead their sons off on wild adventures*, he thought. *I am becoming a land-king now.*

Certainly Hæsta seemed to think so. At this last law-giving, the southern eorl had praised his judgments. Even Hengest, he said, had not understood the land and its needs so well.

And Oesc was still young, and save for that lingering weakness in his left arm, in robust health. There was no reason he should not live as long as his grandfather and see his own grandchildren root themselves in this land. He had taken Rigana and the baby to Aegele's ford so that they could get the blessing of the goddess of the sacred spring.

Suddenly his joy demanded action. The ford was barely an hour away, and then he would see his wife and child, but he did not want to wait so long. The horse's ears twitched as he lifted the rein.

"Wulfhere, that nag of yours is plodding like a plowhorse.

I have a mind to reach Aegele's ford by noon. Do you think you can match me?"

"I'll come there before you!" Wulfhere's eyes kindled.

"Do it and I'll give you the Frankish swordmount that Hæsta gifted me."

"And you shall have your pick of Prick-Ear's next litter if you win—" Wulfhere returned. The other men shook their heads indulgently, but they reined their mounts out of the way as with a shout their young king and his friend set their horses careering up the path.

Bent over the grey mare's neck, gulping in air strained through her flying mane, it was not until Oesc began to cough that he realized the air smelled of smoke—not the smoke of a hearthfire, or soapmaking or the burning of brush or any of the other uses of fire about a farm, but the acrid reek of a big fire, of burning timbers and smoldering straw. He had smelled it too often to mistake, when he was at war.

He straightened, shifting his weight back and hauling on the reins. For a moment the mare fought him, then she pulled up, plunging, just as Wulfhere thundered around the bend behind him.

"What is it? Is your horse—" he began. Then he too caught the scent the wind was bringing and his face changed.

"Go back and bring up the warriors," Oesc said softly. "Leave the baggage ponies to follow as best they can."

"But my lord—"

"I've done scouting. I'll go slowly and take care not to be seen."

Oesc waited until the clatter of Wulfhere's departure faded and the forest grew quiet around him. He could hear neither shouting nor hoofbeats, but the burning must be close for the reek to be so strong. Perhaps Aegele was only burning brush, he told himself, and the men would get a good laugh at his fear. Then a shift in the wind brought him a whiff of roasting flesh, and the mare lurched forward at the touch of his heel.

He slowed again as he started down the slope towards the ford, but now he could hear ravens calling to their kindred. They would not do so unless the fighting was done.

It was strange, some odd, detached part of his mind observed as he rode into the farmyard, how clearly he could still read the signs, though it was nearly ten years since last he had ridden to war.

The attackers had hit the farm without warning. The women had been dyeing cloth. Two squares of blue flapped damply from the rack, but the pot had been overthrown, its contents mixing with the blood on the ground. One of the thrall women lay beside it, her head crushed, her hand still gripping the wooden bat she had been using to stir the pot. But her skirts modestly covered her thighs.

Where is Rigana? Oesc forced the yammering voice within him to be still.

The raiders had not raped or even pillaged—cattle still lowed from the byre. But the hoofprints had already told him that these folk were riding good Roman-bred horses, not the shaggy hill ponies that outlaws would use. He found two more thralls by the byre, and then one of Aegele's men with a sword still in his hand. Outlaws would not have left the weapon, and the strokes that had killed the man had a military precision. This was not robbery, but a raid, conducted by trained warriors with a military objective in mind.

My wife and my son! Dead, or hostages? Once more he shut the voice away.

Methodically Oesc worked his way around the buildings. More men lay with their throats cut in addition to their wounds. The attackers had left no one living to tell the tale. Aegele himself lay just inside the ruins of his house, with his wife beside him. His body was partly burned, but the golden band that marked him as a thane was still on his arm.

Hæthwæge was with them. Could her magic have hidden Rigana and the child?

He left the mare standing and made his way up the path to the shrine. The devastation that had hit the farm had not touched it—more reason for that cold, evaluating part of his mind that kept his rage at bay to conclude British warriors had done this thing. He saw signs of a scuffle in the dirt before the shrine. Blood had been drawn—dark drops speckled the ground.

A breath of wind lifted his hair and chilled the sweat on his brow. He went inside.

The lamps were cold, but a bunch of summer asters, barely wilted, still lay on the stone, and beside it, a baby's teething bone.

"Lady—" he whispered, "they came to serve you. Could you not have protected them?"

Water murmured musically from below, the same song as it had sung for Celt and Roman, and for those who came before. *I am here as I have always been . . .* it whispered, *be still, and know . . .*

But Oesc could not listen. In his ears a furious wind was rising, sweeping both patience and reason away. A swift step took him back to the doorway and the devastated farm below. Wulfhere and his men were just riding in. But he scarcely saw them.

"Rigana . . ." he whispered. The roar of the wind grew louder, though no leaf stirred. *"Rigana. . . ."* Reason was reft away in a great shout that shattered the silence as her name became a berserker's wordless cry. Still shouting, Oesc ran down the hill.

For the next four days they followed the raiders. Messengers galloped off to raise the fyrd while Oesc and his best trackers kept on the trail. It was not difficult. The British had hit other steadings on their way into Cantuware, but in Rigana, they realized they had a prize beyond all booty and were losing no time in getting her away from the Saxon lands. North to Durobrivae led the trail, and then straight west along the old Roman road.

To those they passed, the attackers were no more than an echo of hoofbeats, a rumor in the night. But as word spread through the countryside, folk came from the places they had hit on their way in. By the time Oesc reached the borders of his own lands, his fyrd was over a hundred strong. But the British were a day ahead of them. They had left the road before it reached Londinium and headed cross-country, following minor paths that the Saxons did not know.

Clearly they meant to avoid Venta Belgarum as they had Londinium, but still their way led westward.

A week after Rigana had been taken, Oesc halted his warband at the edge of the British border. Their quarry had gone west and south into Dumnonia, where Oesc had not the force to follow them. But by then he knew whom he was chasing. The warriors who had captured his wife and child belonged to Cataur, prince of the Cornovii and enemy of the Saxon kind.

"What will you do?" asked Wulfhere, his face gaunted by a week of hard riding.

Oesc looked around him. "Beric—" he gestured to a redheaded lad on a roan pony. "Your mother was British, and you speak the tongue well. I will write a message in the Latin tongue, which you must take to Artor. I believe he is in Demetia—the Irish have been raiding again. It is time to hold him to his oath. Rigana and the baby are only valuable as hostages if they are alive. I have to believe that Cataur will take care of her. But he will have to give her up to his king."

"And if he does not?"

Oesc could feel his own features stiffening into a mask of rage. "If Artor does not get her back for me, then my own oaths to him are also void. I will go to my own kind, to Ceretic and Aelle, and together we shall make such a war of vengeance as will drive the British into the sea!"

MONS BADONICVS

A BRISK WIND WAS BLOWING UP FROM THE CHANNEL, BRING-
ing with it the scent of the sea. Oesc took a deep breath, and
for a moment he was sixteen years old and on his way to the
battle of Portus Adurni once more. *And at the end of it I was
Artor's prisoner*, he fought down rage as that old sorrow amplified the new. Cataur still held Rigana and his son.

Struggling for calm, he told himself that this was the same
war that his grandfather had begun, the war to make Britannia Angle-land. His alliance with Artor had been an interrup-
tion, that was all. The thought should have given him
comfort, but the angry knot in his belly still throbbed.

"My lord, you must eat—" said Hæsta, pushing the
wooden platter of swine-flesh toward him. Around the table
of the kings were others for the eorls and the thanes and
lesser warriors, and behind them the rush mats where their
warriors were sitting, chunks of meat and bread before them
and drinking horns in their hands.

Oesc ignored it. "Has there been any word from Beric?"

The thane shook his head. For a moon they had waited,
while the news of Rigana's abduction spread as though carried by the wind. Had Beric found the high king? Had he
even gotten through?

Artor—Artor— his heart called. *Why did you never answer me?*

Perhaps the king was unwilling to go against one of his greatest princes. Perhaps he had not the power to force Cataur to give up his prize.

I would have held to my oath to life's end! It is you who have broken faith with me. . . .

The wind shifted, and Oesc smelled the sweetness of curing grass. It was a moon past midsummer, and all over Britannia men were getting in the hay. The cornfields were ripening, the barley hanging down its head and the green emmer wheat turning gold. Who would harvest them, he wondered, once the Saxons had set the south aflame with war? The men they had sent directly to Cataur had returned with the message that Rigana was his guest, and would remain safe and comfortable so long as Oesc prevented his neighbors from attacking the Dumnonian lands. But if Cataur wanted peace, his own action had destroyed it. Wherever men spoke the Saxon tongue they were calling for revenge.

If Artor, who was acknowledged high king of the Britons, could not rule his princes, it was certain that Oesc could not control the Saxons, over whom he had no lordship at all. It was Ceretic, scenting the excuse that he had been seeking since Portus Adurni, who had summoned the tribes to gather here.

"Oesc, what are you doing?" Hæsta grasped his arm and Oesc realized that he had risen to his feet, his hand on his sword. He looked around him, blinking.

This army was already greater than the one that had challenged Artor eighteen years ago; each day more were coming in. A new generation of warriors had come to manhood, born in this land. They laughed as they ate, boasting of new conquests. His own men of Cantuware, with the West Saxons led by Ceretic and the South Saxons of Aelle, made a formidable alliance. In addition to the kingsmen, from the lands to the east of Londinium had come the Sunnings and the Mennings, the Geddings and Gillings, and more—warriors from a gaggle of clans who were oathsworn to no overlord.

Once more the wind changed. Now the scents were of

horses and leather and roasted meat. Two thralls came past, pulling a cart with a vat of ale. Oesc held out his horn to be refilled and sat down. He took a long swallow, willing his racing heart to slow. For the others, avenging Oesc's loss was only the excuse for a campaign. Their beds were not empty, their children's first words would not be in the British tongue.

Gradually the muted roar of men's voices stilled and he realized that Ceretic was standing. His voice rang across the field as he spoke to the kings and chieftains, chanting names and lineage, bidding them welcome. He knew them all, and their exploits as well. Even as Oesc twitched with impatience, he realized how long Ceretic had been preparing for this day.

"And so, we are come together—" he cried. "Against this army, the Britons will never be able to stand. All that remains is to say who will lead us against this foe!"

"Ceretic! Ceretic hail!" shouted his thanes.

But Hæsta had jumped to his feet as well. "Oesc son of Octha should be our leader! It is his wife who was taken, and he's the heir of Hengest, who brought us to this land!"

"He has not led men in battle—" came the rejoinder.

"But will Ceretic give up his lordship when the war is over? He wants to rule us all!"

"Oesc will be too rash against Cataur and too weak against Artor—"

The meadow erupted in disputation. The British had grown powerful because they all obeyed one high king. Who, Oesc wondered, could command the allegiance of the proud-stomached, hot-headed, independent-minded, warriors who were gathered here?

Oesc kept silent as the arguments went on. He wanted his wife back, but did he want to rule? *Artor won his kingship at the age of fifteen by pulling a God-Sword out of a stone. Shall I attempt the same trick with the Spear?*

He smiled grimly, remembering how even his own house-guard had grown pale when they realized just what the long, swaddled bundle he had taken from Hæthwæge's hut contained. At the time it had seemed right to bring it, but he knew that the Spear was not a token of sovereignty, even though it belonged to the god of kings. Whatever use he might make of it on this campaign, it would not make him Drighten of all the Saxon kind.

Oesc was not sure that anyone could claim that title here. The British were accustomed to overkings and emperors, but no Caesar had ever united the peoples of Germania. It seemed to him sometimes that to do so would be to pervert their very nature. German war-leaders who developed Imperial ambitions always seemed to come to a bad end.

Voices grew louder as tempers frayed. At this rate, the Saxon alliance would not last long enough to bring the Britons to battle. At the other end of the table Aelle was frowning, as if he had heard it all before.

Curse them all! thought Oesc. Rage roared in his ears. Suddenly he was on his feet; when no one seemed to notice, he leaped to the tabletop. Platters danced and food flew, but he kept his footing. Pitching his voice as Andulf had taught him, he cried out—"*Hold!*

"You are squabbling like dogs while another hound takes the bitch away. I want my wife back, and I want Cataur's head—it doesn't matter to me who leads us so long as we win. We need someone with experience, with an authority that all can see. I will pledge myself and my warriors to Aelle of the South Saxons until this war is done!"

A murmur spread through the assembly like wind in the trees. Aelle's head came up and he frowned as if uncertain whether to be grateful. Oesc grimaced back at him. *If you don't want it, all the better! You will be less likely to cling to power.*

"He is right," said Hæsta. "It is the ancient way of our people to choose a war-leader. Aelle is an old wolf and will lead us well."

Everyone looked at Ceretic, whose face had gone dangerously red. But he was a wolf himself, and he could see that the temper of the gathering was against him. He shot Oesc a look of mingled amusement and fury and nodded.

"I agree." He lifted his horn. "In Woden's name I swear it—I and all who are sworn to me will follow Aelle for the duration of this war!"

"Aelle!" came the shout as more horns were raised. "Aelle!"

For a time Aelle listened, then he stood, and gradually the shouting ceased.

"As you have chosen me your leader, I accept the call." His deep voice rumbled through the air like distant thunder. "The Britons have given us fair words, but they cannot uphold them. There is no safety in oaths or treaties. Not until all of Britannia is Saxon will our wives and our homes be secure. Let us go forth in Woden's name, and fight until we have the victory!"

"Look, my lord—from here you can see the Isle of Glass. Beautiful, is it not?" Merlin pointed across the vale, where a scattering of hills rose from a sea of cloud. But only one of them compelled attention. The king reined in abruptly, and Merlin knew he had seen the Tor, its pointed cone dark against a sky flushed rose with morning light, its line pure as some Grecian vase.

"Very beautiful, had I seen it at any other time." Artor's lips tightened and he kicked his mount into motion down the hill. "Does Cataur think that because this is a holy place I will hold my hand? This war is his doing!" His horse broke into a trot.

Merlin held back a little, gazing across the vale. *You will not be stopped by coming to the holy Tor, but perhaps you will be changed.*

The druid had been in Isca when word of the Saxon outbreak arrived. For one terrible moment the events of the first Saxon Revolt had played themselves out in memory. Even before the messenger appeared his dreams had been filled with images of blood and fire. Was it because of them that he felt as if he were repeating actions performed long ago? Or was it only because this was the old enemy, the White Dragon, that had come forth to do battle with the Red once more?

Hengest was dead. This was his grandson, and his foe was not an old king worn out with wars, but Artor. Still, it seemed to Merlin that this campaign was only the culmination of the wars he had fought so long ago, and it was right that one more time he should ride to battle behind a king.

At this season the marshlands were mostly dry. As they reached the bottom of the hill and clattered across the logs of the causeway, cattle grazing in the water meadows looked up with incurious gaze. But mist still hung in the hollows and dimmed the copses, as if they were moving through a series of veils between the worlds.

Artor's face was grim. His control, thought the druid, was no doubt too rigid just now for him to sense any changes in the atmosphere. But the other men, less preoccupied, were looking around them with mingled distrust and wonder. As the Isle grew closer, its rounded slopes rising up to hide the Tor, Merlin felt its power growing steadily stronger, like the vibration of a great river, or the heat of a fire. It had been a long time since he had come here. He had forgotten how, to those with inner sight, the Tor could become in truth an isle of glass through which the light of the Otherworld shone clear.

Open your heart and your eyes, boy, he thought, fighting to control the intoxication of that radiance. The Christian wizard who had brought his followers to this place and built the first church at its base had known what he was doing. The Tor was a place of power.

By the time they reached the Isle, the sun was high. The mists had burned away, and with them, some of the visible mystery. The round church and beehive huts of the monks nestled at the base of the hill, with the community of nuns beside the sacred well beyond them. The lower meadows had sprouted a new crop of tents of hide and canvas, and men and horses were everywhere. The pressure of so many minds buzzed in Merlin's brain.

"Speak with Cataur," he told the king, "and when you are done, however it goes, come to me on the top of the Tor. You will not wish to take the time, but you must do so. From the summit you will be able to see more than the road across the vale—you will see your way." He held Artor's gaze until the angry light in the king's eyes faded and he knew that the younger man was sensing, at least a little, the ancient power that would outlast all of them and their fears.

* * *

"Look at that arrogant son of a swine, parading in here as if he had won a victory instead of plunging the land into war!" exclaimed Cai. "I know how I'd reward him if I were high king!" He frowned as Cataur approached the awning that had been set up to shade the meeting, escorted by Leodegranus, the prince of Lindinis who was in a sense their host here. His hand drifted toward the pommel of his sword.

"Just as well you are not—" answered Betiver. "Artor will have to handle him like a man carrying coals through a hayfield, or we'll have all the west and south aflame. This deed of Cataur's has united the Saxons, but it could break the British alliance."

"And Artor knows it—" Gualchmai shook his head. "He's got a frown on him that would curdle new milk. Still, 'tis not entirely a bad thing. With every year the Saxons have been getting stronger. Do we smash them now, we'll not risk being too weak to do it in a few years' time. . . ."

His younger brother Gwyhir bared his teeth in a grin. He was pale of hair and combative, like his brother only in his height. The third brother, Aggarban, was short and darker. Men said that after the first son, all of Morgause's children had been festival got, of fathers unknown. In the north, where they held to the old ways, no one thought the worse of her. In the south they remembered that she was the king's sister, and if they spoke of it, did so in whispers.

"I hope we will fight—" said Aggarban. "You have had your shares of glory, but I still have to make my name!"

"You sound as if we should thank Cataur for starting this war!" Betiver said bitterly.

Gualchmai shrugged. "I will not blame him. I do admit it has all been a bit unexpected, but ye must bring a boil to a head before ye can lance it. Cataur is only forcing the king to do what one way or another had to come."

Even as Betiver frowned he had to admit that there was a certain hard logic in his words. But he remembered Oesc's fair head next to Artor's brown as they bent over the tabula board or stood at the butts for archery. Oesc had begun as Artor's prisoner, but in the end it seemed to him that they had found a kind of peace in each other's company that Artor had with no one else. The breaking of that bond must surely be hurting both of them now.

There was a little murmur of anticipation as Artor pushed through the crowd. For a moment he hesitated, glaring at the canopy beneath which Cataur waited. Then, without looking to see if his escort followed, he marched towards him. The Dumnonian prince stood up as Artor neared. His sandy hair had grown thinner, noticed Betiver. But the flush on his fair skin was probably from the heat, not shame.

The king's warriors stepped back out of earshot, facing the men of Cataur's houseguard. They could not make out words, but the rise and fall of the two voices came clearly, Artor's deep and tightly controlled and Cataur's higher, with the hint of a whine. But perhaps that was only Betiver's interpretation. Certainly the Dumnonian's face was getting even redder as the discussion went on.

"Say what you will!" Cataur's voice rose. "Giving the woman back now won't stop the war!"

"The war you wanted!" came Artor's shout in reply. The escorts moved closer as he went on. "Send the woman to my stronghold at Dun Tagell. The chieftains of Demetia are still gathering their men. I must go north to join them. Take your own men east and hold Aelle's forces for as long as you can. If you fail me I promise that when I have dealt with the Saxons I will come after you myself!"

He stood, and Cataur got to his feet as well, grinning tightly.

"My lord, we will do all that men can."

The afternoon was far advanced when Merlin felt the energy that pulsed around the summit change and came back from the aery realms in which he had been wandering. Looking down, he saw the pattern of the encampment dislimning as the Dumnonians moved out. Then he became aware of a subtler alteration and knew that Artor was climbing the hill. No other would dare. Even the monks came here only on feast days to make prayers to the Archangel Michael, whom they hoped would bind the old powers that lived in the Tor.

The strengthening breeze set dust whirling in a spiral, and

he smiled. Could one bind the waters that flowed through the earth, or the wind that stirred his hair? Perhaps the monks' prayers kept them from feeling the power of the Tor, but even with his eyes open, Merlin could see the lines of power radiating out from the holy hill.

He turned as the high king appeared at the edge of the flattened oval of the summit, his hair blown, a sheen of perspiration on his brow. But the haze of anger that had pulsed around him that morning was gone. Perhaps he had worked off his fury on the climb.

"Have you brought me here to show me all the kingdoms of the world and the glory thereof?" Artor asked wryly when he had his breath again. To the north and south, hills edged the vale. To the west one could guess at the blue shimmer of the sea. Eastward the land fell away to dim distances veiled by the smoke of burning fields.

Merlin shook his head. "Glory you shall see, but not of this world. Take a deep breath—this air comes pure from the heights of heaven."

"Cataur and Oesc are in *this* world—" Artor said angrily.

"Breathe!" Merlin's voice compelled obedience. The air the king had drawn in to argue with was expelled without words. He breathed in again, more slowly, and his eyes widened.

"What is it? I feel a tingling, and there are little sparkles in the air!"

"Look at me . . ." said the druid.

"There is a haze of brightness around you," whispered Artor after a moment had passed.

"Now, look at the land. . . ."

This time, the silence was longer. The king stood still, trembling, his eyes wide and unfocused.

"What do you see?"

"Light—" came the answer. "With every breath, light flows through the grass and stone and trees. . . ."

"Life," corrected the druid. "It is the Spirit that you are perceiving, that moves like a wind through all that is."

"Even the Saxons?"

"Even through them, though they do not perceive it. He

who understands this mystery is part of the land. This is the power that will carry you to victory."

Nearby, someone was groaning. Oesc roused, smelled horses and old blood and the smoke of a watch fire, and knew he was encamped with Aelle's army. The groaning man must be Guthlaf, one of his houseguard who had taken an arrow through the thigh. But he would live, and they had won the battle. He turned over, wincing as the movement jarred stiff muscles, and gazed upward, where stars winked through a high haze of cloud. The gods had favored them with good weather for campaigning, and barring a few scratches, he had come through the fighting unscathed.

But he was tired to the bone. He tried to remember what it was like to sleep in a real bed with the soft warmth of a woman beside him. He had had Rigana for little more than a year—it was not long enough to offset a lifetime of loneliness. *Is she even alive? Is the child?* By day he could assure himself that Cataur would have no reason to kill her. But in the dark hours he imagined a lifetime spent grieving for her loss.

Even if Cataur had offered to give her back tomorrow, Oesc could not break the oaths that bound him to the war. That was the doom that haunted his nightmares. Living or dying, how could Rigana forgive him for not rescuing her? He had meant their marriage to join their two peoples in harmony, and instead it had led to a new and more devastating war.

It was small consolation to reflect that Cataur must be regretting his action as well. One of Ceretic's warriors was boasting that he had struck the Dumnonian prince from his saddle. The Britons had got their leader safely away, but it would be long before Cataur could fight again. After several preliminary skirmishes, the main forces had met near Sorviodunum, and the Dumnonians, if not quite defeated, had been prevented from retreating westward. Now the larger Saxon army was pursuing them across the plain.

Burdened with wounded, the British would go slowly. Aelle hoped to cut them off before they could join with the forces Artor was raising in Demetia.

Oesc felt a new set of muscles complain as he turned onto his side and closed his eyes once more. But the deep slumber he so badly needed eluded him. Instead he fell into a state halfway between sleep and waking in which he wandered through a landscape of warring ghosts.

At first he thought of the old story of Hild, whose curse set her father and lover to repeat their final battle throughout eternity. But this was a battle of Saxon against Briton, and it was Rigana who walked among them, shrieking imprecations. It seemed to him then that he followed after, begging her to forgive so that peace might come. And then she turned, and her face was that of a wælcyrige, one of the battle hags who choose the slain for Woden's hall.

Oesc halted, shaking his fists at the heavens. *"What do you want? When will you bring this slaughter to an end?"*

And it seemed to him then that a great wind swept across the battlefield, swirling up the bodies of men like fallen leaves and flinging them across the sky. And like the roar of that wind, came the answer—

"When you choose wisdom over war. . . . When you learn how to use the Spear!"

The Britons were retreating. Cataur's appeal had brought Artor's forces down from Demetia to his aid, but the Saxon army was larger than anyone had expected. In the open field, the Britons could not stand against them. Several skirmishes and one pitched battle had proved that in numbers at least, the Saxons had superiority. Every villa in their path had been looted, and the ruins of Cunetio still smoked behind them. But if the defenders were being forced to fall back, at least they were doing so in good order. Their losses had been relatively light—to some, that made their retreat all the more ignominious. Only Artor seemed unconcerned.

When the murmurs became too bitter to ignore, he called his chieftains to council.

They had made camp just outside the hamlet of Verlucio, a staging post on the main road that led from Calleva and the Midlands toward Aquae Sulis. The inhabitants, recognizing that any supplies they did not share with their own side would soon be taken by the Saxons, had been generous with food and drink, and the men were in a more mellow mood than they had been when the day began.

Even Gualchmai, who had been growling like a chained hound, seemed to have been pacified by a skin of wine. But Betiver, gazing at the circle of flushed or frowning faces, still felt a hard knot of anxiety in his gut.

"What is the matter, old friend?" came a voice at his elbow. "You are looking around you like a sheep that has just heard the first wolf howl." It was the king.

Betiver sighed. "It is not the wolves I fear just now, but the sheepdogs. They do not like to be beaten, and they do not like to run."

"And you fear the shepherd will not be able to command them?" Artor's eyes were as bright as if he were going into battle.

Betiver flushed. *He understands what is at stake here, despite his soft words.*

"Have faith. No man can guarantee victory always, but I do have a plan."

"My lord," Betiver answered softly, "I have believed in you since I was thirteen years old."

It was Artor's turn to color then. He turned away rather quickly and took his place in the folding camp chair with the crimson leather seat and back that he used as a portable throne. Gualchmai moved into position behind his right shoulder and Betiver took the left. Gradually, the men gathered before him grew still.

"Let me tell you a story—" the high king said into the silence. "Once I hunted a stag. He was an old beast, and wily, but I was confident that my dogs could run him down. But he knew the ground better than I did, and the chase went on and on. By afternoon, I was far from my own hunting runs. I had no food, and the trail was leading into the hills. But my prey was so close, I could not give up. And then, the ground rose suddenly and I looked up and saw the stag above me on a rock that jutted out from the cliff. Three dogs were killed as they tried to leap up at him. I lifted my spear, but before I could throw, the stag charged. His horns took out two more dogs as he crashed through the circle, and my horse reared and threw me. By the time I sorted myself out, he was long gone, and the dogs that remained to me were quite happy to head home. . . ."

For a long moment there was silence, then Agricola of Demetia let out a guffaw. "Is that why we've been bolting for the hills for the past ten-day?"

"You are trying to draw the Saxons into hostile territory?" asked Cunorix, whose Irish had, in the face of this new threat, been transformed into allies once more.

Artor let the babble of speculation run its course before raising his hand. "Aelle's army is too great for him to carry sufficient supplies. He must live off the land, but if he splits his forces to forage they risk coming upon a larger body of our own men. The farther he gets from his own lands the worse his problem becomes."

"And where do you propose to stand at bay?" a new voice put in.

"Aquae Sulis nestles among hills. In such broken country, the Saxons will find it hard to bring their numbers to bear. There is a hill that overlooks the Abona across the river from the town, above the place where the Calleva road joins the road to Corinium. It stands alone, and its summit is flat, big enough for our mounts and but not too big to defend. That is where I propose we make our stand. We have enough in our saddlebags to hold out for some days, and we can bring river water in barrels from the town. I have sent orders already to the people of Aquae Sulis to flee, to leave what food they cannot carry on the hill, and to take with them every scrap of food they can."

For a moment longer the issue was in doubt. Then Cunorix grinned. " 'Tis a trap, then, that we'll be setting for our foes."

"It is, and we the bait and the jaws of it both!"

Cunorix half drew his sword. "Then I'd best get busy sharpening mine—" More laughter followed, and Betiver relaxed. He should never have doubted, he thought then, that Artor could handle his men.

*　　*　　*

The hill bristled against the pale blue of the sky.

At first Oesc thought the uneven line was brush or treetops, but as they drew closer he could see the stubble of cut tree trunks and bushes on the slopes above. The sides of the hill had once been covered with foliage that might have hidden ascending enemies, but now they were denuded, trunks and branches woven into a spiky rampart around the summit.

He swore softly. "Ceretic was so sure we had them on the run! But if Artor was running, this was his goal—he *meant* to lead us here."

Haesta, who was marching beside him, grunted agreement. "You may know less about leading armies, but you know Artor. Aelle should have listened to you. On the other hand, Artor may not have expected quite so many of us—" He squinted up at the hill. "They're safe for the moment, but where can they go?"

By nightfall, the hill was surrounded, and the Saxon warsongs drifted upward on the wind. On the next morning the first assault was mounted on the southern, and least precipitous, side of the hill. It was also the best defended, and the picked force that had ascended was soon retreating once more.

That afternoon they tried again with a general assault from all sides at once. In the process they discovered the hard way that the Britons had a good supply of arrows and retired with significant, though not crippling, losses. That night they tended their wounds, and in the chill hour just before dawn, sent warriors creeping silently up the western side of the hill. Just as the burning rim of the sun edged the eastern hills a second force charged the eastern side, screaming war cries, and the defenders, springing to the breastworks, were dazzled by the first light of day.

The western force made good use of their distraction, swarming over the piled logs and taking out the sentries, then pulling as much of the breastwork down as they could manage to give those who followed easier entry.

It should have worked. The Britons, waking dazed from sleep, thronged toward the eastern side of the hill, and the Saxons who were infiltrating from the west fell upon them from the rear with silent ferocity. Oesc, who was leading them, was the first to see the figure that reared up before them, glowing with pale light and crying out words of power in a voice that paralyzed the soul.

His warriors, not knowing what had come against them, froze in terror. Oesc recognized Merlin, but for the few crucial moments it took for the Britons to realize where the real threat lay, his knowledge of the druid's powers incapacitated him as completely as it had his men. Then the brightness faded, to be replaced by yelling shapes silhouetted against the rising sun. Now it was the Saxons who were blinded. They turned and ran.

For a moment Oesc glimpsed Artor, clad only in breeches, the dawnlight flaming from his sword. He cried out in challenge, but caught in the midst of his fleeing warriors, he was carried back to the gap in the breastwork and down the hill.

By the end of that day, the disadvantages of maintaining a seige with a large army in hostile territory were becoming clear. Artor and his warriors were surrounded by Saxons, but the Saxons were surrounded by trackless hills from which all sources of food seemed to have disappeared.

"If we are getting hungry, then they must be too," said Ceretic grimly. "And even if they have food, they must run out of water soon. They have horses up there, lads—tomorrow morning we'll attack again, and keep coming until we overrun the hill. Then we'll feast on horseflesh and offer the king's stallion to the gods."

They were fine words, thought Oesc, binding up a gash on his thigh, but if the Saxons did not succeed in bringing the Britons to battle, they would be eating each other soon. His gaze moved to the long, shrouded shape that lay with the rest of his gear. Until now he had not unwrapped it, for Artor had left his Sword in Londinium, safely sheathed in stone. But Merlin had used magic against them that morning. The next time the Saxons attacked, Oesc would use the Spear.

At sunset it was the high king's custom to make the rounds of the breastworks unescorted, stopping at each guard post to hearten the men on duty there. On the evening of the second day of the seige, Merlin fell into step beside him. He had been waiting for the right moment, when the king, driven to the limit of his resources, would be willing to hear his words.

"Have you come to point out my foolishness, as you used to do when I was a boy? I gambled that if I took refuge here, Aelle would be forced to raise the seige, and my pride may have lost not only the war, but Britannia," Artor said bitterly as they moved along the breastwork. "Tomorrow we must try to break free."

"You did not choose so badly. This hilltop has been a fortress before—" Merlin replied.

"What do you mean?" asked Artor. He paused to greet the men who were leaning against the tangle of logs at the post on the eastern side. Torches on tall poles cast an uncertain light down the slope, a garland of fire that was matched by the larger necklace of watchfires below. Between them, dark shapes lay among the stumps; bodies that neither side had dared to retrieve for fear of arrows from above or below.

"Did you think the gods had leveled this summit in foreknowledge that one day you would need a refuge?" Merlin said as they moved on. "Men lived here before the Romans came. That is why the top is flat and the edges so sheer. Your breastworks are built on the remains of the ramparts they raised to protect their village."

"I wish they were here! I speak words of cheer, but this morning we lost men we could not spare."

"What makes you think that they are not?" said the druid. "Now, in the hour between dark and daylight, all times are one. Open your ears and listen—open your eyes and see. . . ."

As Artor turned, frowning, Merlin touched his forefinger to the spot on his brow just between his eyes. The king staggered, blinking, and the druid held him, his own sight shifting. Overlaid upon the shapes of hide campaign tents he saw round houses of daub and wattle with conical roofs of thatch. The ghostly images of earthen ramparts crowned by a palisade veiled the breastwork of piled logs. And among the warriors of Artor's army moved the figures of men and women and children dressed in the striped and checkered garments of ancient days.

"I see ..." whispered the king, his voice shaking. "But these are only memories."

"By my arts I can give such substance to these wraiths as will send the Saxons shrieking. But you must call them—"

"In whose name? To what power that they would recognize can I appeal?"

Merlin drew from his pouch a bronze disc with a woman's face in bas-relief. "This is an image of the Goddess—one of those they used to sell to folk who came to bathe in the waters of Sulis. The ancient ones will know it. Fix it to your shield and summon them in the name of the Lady of this land."

The time for tricks and surprises was over. Today must see an ending—both sides knew it, thought Oesc, tightening his grip on the Spear. Before the sun rose the Saxons had taken up their arms; the first rays glittered on ranks of helmets and spearpoints and shields. The toll was likely to be terrible, but by the end of it the Britons would be broken. He would be avenged.

He wondered why that knowledge brought no triumph. *I will weep for you, my king, but I will not hold my hand. . . .*

Saxon cowhorns blared in challenge, and from behind the ramparts, British trumpets shrilled a reply. On the southern side, where once had stood the gateway to the fortress, he glimpsed a shiver of movement. The tree trunks and brush were being pulled away. Of course, he thought then, this was the only slope on which the horses could hope to keep their footing. The momentum of the hill would aid that of the British charge.

Aelle had given Oesc the right flank. His thanes had formed the shieldwall in front of him, but all around him men edged back as they saw him fumbling with the wrappings that covered the Spear. The dawn wind was rising, tugging at the bindings, whipping back the hair that flowed from beneath his helm.

Are you so eager, lord of the slain? Soon, you shall have your prey!

The last knot came free and the transclucent stone of the spearhead glowed in the light of the rising sun. A tremor ran through the rune-carved shaft. Oesc tried to convince himself it was the wind.

Wood cracked above and a horse whinnied shrilly. Wind gusted, flattening the grass, and suddenly the whole world was in movement, logs bouncing and clattering downward, bowling over the first rank of Aelle's houseguard. The first of the horses followed.

Oesc tensed, balancing the Spear. In a single moment he glimpsed Artor's big black horse with the white blaze among them, and felt his arm swinging back of its own accord.

"To Woden I give you!" he cried. The god-power rushed through him as light flared from the boss of Artor's shield. That same power brought his arm forward, plucked the Spear from his hand and sent it arcing through the air, higher and higher. Surely the wind was lifting it, carrying it where the god required it to go.

Oesc followed it with his eyes, over the horsemen who were cascading down the hill through the opening in the breastwork and straight for the man who had sprung onto the logs beside it, his grey beard flying in the wind. He stared, ignoring the tumult around him, as that white-robed figure seemed to expand, reaching, and impossibly, caught the Spear.

To Merlin, it was a streak of incandescent power. He reached out with body and spirit, knowing only that he must keep it from plunging into the mass of men behind him. And then, like a striking eagle, it came to his hand, and agony flared through every nerve and limb. He wheezed as the air was squeezed from his lungs, breathed again in a great gasp and felt the pain replaced by ecstasy.

Consciousness whirled upward as through the gateway thundered wave after wave of men and horses. With awareness at once precisely focused and impossibly extended, Merlin heard each battle cry and knew the name of the man who uttered it. He heard the silent yelling of the wraiths who rose from the earth as Artor called them, felt them flow down the hill, and heard the terrified babble of the men who fell before them. He heard, as once before at Verulamium, the battle-shriek of Cathubodva's raven that weakened the sinews and fettered the will, as Artor swept back and forth across the field, scything down men as a reaper cuts grain.

He knew all words in all languages, and the language of the earth itself, the song of every blade of grass and leaf on tree.

And he heard, with a clarity beyond mortal hearing, a Voice that whispered, "*All those who battle on this field I claim— my speech will fill the mouths of their children's children; my law will rule this land. But today, to your king I give the victory. . . .*"

Oesc fought an army of shadows, with shadow-warriors at his side. Some of them had faces he knew—men he had led to battle, and men he had known as a child. It was when he saw Octha his father among them that he understood that this battlefield was not the British hill he had left, but the plain before Wælhall. He stopped then, and put down his sword. His father saw, and turned to him, gesturing towards the foe.

"*Is this all,*" Oesc cried, "*Is there no other way but war?*" As he spoke the shadows faded, and he fell down a long tunnel and back into his body once more.

At least he assumed it was so, for he was very cold. With an effort he drew a breath, and felt the first tinglings of pain. With sensation came hearing—the cries of wounded men, and someone speaking nearby.

"Oesc, can you hear me?"

With another effort of will, Oesc made his eyes open. Artor was bending over him, his hair matted by the pressure of his helmet and the smudges of fatigue shadowing his eyes.

"My lord. . . ." It was barely a whisper. "He took Rigana. Why didn't you answer me?"

"I didn't know!" Artor's face contorted. "By our Lady I swear that you were on the march before I knew." He reached out to take Oesc's hand.

Oesc tried to return the grip, but nothing seemed to be happening. "I can't . . . feel . . ."

He sensed movement and saw that Artor was cradling his hand against his breast, but he felt nothing at all.

"A horse fell on him," said another voice. He could not turn his head to see. "I think his back is broken."

There was a moment of shock, and a rush of bitterness as Oesc understood that he would never hold Rigana in his arms, never see his son grow to be a man, never again watch the rich grasslands of Cantuware rippling in the wind from the sea. All his hopes, his ambitions ... whirled away like dust on the breeze.... He fought for control.

This, then, was the Wyrd that the runes had foretold for him, the outcome of all the choices he had made. It was the gift of a hero to know when the time had come to cease fighting. To choose whether his spirit should dwell with the gods or stay to guard his people was the gift of a king.

"I don't remember that ... only the fighting...." With difficulty, he drew breath once more. The cold had increased; he didn't have much time. "My lord ... find Rigana and my son...."

"They are safe—" Artor said quickly. "I will bring them back to Cantium. And you—" His words failed.

Oesc remembered the shrine at Ægele's ford and the promise he had given there. "Make my mound next to Hengest's, and I will guard the land. I am ... its king. But you ... are different. You belong to all ... Britannia."

A sudden flush of color came into Artor's face, as if only now was he realizing that with the Anglians tamed and the southern Saxons broken, for the first time in his reign he was truly the high king. He cleared his throat.

"Eormenric shall have your high seat, and while I live no one will dare to challenge him!"

Oesc managed a smile, and after another moment, the breath to speak again. "Only one last gift ... to ask...." Sudden anguish filled Artor's eyes, but Oesc held his gaze until he nodded acceptance. "Now...."

Light glinted from the king's dagger. Still smiling, Oesc closed his eyes. There was a swift pressure, but no pain, only the sweetness of release as his heart's blood flowed out to feed the earth and he gave his breath back to the god.

PEOPLE AND PLACES

A note on pronunciation:

British names are given in fifth-century spelling, which does not yet reflect pronunciation changes. Initial letters should be pronounced as they are in English. Medial letters are as follows.

SPELLED	PRONOUNCED
p	b
t	d
k/c	(soft) g
b	v (approximately)
d	soft "th" (modern Welsh "dd")
g	"yuh"
m	v
ue	w

✝

PEOPLE Iꟼ THE STORY

CAPITALS = major character
* = historical personnage
( ) = dead before story begins
[ ] = name as given in later literature
Italics = deity or mythological personnage

Ægele—thane holding Ægele's ford for Hengest
*AELLE—king of the South Saxons;
AEethelhere—one of Eadguth's thanes
Aggarban [Agravaine]—third son of Morgause
Alfgifu—daughter to Ceretic
(*Ambrosius Aurelianus—emperor of Britannia and Vitalinus's rival)
(Amlodius—Artor's grandfather)
Andulf—a Burgund bard in the service of Hengest
(Artoria Argantel—Artor's grandmother)
ARTORIUS/ARTOR [Arthur] son of Uthir and Igierne, high king of Britannia
(*Augustinus of Hippo—St. Augustine, originator of the doctrine of predestination)
Baldulf—a Jutish warrior settled in the North
Belinus—prince of Demetia
BETIVER [Bedivere]—nephew to Riothamus, one of Artor's companions
Brigantia [Brigid]—British goddess of inspiration, healing, and the land
Byrhtwold—a thane in the service of Eadguth and Hengest
CAI—son of Caius Turpilius, Artor's foster-brother and companion
Caidiau—commander of the western forts on the Wall
Caius Turpilius—Artor's foster-father
CATAUR [Cador]—prince of Dumnonia
Cathubodva—Lady of Ravens, a British war goddess

*Catraut—prince of Verulamium
*CERETIC [Cerdic]—son of Maglos of Verulamium, king of the West Saxons
*Chlodovechus—king of the Franks in Gallia
*Constantine—son of Cataur
*Cunorix—a hostage from the Irish of Demetia, later leader of Artor's Irish allies
*Cymen—Aelle's eldest son
Cyniarchus—son of Matauc of Durnovaria
*Cynric—son of Ceretic
*Dumnoval [Dyfnwal]—daughter's son of Germanianus and Ridarchus's brother, lord of the southern Votadini
Docomaglos [Docco]—prince of Dumnonia, second son of Gerontius the elder
*Dubricius—bishop of Isca and primate of Britannia
Eadguth—king of the Myrgings, Oesc's maternal grandfather
Eadric—one of Hengest's thanes
Ebrdila—an old priestess on Isle of Maidens
Eldaul [Eldol]—prince of Glevum
Eldaul the Younger—his son, one of Artor's ministers
Eleutherius—old lord of Eboracum
(*Eormenaric [Ermanaric]—king of the Goths at time of Hun invasion)
*Eormenric—son of Oesc, heir to Cantuware
Fastidius—a priest in Artor's service
Freo [Freyja, the Frowe]—*Germanic goddess of love and prosperity*
Frige [Frigga]—*Germanic goddess of marriage, queen of the gods*
Ganeda [Ganiedda]—Merlin's half-sister, wife of Ridarchus
Geflaf—chief of Eadguth's sword-thanes
*Germanianus—prince of the South Votadini
*Gerontius the Younger—son of Docomaglos
(Gorangonus—prince of Durovernum, grandfather of Rigana)
Godwulf—oldest of the Saxon priests, formerly one of Merlin's teachers
(Gorlosius—elder son of Docomaglos, father of Morgause)
(*Gundohar [Gunther]—king of the Burgunds, killed by Attila)
Goriat [Gareth]—fourth son of Morgause

Guthlaf—a warrior in Hengest's hall

GUALCHMAI [Gawain]—first son of Morgause

Gwyhir [Gaheris]—second son of Margause

Hæsta—a Jutish chieftain who settles in Cantuware

HÆTHWÆGE—a wisewoman in the service of Hengest

*HENGEST—mercenary warrior, later king of Cantuware (Hildeguth—Oesc's mother)

Hrofe Guthereson—eorl holding Durobrivae

Hyge and Mynd [Huginn and Muninn]—Woden's ravens

*ICEL—king of the Anglians in Britannia

IGIERNE—Artor's mother, Lady of the Lake

Ing [Yngvi]—Germanic god of peace and plenty

Johannes Rutilius—count of Lugdunensis, father of Betiver

Leodagranus [Leodegrance]—prince of Lindinis

LEUDONUS [Lot]—king of the Votadini

Matauc [Madoc]—king of the Durotriges, lord of Durnovaria

Maglos Leonorus—king of the Belgae, Ceretic's father

Mannus—mythic ancestor of the Ingvaeones

MORGAUSE—daughter of Igierne and Gorlosius, queen of the Votadini

MERLIN—druid and wizard, Artor's advisor

*NAITAN MORBET—king of all the provinces of the Picts

Norns—Germanic goddesses of fate

*OCTHA—son of Hengest, Oesc's father

*OESC—son of Octha and king of Cantuware

(*Offa—king of Angeln, enemy of the Myrgings)

(*Pelagius—fourth-century British theologian who believed in salvation through good deeds)

Peretur [Peredur]—son of Eleutherius, lord of Eboracum

*Ridarchus—king at Alta Cluta

RIGANA—granddaughter of Gorangonus, wife of Oesc

*Riothamus—duke of the Britons of Armorica

(Sigfrid Fafnarsbane [Siegfried]—hero)

Thunor [Thor]—Germanic god of thunder

Tir [Tyr]—Germanic god of war and justice

(*Vitalinus, the VOR-TIGERNUS, overking of Britannia)

(Uthir [Uther Pendragon]—high king of Britannia, Artor's father)

(Wihtgils, Witta, Wehta—Anglian kings in Hengest's line)
Woden (and Willa and Weoh) [Odin, Vili, Ve]—Germanic god of magic, war and wisdom
Wulfhere—one of Oesc's sword-thanes

†

PLACES

Aegele's ford—Aylesford, Kent
Abus—Humber
Afallon [Avalon]—Glastonbury
Alta Cluta—Dumbarton Rock
Ambrosiacum—Amesbury
Anderida—Pevensey, Kent
Anglia—Angeln in northern Germany
Blackwater—River Dubglas, probably the Witham in Lincoln
Calleva—Silchester
Camulodunum—Colchester
Cantium/Cantuware—Kent
Cantuwaraburh—Canterbury
Cluta fluvius—the Clyde
Cornovia/Kernow—Cornwall
Demetia—modern Pembrokeshire
Deva—Chester
Dubris—Dover
Dumnonia—the Cornish peninsula
Dun Breatann—Dumbarton
Dun Eidyn—Edinborough
Dun Tagell/Durocornovium—Tintagel
Durobrivae—Rochester
Durolipons—Cambridge
Durovernum Cantiacorum
Durnovaria—Dorchester, Dorset
Eburacum—York
Fifeldor—"Monster Gate," the mouth of the Eider, Germany
Giant's Dance—Stonehenge
Glevum—Gloucester

Guenet—Gwynedd
Icene—River Ictis
Isca Dumnoniorum—Exeter
Isca Silurum—Caerleon
Isle of Glass—Glastonbury, Somerset
Jute-land—northern Denmark
Liger—River Loire
Lemanis—Lympne, Kent
Lindum—Lincoln; Lindensis—the country around it
Londinium—London
Luguvalium—Carlisle
Lugdunensis—Lyons, France
Maridunum—Carmarthen
Meduwege—the Medway River
Mona—the isle of Anglesey
Myrging lands—between the Eider and the Elbe
Novantae lands—Dumfriesshire and Galloway
Portus Adurni—Portsmouth
Regnum—Chichester
Rutupiae—Richborough, Kent
Rhenus—River Rhine
Salmaes—the Solway
Saxon lands—between the Ems and the Elbe
Sorviodunum—Old Sarum (Salisbury)
Stratcluta—Strathclyde
Tamesis Fluvius—Thames River
Tanatus Insula—Isle of Thanet, Kent
Tava Fluvius—the Tay
Treonte, Trisantona—the Trent
Vecta Insula—Isle of Wight
Venta—later Gwent, modern Monmouthshire
Votadini lands—southeast Scotland, from the firth of Forth to
    the Wall
Venta Belgarum—Winchester
Venta Icenorum—Caistor St. Edmunds
Venta Silurum—Caerwent
Verulamium—St. Albans